Retribution Rails

Erin Bowman

HOUGHTON MIFFLIN HARCOURT

BOSTON   NEW YORK

www.hmhco.com

The text was set in ITC Cheltenham.
Map artwork by Sophie Kittredge.
Bird art on map by Teagan White.

Library of Congress Cataloging-in-Publication Data
Names: Bowman, Erin, author.
Title: Retribution rails / Erin Bowman.
Description: Boston ; New York : Houghton Mifflin Harcourt, [2017] |
Companion to: Vengeance Road. | Summary: Ten years after the events of
Vengeance Road, Reece Murphy, who has been forced to join the Rose Riders
gang, must work with aspiring journalist Charlotte Vaughn to get free.
Identifiers: LCCN 2016058459 | ISBN 9780544918887 (hardback)
Subjects: | CYAC: Frontier and pioneer life—Fiction. | Adventure and
adventurers—Fiction. | Robbers and outlaws—Fiction. | Revenge—Fiction. |
West (U.S.)—History—19th century—Fiction.
Classification: LCC PZ7.B68347 Ret 2017 | DDC [Fic]—dc23
LC record available at https://lccn.loc.gov/2016058459

Manufactured in the United States of America
DOC 10 9 8 7 6 5 4 3 2 1
4500674585

For Casey—
My wildest adventure

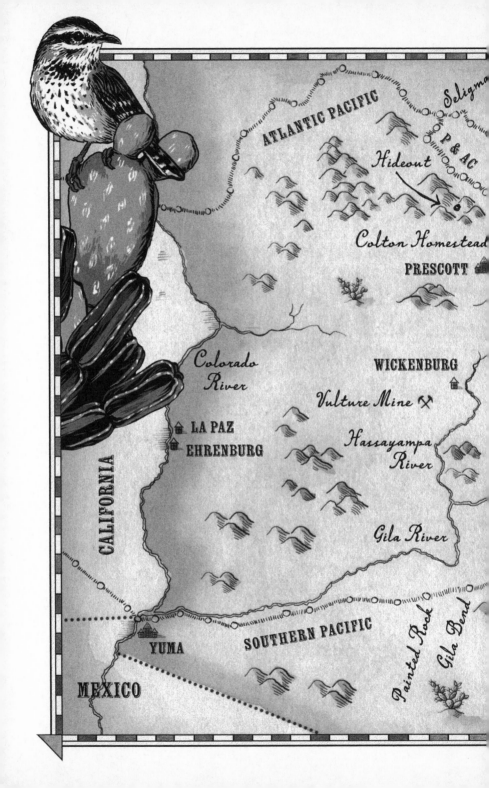

Before you embark on a journey of revenge, dig two graves.

— CONFUCIUS

CHAPTER ONE

REECE

There's a nice stretch of rail between Painted Rock and Gila Bend, and that's where we'll take the train.

Diaz and Hobbs are hunched over the track, sweating and cursing beneath the Territory's winter sun as they work to uproot another spike. Hobbs is yapping advice in a tone that's earning him rude gestures from Diaz. Besides their banter and the clank of tools hitting metal, the morning's silence is damn near deafening. No cactus wrens singing. No breeze. Not even the far-off whistle of the train we know's coming.

A robbery ain't how I envisioned spending my eighteenth birthday, but after three years riding with this crew, I've learned to expect nothing and be ready for anything.

Boss checks his pocket watch and tucks it away without comment. Means we're still on schedule. For now.

"Well, Murphy?"

"Nothing yet, Boss."

I been sitting in the saddle 'longside him all morning, checking the horizon with his binoculars. The train's due in Gila Bend at quarter past twelve, meaning it should be chugging our way 'round high noon. We heard it's carrying a mountain of money to a bank in Tucson. Payroll, plus general funds being transferred. Has something to do with the approaching new year. Exact details don't matter to us. Boss's got an informant, and his info ain't steered us wrong, save for one skirmish a few months back, so when we hear money's on the move and can be lining our pockets before the sun sets—three days, even, before the calendar reads 1887—we follow the lead.

"How 'bout Crawford?"

I turn my attention east. The Gila carves through the parched Arizona soil in the distance, but on a slight rise before its banks, a mass of cattle're grazing. The rest of our boys—Crawford, Barrera, DeSoto, and Jones—are out there among the beef. The herd belongs to some rancher, but when the train breaks the horizon, Crawford and the others'll get 'em moving, coaxing 'em this way till they're stampeding for the tracks. If'n things go smooth, the rail Hobbs and Diaz are wrestling with won't matter. Conductor'll see the herd and shout for the brake. Then we'll step onto the cars as the dust settles, taking 'em by surprise. But if the herd don't cooperate or their timing ain't agreeable, a busted track ain't the worst way to stop a train. We done it before.

"He's still getting in place," I say. The hillside ain't

speckled with nothing but tan hides and dull-green shrub, and Crawford's supposed to turn his jacket out when he's ready. It's got a red lining.

"Lemme have a look," Boss says, reaching.

I surrender the binoculars and watch as he observes the herd. His brows're pulled down tight, his expression stern and focused. It ain't a rare look. I think I only caught him laughing twice in the three years I been forced to ride with him.

"Were I wrong?" I ask after he hands the binoculars back.

"Nah. Didn't think you would be, but a boss's gotta check or he ain't much of a boss."

My chest puffs up a little, then deflates from the shame. I ain't sure how it's possible to admire and despise someone in the same breath, but that's how it is for me with Luther Rose. I can't forget the scar he put on my forearm —the half-finished rose brand of pink, puckered skin— or what his men did to the Lloyds that day they dragged me into their crew. Or the waste Boss lays at his feet day in and day out, never seeming to feel an ounce of remorse or guilt. None of the Rose Riders seem to. And yet, this is my life now. This is how I gotta live. I'm here 'cus I got something Boss wants, and I'm gonna be his prisoner till he gets it. Surviving is easier if I pretend I'm one of 'em.

And if I make Boss happy in the process.

Luther Rose runs a tight outfit, after all, as savage and unforgiving as his half brother, Waylan. Back when he were still alive, the gang hit the stagelines, not the rails, and local folk didn't even know Waylan had a sibling. It were a secret within the gang. Waylan never wanted his kin to be a target, and since they had different mas and didn't bear a striking resemblance, he had Luther act like any old member of the crew. It was only after his passing that Luther made his true relation to the late Boss known. It helped strike fear. Now people quake at the mention of Luther Rose just as much as they did when hearing of Waylan a decade earlier. The gang's as feared as ever.

Hell, I was scared of 'em as a kid growing up with the drunk I called a father in Ehrenberg, and I was downright terrified when they rode into my life three years back. Most days, I'm still on edge. The trick is, I try not to show it. You display yer weaknesses 'round these type of men and they'll eat you alive.

The shriek of an engine whistle shatters the afternoon quiet.

"Soon now, Murphy," Boss says to me. A plume of dark smoke puffs 'long the horizon. "Soon."

I check for Crawford and find a swatch of red, hear the gunshots popping next. The herd starts lumbering.

Diaz has finally pulled the last spike, and now him and Hobbs are wrestling with the rail, yanking it so it don't line up with one farther down the track. Soon as it's free, they circle back on their horses, pulling up behind me and Boss.

The stampede comes on, our boys riding 'long the outskirts to keep the cattle confined and on target. My mare, Girl, is already getting spooked. She ain't never liked trains, and she twitches beneath me. I squeeze her tight with my thighs, trying to assure her all's well, but if I had it my way, I'd clear out a little, let the beef run their course, and swoop in when the train brakes for the animals. But Boss is sitting proud in his saddle, unfazed and barely blinking, so I try to do the same.

The engine's bearing down on us like a bullet come outta the barrel, a blot of black on the horizon that flies straight and true. It ain't slowing, but neither are the cattle. Crawford and his men draw rein on the north side of the rails, letting the herd lumber on. Dust billows 'round the beef.

Beyond the dirt cloud, the train keeps blowing its whistle.

"Boss?" Diaz warns at a shout.

But Boss just holds up a hand.

Right when I'm certain *this* is the time a train'll derail and go flying, the brakeman applies the brakes. The clamped-down wheels screech and scream, running over the rail. The shrill cry is like a pickaxe to my skull, the worst kind of headache. I got my bandanna up over my mouth and nose to protect from the dust, and I can still smell the metallic tang of the hot steel, the engine's coal steam.

For a good half minute our world is nothing but dust and heat and screaming brakes. Sparks fly. With one final exhale from the engine, the train goes still. The herd continues south, taking the dust with 'em.

I fan dirt from my eyes.

The dark outline of the train engine sits a few yards

ahead, air rippling 'round it. It's a giant of a locomotive, a towering black behemoth that came to a stop just yards from our busted bit of rail.

A figure leans out from between cars, flapping a pale kerchief so he can see if the herd's cleared out.

Boss draws his pistol.

The poor bastard don't even have a chance to yell out a warning. The moment his eyes find us, going wide and fearful, Boss pulls his trigger. The man's head snaps back, and he topples from the train, landing beside the track.

"Let's move!" Boss orders.

We draw our pistols, tip our hats low so all you can see easy between the brims and bandannas is our eyes. And then we're storming the train.

CHAPTER TWO

CHARLOTTE

It is not my first ride in the elegant passenger car of a Southern Pacific locomotive, but when the engine comes to an unexpected stop and a pistol is discharged outside, I'm certain it will be my last. Lord knows trains do not make unannounced stops between depots for any good reason.

"Sir," I say, nudging the sleeping lawman beside me.

He does not budge.

Since leaving Yuma, the engine's been pulling us northeast, following the Gila River as she chugs toward Tucson. It's provided a beautiful view of the southern plains, and had I known that the lawman intended to sleep the entire trip, I'd have requested the seat by the window. There's little view now that the glass is caked with dust, but if I peer with determination, I can see a barren hillside and a wisp of the river in the distance.

This is what I get for chasing a story.

"Your father sank a small fortune into the Prescott rail project, Charlotte," Mother said to me before she left for the capital yesterday. "He'd want me to see the final spike driven, maybe even say a few words on his behalf. Sit tight, and I'll be home in but a few days' time."

Uncle Gerald's been running the family mine since we moved to Yuma a decade ago. Always in the habit of stealing the accomplishments of others, he'll surely "say words" on Father's behalf. But it won't end there. Father has been in the ground only a single week, and Mother has already confided in me her fears that Uncle Gerald might try to demand her hand in marriage in order to gain ownership of the mine. He'll argue that this is his way of supporting us, that the business will need a re-spected man at its helm, but we both know he just wants the money.

Mother's gone to Prescott to have a firm discussion with him about the will and what to expect—a lovely way to spend the holiday season.

And I've gone after a story, for while Mother doesn't think Uncle Gerald would stoop so low as to hold me over her head, I worry otherwise. *Don't you want to be able to provide for Charlotte?* he'll croon. *Wouldn't it be a pity if something happened to her?* But if I get my big break —a story with my name attached to it, a career reporting for a paper—I'll be able to take care of myself. I refuse to be a burden or a bargaining chip.

But now, sitting near the back of the train's first-class car, I fear I'm about to pay for my stubborn determination.

To my rear is a locked car carrying valuables, and farther back are the rest of the passengers, where I can hear muffled demands shouted.

Way up front, our car door bangs open, and I lurch for the suitcase at my feet, feeling blindly until my fingers graze the barrel of Father's most prized pistol. I'd taken it with me for protection, never thinking I'd truly need it. I snatch it up and press it to my ribs, hiding the weapon beneath my jacket.

"Hands where we can see 'em!" a man shouts as he climbs into view. A sweat-stained bandanna is drawn over his nose, and his hat is angled low across his brow. "Hands up, and no one gets shot."

Throughout the car, passengers slowly reach for the ceiling, but I can't bear to let go of Father's pistol. I hunker down in the seat, breathing heavily, considering that if I appear small and frightened, the robber might not think twice about my hands being deep inside my jacket.

Another man steps into view—slighter than the first, but just as tall, and just as hidden behind his attire. He ducks past the first man and moves up the aisle.

"Murphy!" his companion calls, and tosses him a burlap sack.

The man named Murphy catches it. "Valuables," he says, angling toward the nearest seat.

"Watches and purses!" the other adds from up front. "And yer jewelry."

I nudge the lawman with my leg. Nothing. He's still slumped against the window, a dark handkerchief clutched in his lap. He'd been coughing quite a bit when we boarded the locomotive in Yuma. Could be he's like Father, fighting a losing battle with tuberculosis.

"That band on yer finger," the stockier robber says from up front.

"But it's my wedding ring," comes a retort.

"Do you wanna die today?"

The woman breaks down, gasping and sobbing, but the man refrains from loosening bullets. How the lawman can sleep through this, even with his condition, is beyond comprehension.

The man called Murphy moves on to my row. I blink at the burlap sack dangling in my peripheral vision, squeeze the grip of the pistol beneath my jacket.

"Yer valuables," he grunts at me. He's wearing filthy trousers and a pale blue work shirt stained with a ring of sweat around the collar. The bandanna over his mouth matches his shirt, but it's his hat that compels me to pause. A deep, rich felt material, broad-brimmed but high, with an intricately braided strip of leather encircling the crown. It's too showy for a man of crime, too proud. Surely stolen. But I make note of it all, committing the details to memory. A description of these men is the first thing we'll be asked for when we chug into town, robbed dry.

"I don't have anything worth giving, mister," I say, avoiding eye contact. I can feel him staring, though, and when I venture a look, his eyes are working a line over my entire person. The small suitcase at my feet, the visible portion of my black mourning dress, the fine winter jacket draped across my shoulders, my chin, nose . . .

"Yer earrings," he says.

The small pearl studs were a gift from Father when I turned sixteen last month, and I refuse to give a piece of him to some no-good train robber who makes a living taking what others have rightly earned.

"The earrings," he says again. "Put 'em in the bag, and no harm done."

Like hell.

Suddenly I'm mad at the world. Father, for leaving me and Mama. The Law, for not being able to rein in these bands of robbers that continually plague the good folk riding the rails. The devil, for creating men as desperate and dark as the one standing before me.

My fear betrays me, and my lip trembles. I bite down on it, snuffing out the quiver. An expression flickers over the robber's face, something that suggests he has no problem stealing, but doesn't particularly like being reminded that his victims are human. That they fear and shake and cry.

But perhaps that can be used to my advantage.

There are only two robbers in this car, and if I'm able to surprise the man named Murphy—drop him with a bullet—surely someone else will spring to action. Certainly the lawman will wake from a gunshot fired in such an enclosed space.

A bullet goes off in the payload car, startling me so thoroughly, I nearly drop Father's pistol.

"Hurry up, dammit," the robber snarls.

"All right," I say, cocking Father's pistol beneath my jacket, intent on giving Murphy a pearl-shaped bit of lead.

But as I draw the weapon, the door to the cash car bursts open and several men tumble into ours. The one in the lead sees the barrel of my gun appearing from beneath my jacket, and he dives at Murphy, knocking him to the aisle floor. My shot goes into the man's shoulder.

And that's when the lawman finally wakes.

Dropping his kerchief and drawing his pistol, he shoves me toward the window and opens fire on the robbers. I flinch at each shot, grabbing my ears as the car explodes with thunderous noise. Around the lawman's legs, I can see a bit of the aisle: Murphy struggling to free himself from beneath the man I hit—a man he's now calling "Boss."

The lawman lets out an *oof* and slumps into me. There's shouting and more gunshots, then silence. My ears still ring, barely able to hear the pound of fleeing hooves.

I peer out the window and find the gang on the move, their steeds kicking up dust as they fly for the river.

"Sir?" I say, turning back to the lawman. He shifts his weight off me awkwardly and lets out a low wheeze. "Sir, are you all right?"

The pistol slides from his hand, landing on the floor of the car with a clatter. His eyelids flutter.

"See it through for me, miss," he says. "Please?"

I grab at his front. He is slick, wet. The breast pocket of his vest is glistening with blood. "What?" I gasp out. "See what through?"

But his only response is a ragged, uneven breath as his blood seeps through my fingers.

CHAPTER THREE

REECE

By the time we cross the Gila and kick the horses into a true sprint, flying north, the reality of the situation crashes into me.

That fair-skinned, wide-eyed, lip-trembling girl nearly sent me to meet my maker.

I know exactly where I went wrong, why I didn't catch sooner that she were pulling an act. I'd been keeping my gaze down as I moved up the aisle, trying to avoid looking folk in the eye if I could manage it. In part 'cus it ain't never worth being recognized, even with the bandanna up high and our hats down low, but also 'cus I *hate* the look I get during jobs. The fear and horror, the desperate anguish. I know what they're feeling 'cus I lived it myself. When I'd finally fled my drunken father at thirteen and found work on the Lloyds' farm near La Paz, I thought I were safe. The Colorado ran nearby. The earth were rich and fertile. It was heaven. For nearly two blessed years I wasn't *boy,* or *bastard,* or *son of a bitch,* but Reece Murphy, a kid that just might be able to make something of himself. I vowed to be a farmhand for the Lloyds long as I could manage. But then Boss and his boys came galloping onto their claim the summer before I turned fifteen, and it all went to hell.

It were the hottest day I ever saw. Longest, too. They killed the whole family—Billy included, who were only seven—and they took their time doing it.

I don't know what made 'em choose that claim. Maybe they were bored. Maybe they needed money and the Lloyds were the easiest, closest hit. Alls I know is I'd've been strung up also if it weren't for the coin Diaz found while emptying my pockets.

"Boss, you seen this?" he said. "Ain't this yer brother's?"

He tossed the coin over, and Luther—who were in the process of carving that blasted rose into my forearm—paused to snatch it outta the air. He went dead still when he done saw it proper. A fury spread over his face, not unlike the look that crawls over my pa's when he's had too much whiskey.

"Where'd you get this?" Boss snarled, holding the coin an inch from my nose. It were a gold piece a touch smaller than a half-dollar, featuring a wreath on one side and Lady Liberty on the other. It looked a bit like a three-dollar piece, but there was no currency amount on either face. I reckon it coulda been worth a cent or a hundred times that, but I'd held on to it simply 'cus I'd never seen another like it.

"A cowboy gave it to me last week," I answered.

"What cowboy?"

"I don't know."

Boss backhanded me 'cross the cheek.

"I swear, I don't know," I said again. "He were a stranger. I ain't never seen him 'cept for that once."

And it were the truth. The cowboy'd stopped at the Lloyds' one afternoon, looking to repair his steed's faulty shoe. Mr. Lloyd gave the man a drink from the pump and a bite to eat. I took care of his horse. The next day, he'd flicked the coin at me with a gruff "Thanks" and rode south. That was it. In our lives for a day, then gone forever.

But Boss still moved his knife to my neck like I were lying. My pulse pumped so hard I could feel the blade more firmly with each heartbeat.

"Think you'd recognize this cowboy if'n you saw him again?"

"Y-yes," I stuttered, just wanting it to end—the pain in my forearm and the crackle of building fire and the women's screams coming from somewhere behind me. "I could point him out," I promised. "I'm s-sure of it."

And just like that, Boss was sheathing his knife and I were being hauled onto Diaz's horse.

I looked back only once as we rode out. Inside the corral, in the mouth of the Lloyds' blazing barn, four dark shadows hung swinging.

I was a wanted criminal after that day, charged with the murder of the Lloyd family. I weren't Reece Murphy no more. I was the Rose Kid. Infamous. Feared. I slaughtered that poor family, ran, and then joined up with the Rose Riders so I could continue doing evil. Least that's the story that got printed, the tale folks chose to believe. Sometimes I wonder if Boss or his boys've let lies slip, too, planted yarns and encouraged the rumors. It sure don't hurt the gang's image. If nothing else, it makes 'em even more fearsome. Makes the kid they got riding in their ranks out to be a true villain, not a fool held hostage. Fear can be more persuasive than facts.

It's why I bought that girl's act, after all. By the time I had the nerve to look her in the eye, I only saw a scared girl trembling in her coat, not a spitfire opponent with a pistol hidden from view. I'd even been close to telling her not to cry, that I weren't gonna hurt her, that if she just handed over the earrings, it'd all be over, but Boss had been nearly done in the cash car, and I didn't want him to catch me being sympathetic.

It all went to hell after the girl's pistol discharged. Boss toppling into me. Hobbs just behind him, firing like mad with the cash slung over his shoulder. Jones shouting for us to get a move on from the front of the train.

It's moments like this—fleeing a train job gone wrong, with my cheeks chapped from the cold and every bone in my body bracing for Boss's rage when we stop—that I wonder what in tarnation I'm doing.

I truly believe he'll let me go if'n I find that cowboy for him. He's vicious, but he's still a man of his word. A handshake means something among men, even outlaws, and over the years the small promises Boss's made me, he's kept. Like getting me new boots when I outgrew mine, and other small decencies. It ain't him keeping his promise that worries me. It's the cowboy. He's starting to feel like a ghost, an impossible whisper of a man.

I ain't never gonna find him. I'm gonna be stuck riding with these boys forever.

I almost wish that girl'd managed to shoot me.

We ride hard all day, and when we stop at dusk, Boss damn near falls from his saddle. He's lost a good amount of blood, but he don't check the wound or even if we got the payload out safe. (We did.) He just stumbles straight for me and delivers a blow to my chin that sends me sprawling.

"Goddammit, Murphy! You got air between those ears? You don't let no one reach into their jacket like that, not even some shaken, near-blubbering lady. Yer gonna get us all killed, kid!"

He kicks me in the side, and I don't even bother trying to shield myself from the blow. He took a bullet for me.

Boss turns toward Hobbs. "The damage?"

"None. We got all the cash out."

"And the lawman?"

"Got him taken care of, too."

It's good news for us, but Boss don't look none the more relieved.

"Rest while you can," he announces. "Word of that robbery'll be telegraphed 'cross the Territory. With luck, there'll be reports of unidentified men attacking, nothing more, but we're riding hard for a while. The farther we get from the Southern Pacific, the better."

As the others start seeing to their bedrolls, Boss crouches down beside me. The tang of sweat and blood drips off him. If fury's got a scent, he's wearing that too.

"You do something that dumb again, and I'll finish that rose on yer forearm, Murphy. I swear it on my brother's grave."

The little I know 'bout Waylan's death suggests he died in the Superstition Mountains east of Phoenix and were left there to rot, not buried. There ain't no grave to swear on. But I keep quiet.

"It ain't like I want to," Boss adds as he straightens. "It's just I can't have you dying on me, son. You got that?"

I know it's less 'bout me meaning something to him and all 'bout him wanting answers—'bout tracking down who killed his brother, which starts with questioning the cowboy only I can identify. But when he leaves to tend to his shoulder, I say a prayer that the cowboy wanders 'cross my path soon. I'll gladly give up one more soul to cut free. I can deal with that last bit of blood on my hands.

Since running from home, I've spent more time in this gang than not, and while I know everything we do is wrong and wretched and cursed, it's starting to feel normal. It's starting to be all I know. I barely trust my own two hands these days, so I gotta find that cowboy before I start feeling like this is where I belong. I gotta walk away from the Rose Riders before I start liking the way it sounds to hear Boss call me "son."

CHAPTER FOUR

CHARLOTTE

"*Is there a doctor* onboard?"

The passengers are in an uproar, some sobbing while others rant about stolen purses and lost jewelry.

"Dammit, is there a doctor onboard?" I shout.

An elderly woman twists around to face me. She's pinching a set of rosary beads, her lips still curled around a prayer. I think she might scold me for such foul language, but then she notices my bloody hands gripping her headrest. I've stained the wood, left red smears on the velvet upholstery.

"Leonard," she says, turning to the man with her. "Leonard, I do think your assistance is needed."

Leonard leans on a cane as he moves up the aisle, a medical bag hanging heavy from his free hand. He kneels beside our seat, observing the lawman over the rim of thin wire spectacles.

I didn't even know his name. He'd made a bit of small talk, shining the badge on his vest when I sat down beside him. I told him I was a journalist with the *Prescott Morning Courier*. A half-truth. I don't write for the paper in any official capacity, but the lie made me appear older than my sixteen years, and the last thing I desired was for him to question why I was traveling without a chaperone and insist on escorting me home.

The doctor feels for the man's pulse. I don't need to watch more than a minute to know there's nothing he can do for the lawman. I see the verdict on his face. One side of his mouth pulls down; then he licks his lips and swallows, glances at me quickly. He hasn't even opened his medical bag.

"Are you traveling with anyone else, miss?"

My bloody hands are resting on the skirt of my dress, its fabric wet in places.

"Miss?"

I glance up. "No, sir."

"A young lady like yourself shouldn't be traveling alone," his wife says. Then, almost in afterthought, her gaze jerks back to the deceased man and she adds, "God rest his soul."

"I'm sorry to say there wasn't much I—or anyone— could have done," the doctor says. "He passed on almost immediately."

My head bobs in a bit of a trance.

He's dead. Those outlaws killed him.

The car lurches. I hear someone mutter, "There was

a disengaged beam, but the crew fixed it." The engine starts chugging, the wheels and rods rolling faster and faster until the scenery outside begins to blur.

I glance at the lawman.

His eyes are closed—the doctor's doing—and if it weren't for the blood all over his front, he almost appears to be sleeping again.

See it through for me. Please.

I flip open my journal and began scribbling down everything I can remember about the gang. Murphy's hat and blue bandanna. His companion's stockier build. The boss's graying hair and sunken eyes.

I'll see it through. I'll see the Law gets the cleanest description possible and that the hounds are sent after those devils.

When the locomotive chugs into Gila Bend, a flurry of activity awaits us. Word of the robbery was sent ahead by telegraph, and a posse is being rounded up to go after the gang.

The train is held at the depot while a deputy sheriff asks to speak with anyone who might be able to give a description of the robbers. I provide all I can remember, and the man taking down my description startles at the details of Murphy's hat. He moves on to another passenger before I can ask him if they've had trouble with these characters before. It's only after they've departed and the train is moving east again that I overhear Leonard and his wife conspiring; the young man named Murphy is actually Reece Murphy. The Rose Kid.

My stomach twists, and I slump in my seat.

I'd assumed Murphy was his first name, not last, and this new possibility laces my limbs with goose flesh. The Rose Kid rides beneath the equally heartless Luther Rose, and the men who make up the Rose Riders are among the Territory's most vile and bloodthirsty lowlifes. Thieves, murderers, rapists, devils. There is not a tale I've heard of their crimes that does not make me shudder. What happened during the robbery now seems jovial. Things could have gone much, much worse.

I'm still quite shaken when I reach Maricopa, where a stagecoach can take me north to Prescott. The doctor is continuing east to Tucson, and his wife makes sure to chastise me on the dangers of traveling alone and my "sinful, improper ways."

I assure her I will most certainly be fine, that family is waiting for me in Prescott, and besides, Nellie Bly travels without a chaperone. In fact, she's currently down in Mexico, reporting for the *Pittsburg Dispatch*. Leonard's wife has either never heard of the young female reporter or simply doesn't care enough to change her opinion of me, for she watches with a scrutinizing gaze as I step onto the depot.

I'm not sure why I'm surprised.

Father told me long ago that I could do anything I set my mind to, but it would behoove me to be prepared for resistance at many turns. My journalism career began by summarizing the proceedings of the P&AC rail—or, rather, the particulars Father was privy to. He'd mark up my words and I'd redraft them, and if he approved of the result, he'd send them on to Uncle Gerald, who would in turn send them along to an acquaintance, John Marion, editor and founder of the *Prescott Morning Courier*. On the occasions that my pieces were printed, they were always credited to Uncle.

When I confronted him by post, he simply replied that it is not a lady's place to report on issues lest they pertain to ladies themselves—fashion and gardening and all else oft found in the "women's pages." He was doing me a favor by submitting the work to Mr. Marion as his own. No one would even read my stories if they saw my name on the byline.

Well, I beg to disagree. I will write one darn impressive story about the completion of the Prescott and Arizona Central line, and while Uncle Gerald is busy trying to pressure Mother into an unwanted marriage, I will march into Mr. John Marion's office, smack my piece down on his desk where he can't ignore the words before him or the person who wrote them, and demand credit.

If I'm lucky, I'll get a job, too.

I find my way to the stage stop, only to be told I've missed the day's lone coach to Prescott. It's rotten luck on an already horrid day, but moaning about it will change nothing. This is a lesson Mother has hammered into me, and I exhale hard—just as she taught me—and follow it with a smile. *Things always look better when you smile,* she says. I can admit that forcing my lips upward brightens my spirits, even if only minimally.

I purchase fare for a coach that will depart the following morning, then go about locating a boarding house for the night, which all but drains my purse.

I exhale again, but it's harder to produce a smile a second time.

When I collapse on the bed, still wearing my jacket and bloodstained dress, I can't help but worry about Mother. Has she spoken with Uncle yet? How did he take the news that Father left the Gulch Mine to Mother and me, not him? Lord knows he'll feel entitled to it. He's overseen operations this past decade while Father pursued additional business opportunities — mainly buying up lumberyards along the Colorado and selling cheap fuel to steamboat companies that agreed to ship his copper at discounted prices in return. The P&AC will help with those freighting costs also, which was why Father invested so heavily in the project when construction finally began.

I'm struck again by the sudden sting of reality. He's gone. He spent years slowly leaving us, but I still wasn't prepared for his absence.

It is such a shame that he passed before the rail's completion. I will have to write one heck of a story about the celebratory gala. Perhaps there are newspapers in heaven.

CHAPTER FIVE

REECE

We head north at dawn, following the dry riverbed of the Hassayampa.

I'm riding in Jones's shadow 'cus the bruises I got on my side and jaw sting enough to keep me away from Boss. Not that he ain't looking my way constantly. He prolly figures I can bring trouble upon us just by breathing wrong after that mess on the train. His constant watching makes me anxious, but I know better than to complain.

Jones senses my mood, though, and does his best to keep me smiling. "What'cha gonna do with yer cut of this purse?" he asks.

Everyone gets a percentage, but not me. Not till I find that cowboy. Boss keeps a tally of what I've earned on the inside cover of his Bible, and in the meantime I just get scraps—enough to buy myself a drink or a shave in town, but nothing nobody could live on. It's just one of the many ways he keeps me tethered.

"I don't get a cut, remember?" I remind Jones.

"After, then," he says.

"I barely got time to think 'bout today, much less after. What about you?"

"Gonna buy a nice plot of land someday."

"When's that gonna be?"

He shrugs, but it's somewhat normal talk, and it warms a part of me that often feels hollow and dead.

Since fleeing the Southern Pacific, we been riding hard enough to make good time, but not so hard that we run the horses ragged. Boss leads and DeSoto, like the quiet shadow of a man he is, brings up the rear. The day of the robbery we stayed well west of Phoenix, and we ain't stopped riding with the Hassayampa since we came upon the river. Today our target is Wickenburg, a mining town on the decline, with no rail and a decent ride from any of the existing tracks, even by coach. A good place to see if there's a new bounty out on us.

Diaz pulls up 'longside me and Jones. "Boss wants you riding up with him, Murphy." He leans closer and adds, "Happy birthday, by the way."

"A day late," I shoot back.

"Well, we were kinda busy robbing a train."

"Ain't that how everybody celebrates turning eighteen?"

Diaz grunts. "There's usually whiskey involved. And women. You shoulda had some fun on that train, treated yerself to that pretty blond thing."

Jones chuckles, but I frown.

"You don't like gals that can pull a pistol on you," Diaz says. "I get it."

"That she drew on me says an awful lot about how far she wanted me from her."

I don't add that there ain't time for that sorta disgrace during a train job, which Diaz knows as well as any. Still, his lip curls.

"Do us all a favor and buy yerself a poke when we get to town. All that righteous talk is making me sick." He heels his horse and trots ahead.

I spit a few times, though there ain't nothing in my mouth.

Come midafternoon we get our first sight of Wickenburg. It rises outta the desert, several blocks wide and rarely over a story tall, most of the buildings as barren and plain as the dry stretch of earth they sit on.

Boss gives orders for a staggered arrival, which we do often in situations like this, entering town in small groups or even pairs. It distracts from prying eyes, and if word of our train job's done traveled cross the Territory 'long with our description, we wanna look nothing like a band of eight on horseback.

Boss barks out orders from the saddle, voice gruff. "Crawford, Barrera, and DeSoto—y'all ride in together, but find a farrier. Replace a shoe or two if needed. Whatever makes you look like folk just passing through and needing some care for yer horses. Jones, you can ride in, but come dusk." He turns to Diaz and Hobbs. "You two follow me, but hang back a half hour or so. Don't be too on my tail. And Murphy?" Boss raises a hand. "You ready?"

I ain't surprised to hear I'm riding with him. After yesterday, he ain't gonna let me outta his sight, and if any of our gang's to look unsuspicious, it's the two of us together. Me, eighteen. Him, fortysomething. We could be father and son, stopping for a rest. We don't got too much in common by way of features, but what do I know? I ain't looked into a proper mirror in months. Could be the spattering of freckles that cover my nose have up and fled, that my hair's gone suddenly streaked with gray and now I look like the bossman's twin. My hands've done things I didn't think 'em capable of these last three years. Maybe I won't recognize the person who wields 'em no more.

I give Girl a nudge in the ribs. She's a good horse, quiet and obedient. A day after I got dragged into the gang, Barrera stole her for me in the thick of the night. She came from a homestead not far outside La Paz and was prolly someone's livelihood.

"What's her name?" I asked Barrera.

"Hell if I know. She responded to Chica all right as I led her from the barn, though."

It's a sorry name for a horse, but most folk in the gang were only calling me "kid" back then, so I figured a label were better than nothing. I started calling the mare Girl, and while we rode, I mulled over better names and how I might try to make a run for it.

Three years later, she's still Girl and I'm still riding with these bastards.

I tried running once. The results weren't pretty.

The only way out is through the cowboy.

As we ride, I try to be like Boss: at ease in the saddle, confident, relaxed. We peel off the Hassayampa and cut west to enter the town. Both sides of Wickenburg's main street boast adobe and frame buildings, homes and businesses full of people that got no notion of the kind of men riding into their world.

Boss tips his hat at a lady beating rugs outside a boarding house, smiles at a pair of kids waiting in a wagon hitched to a horse outside a general store. ETTER'S, it says on the front of the double-peaked roof. We'll be stopping there before we leave, no doubt. Boss could use some new bandages for his bad arm, and our eating's been meager the last two days. Barrera's one hell of a cook, but he can't make a feast outta nothing.

We trot a bit farther down the street, finally stopping outside a saloon. The dressing on Boss's arm's hidden from view beneath his long gray coat, and most folk would never guess he were shot yesterday, but I can see the signs. He flinches a touch as his leg swings over the saddle, grimaces as he ties his mare to the hitching post.

I secure Girl, too, aware of Boss's intentions without asking after 'em. We'll chat up the locals, ask 'round for news. If'n it appears folk are aware of the train job or too keen-eyed 'bout newcomers, we'll stock up on what we need and leave quick as can do. But if the robbery news ain't reached here, if the locals're warm and welcoming . . . Well, a bed at that hotel we passed and a night with the working girls ain't something Boss is gonna deny the crew.

I follow him outta the weak December sun. Inside, the saloon's empty 'cept for a bartender cleaning glasses and a couple drunks playing cards. Light from the street seeps in, doing little to brighten the dingy space.

The bartender looks up from his work as the doors swing shut behind us.

"Whiskey for me and my boy," Boss prompts.

He leans into the bar, easy, and as the man sets two glasses on the counter, I catch my reflection in the mirror behind him. I look tired and beat. My freckles are barely any darker than my tan skin these days, but I ain't lucky enough to have lost most of my father's Irish features. My Mexican mama—whose folks called this land home long before wars and shifting borders decided it were Arizona Territory—looks his opposite, but it's so clear I'm *his* son. I got the same square jaw and hair just a few shades darker than his straw blond. The only bit of me that *don't* look like him is my eyes. They're darker, like my ma's, but have gone all pinched these last few years. From squinting in the sun, likely, or from all I've seen and keep trying to blink away.

The bartender pours, then puts the stopper on the decanter. "You folk ain't from around here," he says as he slides the drinks over. It's a fact, not a question.

Boss throws back the whiskey and nudges the glass forward for more. "Just passing through."

"Hear 'bout that train robbery outside Gila Bend?"

"Can't say we did. Been in the saddle this past week. Who done it?"

"No word on that yet. Not much word, in general. I only know some fellas on horseback made off with a hell of a fortune. And that a lawman's dead on their account."

I spin my glass a few times, finally take a sip. I ain't never been able to down whiskey the way the boys do. It burns too much, and that ain't a sting I wanna get used to. Not ever. I seen what it can do. The best men can go mad, and the wicked ones only fall farther. I ain't got a memory of my father where he weren't drunk, but I do remember a time when he at least apologized for lashing out at me, when he still saw a fault in his ways. By the time I ran, even that shadow of humanity had long since flown, leaving me with a demon who knew just three things: how to drink, how to insult, and how to beat.

"Shame," Boss says. "First the coach lines, now the rails. Ain't no way to travel safe no more."

"Ain't that the truth." The bartender pours himself a glass and clinks with Boss. They both gulp down the poison.

The doors creak behind us.

I peer over my shoulder and spot Diaz and Hobbs entering the saloon. They nod at the bartender by way of a welcome but then move to a nearby table.

I stay focused on my whiskey. Boss goes on making small talk with the bartender.

I've managed to empty half my glass when a couple more gents trickle into the saloon. One of 'em tips his hat at the bartender. "Martin," he says. That he knows the bartender by name means he's gotta be a local, someone familiar, but the bartender's expression's gone suspicious and cold. His eyes dart between the newcomers and us. The air feels tight suddenly, tense. Like a coiled trap ready to spring.

Boss senses it too.

"I reckon we'll be on our way." He pushes a handful of coins 'cross the bar. It covers what we drank and then some.

But the bartender goes for something behind the counter.

Me and Boss reach for our pistols.

"Keep those fingers where I can see 'em," a voice behind us says, "and turn around nice and slow."

We pause, carefully move our hands away from our holsters. I turn like I been told, though Boss spins something quick. Flirting with death is his favorite game.

In the mouth of the saloon stands a skinny man with an equally skinny mustache. His jacket falls to his knees, and he has a pistol drawn, aimed right at us. There's a second man near the poker table, a third not far to my right. Two more hovering by Diaz and Hobbs. They all got their guns out.

"I ain't following," Boss says, slow. "What's the meaning of this?"

The skinny fella pulls his jacket back to reveal a silver badge on his vest. A deputy sheriff. "You boys are under arrest for the robbery of a Southern Pacific train outside Gila Bend on Wednesday."

"You got the wrong men, partner," Boss says. "I suggest you move on."

"And I suggest you skin those pistols and come quietly. Else we'll be taking dead men from this saloon."

Boss is as fast as a rattler when he draws, but this is an awful lot of guns, the whole of 'em already pulled and spread through the room. Plus, there's the bartender behind us, who I'm certain's drawn a shotgun from below the bar by now and is likely aiming it at our backs. That puts our rivals at six strong. Even on a good day, without a bullet wound to the shoulder of his shooting hand, Boss can't beat these kinda odds.

"You arrest all innocent men passing through yer town?" he asks.

"You're innocent like I'm a U.S. Marshal. Besides," the deputy adds, "we got a witness."

The doors shove in, and a silhouette enters, falls in line beside the deputy. Then the doors quit swinging and her features come into focus. The front of her dress is stained with blood, her pale hair a disheveled mess, but there's no mistaking her.

It's the girl from the train.

CHAPTER SIX

CHARLOTTE

"It's them," *I say* firmly. "No question."

I recognized the Rose Kid's hat the second it glided past the window of Etter's. The ride to Wickenburg had been rough and backbreaking, so when the coach lurched to a stop and the driver announced we'd have fifteen minutes while the horses were changed, I gladly opted to stretch my legs. I roamed aimlessly, truly feeling the absence of Father for the first time since his passing. It had been a horrid few days leading up to Christmas, the house a flurry of unpleasant conversations regarding funeral arrangements and business propositions, but even since Mother left for Prescott, I've yet to be truly alone. The train had been a distraction, same with the coach. But as I stood before a row of tobacco in Etter's, the scents conjuring up memories of Father sitting in his rocking chair and smoking a pipe while reading the paper, a familiar hat drifted by the window.

Brown felt.

High crown.

Braided leather rope.

I pressed a hand to the glass and peered closer. Familiar jacket, too: plain and tan, hanging to his knees. And that pale blue shirt still stained with sweat. The Rose Kid was riding into town alongside Luther Rose. I bolted from the general store and fetched the deputy in a hurry.

"That one tried to take my earrings," I say, pointing to the Rose Kid. With his hat and bandanna no longer hiding his features, I can see him clearly. There is a slight resemblance to the wanted posters, but the drawing gives him too many freckles. It doesn't render him as young as he truly is, nor does it accurately capture the emptiness in his eyes. They are vacant and unfeeling. It's a kind of hollowness I imagine only a killer can have.

Luther Rose leans nonchalantly against the bar, something akin to a smile on his lips, his jacket hanging open to reveal a pair of twin pistols. Two other men sit at a nearby table, smoking cigarettes. I recognize them from the train as well. They'd been with Rose when he tumbled from the cash car.

Present in this Wickenburg saloon is one half of the Rose Riders. My skin prickles again. Had I known their identities during the train robbery, I don't think I'd have had the nerve to try to fire on anyone.

"I meant to shoot him," I say, pointing to the Rose Kid,

"but I hit the boss instead. And one of them is the coward who killed the lawman." I flick a hand toward the table where the other two sit. I don't even know if it's true. The lawman had been blocking most of my view, but I only care about watching these men hang.

Mother always says I am her firecracker, that I'm nothing but sugar and sweetness until I'm crossed. *It's admirable, in some regards,* she says, *but it will make you a foul reporter.* I never quite understood what she meant, but I think I do now. Because as I stare at the men before me, I feel something harden in the pit of my stomach. I want them punished for their crimes. I do not care if I'm giving a false statement, and that's the crux of the problem, really. Nothing is more important than the truth when it comes to journalism. If I cannot confirm something, it should not be printed or lauded as fact, yet here I stand, naming the lawman's murderer when I cannot back it up.

I press the thought aside. There is something I do know as truthful, and it is that if this man didn't kill the lawman, he's still killed others. All the Rose Riders have. These are not men who have made their first offense. They are guilty countless times over, and they are undeserving of mercy.

I do not understand how they can stand here so calmly. Luther Rose is sporting a crooked smile, the men at the table lounge lazily in their chairs, and the Rose Kid —he's perhaps the most terrifying of them all because he's completely emotionless. His face is a blank canvas, his eyes empty. A palm rests casually on the butt of his still-holstered pistol.

"Where're the others?" the deputy asks.

"What others?" Luther Rose answers.

"Don't play dumb with me."

"There ain't any others. Now you gonna bring us in or you gonna keep wasting our time?"

His lie is blatant. It's a known fact the Rose Riders are eight strong, and the Rose Kid's accomplice—the one who tossed him that burlap sack—is not here. But there is not much that can be done about this at the moment. The deputy, who introduced himself as Clarence Montgomery, rounded up a posse of townsfolk on our way to the saloon. It was frantic, a desperate plea made to any man we passed, and they need to contain the threat before them before they go searching for the rest of the gang.

The lawman's posse outnumbers the four Rose Riders, but they also look mighty skittish. The fellow standing near the Rose Kid can't even hold his pistol without the barrel visibly quivering.

Luther Rose sizes up the number of guns spread through the room. The Rose Kid appears to be counting exits. The other two sit tall and springy.

If these men are half as fast as tales make them out to be, it might be a close fight, even with the posse's guns already drawn. It will come down to a gambling matter: Is Luther Rose willing to sacrifice some of his men's lives in the hopes of walking out with his?

His gaze flicks to the men at the table, then to the Rose Kid. "Stand down, boys," he says.

"But, Boss—"

"I said stand down!"

I'm nearly as shocked as Rose's men, but the surprise fades quickly, replaced by a wave of smug satisfaction. I watch a Wickenburg local yank the Rose Kid's hands behind his back. They'll die for what they did—what they've done—and though it doesn't erase the damage they've leveled, it's a small victory.

Too often bad men walk free.

Cuffed and stripped of their weapons, the gang is led onto the street and down to an enormous mesquite the locals refer to as the Jail Tree, where they are secured to iron holds that have been driven into the trunk. It is a preposterous method for detaining prisoners, but I remind myself that it is only temporary. The men are sure to hang, just as soon as Deputy Montgomery gets word from the capital.

He runs off to send a telegraph, and though I hope his next course of action will be to search the town for the rest of the gang, I do not have time to linger. I race for the stage stop. When I round the corner at Etter's, my heart drops.

The coach is gone, and the passengers I'd been riding with are nowhere to be seen.

"Where's the coach bound for Prescott?" I ask a wiry man working the ticket counter.

"Why, that left a solid ten minutes ago, miss."

"It *left?* But I'm supposed to be on it!"

"Well, I regret to inform you that yer still here." He smiles as though he's made a fantastic joke.

"When's the next coach?"

"Tomorrow, at noon."

"Tomorrow?" The rail is supposed to be finished by the end of the year and it's already the thirtieth. If I miss the ceremonies, I can't document the speeches or take notes for a story. And without a fabulous story, securing a job with Mr. Marion's press will be impossible.

The man chortles. "You in the habit of repeating everything you hear, or am I speaking a whole lot softer than I realize?"

"Your sense of humor is sorely lacking," I snap, and immediately regret it. His expression has darkened, and he no longer seems interested in helping me.

I force a smile. It does not help to lift my spirits at *all,* but the man's grin returns. "You'll be all right, doll," he says assuredly, and pats my hand. "Keep yer chin up. It's a good look on you."

So much for things always looking better with a smile. Perhaps what Mother meant is, men like women best when they smile.

I walk away grumbling under my breath and eventually sit on the edge of Etter's porch, my disheveled skirt fanned around my ankles. Having spent most of my money at the Maricopa boarding house last night, my purse is all but empty. I don't have enough for another coach fare. I likely do not even have enough for accommodations this evening. I might very well be stuck here.

I could write to Mother in Prescott, but she has enough

on her plate. Besides, she'd only come collect me like a stray dog and tow me home with my tail between my legs. She'll claim I have been brash and reckless, but staying put in Yuma as she'd ordered would have helped no one, not if Uncle Gerald responds as I predict.

I blow a sweaty tendril of hair from my eyes. *What would Nellie Bly do?*

For one, she wouldn't sit around pouting. If she didn't have the coin to buy her way, she'd barter herself into a favorable position. I touch my pearl earrings longingly.

Someone marches by my line of vision. I look up, my hand falling away from my jewelry, and spot Deputy Montgomery striding back toward the Jail Tree. There is a briskness to his gait that is concerning.

I leap from the bench, worries of lodging and coach fare falling aside as I hurry after him.

CHAPTER SEVEN

REECE

I'm gonna hang. Just a day past eighteen, and I'm gonna be strung up and sent swinging, all 'cus of that doe-eyed train girl.

They know we're the Rose Riders by now. Boss and me are the most wanted outta the bunch, and we match descriptions given in telegraphs and papers and on wanted posters. Diaz and Hobbs are matches for other boys known to ride with the gang. Between the four of us, we got a list of crimes longer than the Southern Pacific's rails, and a fine bounty, too. Ain't no way we'll be shown mercy.

I reckon alls I can do is pray my neck breaks during the drop, that it's quick and clean. I got no desire to be one of those bastards who kick and flail, trying to swim themselves free of the noose while they slowly suffocate.

"Quit it, Murphy," Diaz grunts.

I try to calm my flighty fingers, but I'm too riled. After stripping us of our pistol belts and weapons, they marched us to this godforsaken mesquite one of the locals called the Jail Tree. That Wickenburg don't have a proper jailhouse gave me hope—at first. There's a knife in my boot they never found, but then they cuffed the four of us, securing us to iron chains hammered deep into the tree's trunk, and my hope all but shriveled. I sure as hell can't reach my boots. The chains are so short, all I can do is stand, shackled hands held up near my chin.

"They'll come for us," Diaz adds. "Crawford and the others."

Boss don't say a word. He must got a plan if'n he willingly let us be taken. We wouldn't've all got outta that saloon alive trying to fight 'em, but it's best to go down swinging. Least that's the sermon he usually preaches. But right now he's got his head reclined 'gainst the trunk of the Jail Tree, looking calm as a daisy as he peers through the thin foliage and into the darkening sky above. He might as well be whistling a tune, running a poker chip over his knuckles, flipping the coin he took from me.

That damn coin. I wish it never fell into my hands. Maybe more than that, I just wish we'd cross paths with that cowboy already so I can point a finger and move on with my life.

I pity the poor soul who killed Boss's brother. Boss don't got kind plans for him.

"Murphy, I ain't kidding!" Diaz growls.

I make a fist and smother it into my palm, clasp my

fingers tight to quit the shaking. The chains still rattle, just not as much.

Diaz is prolly right. My worrying's a waste. The others'll come, but only 'cus of Boss. If he hadn't been with us when we got brought in, we'd be goners. *They were dumb enough to get themselves caught, so they don't deserve to ride with me,* Boss'd say if the tables were turned. Jones has told me stories 'bout men getting pinched and Boss just riding on out. Sacrifice one to save many.

I look at my chains. Four of us shackled here. Men standing in the street, all too eager to see our demise. They been standing there the last half hour or so, waiting on a telegraph from the capital and betting on our sentences. Odds seem to be on hanging, based on what I can overhear. Firing squad is a close second.

"Deputy Montgomery?"

My head snaps up. The train girl is chasing the lawman as he strides toward the gathered men, coattails flapping.

"Deputy!" she tries again.

I still ain't sure what she's doing up here, so far north of the line where we encountered her, but I'm again struck by how serious she looks, how far from meek and crying. Her brows are drawn 'bout as viciously as a poker player done calling a bluff, and though her cheeks are pinched with cold from the run, she ain't breathing heavy. I'm starting to suspect that she had every intention of shooting me from the moment I shook that burlap sack in her face. She were just waiting for the right moment.

The deputy ignores the girl and instead addresses the

men. "I just heard back from Prescott. They're calling for a trial."

"A trial?" she gasps out, nearly barreling into the deputy when he comes to a quick halt. "They'll be found guilty. Why delay?"

"It ain't my decision, Charlotte. Now I know you're upset from what you witnessed on that train, and you want justice here and now, but word is we're to make an example of these boys. A formal trial, a public hanging. Enough to scare the rest of the band into dismantling, and hopefully sending a clear message to any other gangs looking to target the rail. This criminal life won't be tolerated."

"I don't imagine the trial will happen here, in Wickenburg?"

"We'll move them to the capital tomorrow morning at first light. In a locked coach. Escorted by a half dozen men, myself included." He looks over his posse. "I'll need volunteers."

A couple hands go up.

"Escorted!" the girl named Charlotte erupts. "Are you an idiot, Deputy?"

"Pardon?"

Diaz laughs beside me, and even I can't help but smile. I'm surprised the lawman's let her go on this long. He looks far from pleased.

"Where's the rest of the gang, sir?" the girl continues. "You think your men are going to be able to best a handful of Rose Riders once you leave the safety of these streets? A locked coach and a few escorts will not protect you on those plains. The men you *don't* have in custody will free the men you do, and then we're right back where this all began."

"The decision ain't mine. I got folk above me saying to bring them to Prescott. I promise you we're taking every precaution."

She grunts in a very unladylike fashion and says, "Mark my words, Deputy, this plan will not unfold as you figure. And the blood will be on *your* hands." Then she picks up her skirt and shoves past the men.

"Charlotte!" the deputy calls after her. She keeps marching. "Miss Vaughn, my hands are tied."

"Ah, let her go," one of the men says. "Girl don't know her place."

"She don't," Boss agrees. "But she's right."

The deputy and his posse are too far away to hear Boss's comment, and they hurry off to discuss our transport and hanging, unaware of the wolflike smile he flashes at the mesquite's branches.

"The boys'll come, won't they, Boss?" Hobbs asks.

"I reckon so. Tonight, since the townfolk are expecting it during the move."

And if they don't come? I wanna ask. *If'n they turn their backs on us and leave us to hang?*

"I thought I saw a red coat riding for the river when they chained us here," Diaz adds.

Boss nods in agreement.

It makes the ghost of a noose I already been feeling 'round my neck loosen slightly. If Crawford's left town with the others, it means the deputy ain't aware how near the rest of our men truly are. They'll be able to regroup, make a plan. We just might make it out alive.

"For yer lip," Boss says, passing me his kerchief.

I grab it with my bound hands, touch the pale cotton to my mouth. It comes away bloody. Skin musta split when we were taken into custody. The posse sure weren't careful with their elbows.

"Rest while you can, Murphy," Boss adds. "There won't be time for it later."

CHAPTER EIGHT

CHARLOTTE

I march off, silently cursing the deputy's senseless plan, when the solution hits me. I know what to barter. I turn on my heel and race after Deputy Montgomery.

"Sir, I beg you to reconsider," I call out to him. He has just set foot on the front porch of what I assume to be his residence. The step creaks beneath him as he pauses. When he turns to face me, expression weary, I do not miss how his eyes skirt over my shoulder, finding the Rose Riders across the way, still secured to the Jail Tree. There is worry in the deputy's eyes. He knows there was truth in my earlier argument.

"I implore you," I continue. "If you had the whole gang in custody, transporting them would be one thing. But this is a fool's errand. You must consider alternate means."

"Alternate means?" He leaves the steps for the street,

staring down at me with his brows raised precariously high. What I wouldn't give to be a foot taller, to look men in the eye. "I have five men in agreement to ride with me tomorrow, and a judge expecting the gang delivered by coach. You're what, a girl of fifteen? Pardon me for not taking the advice of a child with such little worldly experience."

"I'm sixteen," I retort, "and I'm a journalist."

"That so?"

I nod surely. "I was traveling to Prescott to report on the nearly completed Prescott and Arizona Central line, and I'll be sure to cover this debacle, too, once it goes south. Then again, if you do *anything* unexpected—like moving the criminals tonight, or before dawn—maybe things won't go south. Maybe there will be only successes to report."

Deputy Montgomery's expression shifts from contempt to tolerance.

"That's an idea," he says, mulling it over. "It'll be too dark in the dead of night for a move. Not much moon this time of the month, plus our lanterns would give us away for miles. But near dawn . . . Perhaps we'll leave early, an hour before first light. The rest of their gang will likely be still sleeping, expecting the move later." He rubs his chin. "We could be well out of Wickenburg by the time they look to strike, on high ground and climbing the mountains, able to shoot down on them as their horses battle the slope."

"That sounds like a solid strategy, Deputy." I give him the most charming grin I can muster. Let him believe it's his plan. Let him think he's the hero saving the day. I'm plenty used to men taking credit for my ideas—and my bylines—and I merely need him in a fine mood for what I'm about to suggest. I put on my most confident face and say, "I will ride in the driver's box."

Deputy Montgomery nearly trips over his own feet. "Pardon?"

"Alongside the driver. Or up top."

He stares in dismay.

"Think of it this way, sir: I'll be quiet, sit out of the way, and once you pull that coach up to the depot in Prescott, I'll have a documented account of your heroic efforts. There'll be a printed story featuring the good men of Wickenburg and how their deputy sheriff Montgomery captured four Rose Riders, including Luther Rose and the Rose Kid. How he exhibited great bravery and commitment to the feat of delivering them to trial, how he is the embodiment of the badge he wears."

Deputy Montgomery inflates a little, his brows rising with agreement. He unconsciously shines the badge on his vest with his thumb.

He must know the power of such a story, for I surely do. With a firsthand account of the transportation of the notorious Rose Riders from Wickenburg to Prescott, no one will be able to ignore my journalistic pursuits. Not Mr. Marion, or Uncle Gerald, or even Ruth Dodson of the *Yuma Inquirer.* She'd turned me away earlier this summer, when she opened shop and I came inquiring about a job. Run exclusively by females, the press sounded like heaven on earth, but her budget was tight, her staff full.

I understood being turned away. But I'll have my pick of publications now. In Yuma, Prescott, anywhere in the Territory.

"I won't be telling my men about it," Deputy Montgomery says after some consideration. "They won't take kindly to a lady being involved in such a situation. I ain't fond of it myself. But if you appear at the stage depot an hour before dawn, ready to make the trip, I won't turn you away."

And just like that, I've hitched myself a ride to Prescott and snagged the story of a lifetime.

It takes all my conviction not to grin like a fool.

Draining my purse entirely, I secure a room for the night at a place called Ma's Boarding House. Who Ma is, I'm not one to know, as it's a young man who takes my money. He introduces himself as Jake. I'd wager I'm a year or two his senior. He's lanky and lean, but already taller than I am. His wool cap looks new, but a pale starched shirt held in place by faded suspenders and tucked into too-big trousers have seen better days. Though I have two hands of my own and am perfectly capable of carrying my suitcase, he insists.

The boarding house is neither big nor fancy. The first floor isn't much more than a long hallway lined with rooms. The rug is worn from foot traffic, and candle sconces mounted between most of the doors attempt to liven up the dimly lit space.

"Second floor's for Ma and me," Jake explains, which I take to mean his ma is *the* Ma. He gestures beyond the stairs, down the narrow hallway. "Washroom is first door on the right, kitchen the first on the left. You got the far room, at the end of the hall. Dinner's in half an hour."

He leads and I follow. Most of the doors are ajar—no occupants for the evening—and the kitchen, which already smells of fresh bread and stew, isn't abuzz with chatter. The floorboards audibly protest our weight as we make our way down the hall.

"Is it always this quiet?"

"Used to house a lot more miners, but Vulture Mine's got plenty of quarters of their own these days, plus a Chow House and Rita's brothel." He says the last bit with an air of excitement. "I only stay here 'cus Ma needs the extra hands on the days I ain't working."

We stop outside what'll be my room, and he sets my suitcase down.

"You need anything, you just holler." Jake leans in close and drops his voice to a whisper. "I don't say that for most folk, but most folk ain't so pretty."

He then blushes so quickly, I reckon he means it.

"Thank you—" I call after him as he darts down the hall. "For carrying my bag and all." But he's already gone.

My room's plain, but clean. A single four-post bed, a reading chair, a short wardrobe with a folded towel set on top. Against the far wall is a single window. I pull open the shutters and am rewarded with a sad view of a small alley littered with crates and barrels. In the distance, I can make out the peak of the roofline of the stage stop.

I set my suitcase on the wardrobe. I have a second set of mourning clothes packed, but don't intend to change until Prescott. The coach ride north will only dirty my skirts with dust anyhow. The blood-spattered state of my current attire, however, will not do. I snatch up the towel and head for the washroom.

There's a mirror above the basin, and I startle at my reflection. Stray tendrils of hair fall wild around my face, and I work the pins as best I can, re-taming the mess. Then I wash my face and hands in the basin. Dirt from the coach lifts free, followed by blood once I go about scrubbing at the stains in my skirt. It could very well be *my* blood that is spilled tomorrow. The deputy's and his posse's too.

Whatever is wrong with midwifing? I hear Mother chide in my ear. *It's a respected line of work. I can teach you all I know.*

She has been offering this ever since Cousin Eliza sent me a copy of Nellie Bly's first piece and I set my heart on journalism. There is nothing wrong with Mother's profession. She is appreciated within the community. She seems to love her work greatly. It is because of this love that I am baffled at how she is unable to see that I love something else. She claims I will be met with nothing but disappointment and resistance as a journalist. So far, she's been proven right. But I've assisted her in several births, and it is not for me. It is thrilling, yes, but the whole time I am wishing for it to be over, whereas with writing, as soon as I stop, I want to start again.

"Let her chase this, Lillian," Father once said. "She is

not you, and there are worse things a young woman can do with her time."

Such as going against one's mother's orders, sneaking from home, traveling without a chaperone, and volunteering to assist in the escort of the Territory's most notorious band of outlaws, all for the sake of a story.

I fumble for the soap, fish it from the cloudy water.

A story that will help you and Mother, I remind myself.

I will not be swayed by fear. It is fear that fosters silence, that breeds ignorance, that causes half-truths to be printed over fact. It is fear that has kept me dutiful so far. No more.

If my career will not come waltzing to me, I will hunt it down myself. I will claim it for my own.

I scrub at my garments until my fingers are raw.

CHAPTER NINE

REECE

The first sign of our salvation comes as a whistle in the night.

It sounds a bit like the cactus wrens that feast on insects on the plains, but that bird only sings with the sun. This is our crew, whistling. This is the call Boss teaches all his men when they agree to ride with him. For emergencies and mishaps. In case you get separated from the group. To announce yer near without the enemy being none the wiser.

It's a dark night. The slivered moon's doing little to light the land, but Diaz peers down the street. Hobbs sits a little straighter. And Boss don't twitch a muscle. He's still staring at the lone man the deputy left watching us. Some guard. I ain't got a notion how he's meant to keep an eye on us when he's sound asleep in his rocker.

The local men brought the chair outta one of the houses 'round dinnertime and set it up a few paces from the Jail Tree. They been taking turns watching us since. Most have kept their eyes keen, their focus unshifting, as if they think us slippery enough to wriggle from our cuffs and saunter for the horizon. If we could, we'd've done it by now.

But this sleeping guard . . . His chin's slumped to his chest, his hat tipped low over his eyes. A wool blanket's wrapped 'round his frame so tight, he don't even got a hand on his pistol. He's gonna pay for it dearly.

I hear movement somewhere nearby. Boots crunching 'gainst dirt, paces quick and sure. I can see it in my mind: Our men creeping up the side streets, setting diversions and distractions, stationing themselves with purpose. They're circling the city like wranglers rounding up a herd—Crawford and DeSoto and Barrera and Jones. Four men can do an awful lot of damage when leveraging the element of surprise.

Their attack begins quietly, with nothing but a flicker, down near the general store. Faint. Glowing. 'Bout half a block away. Several buildings obstruct my view, but it only takes a few minutes for those flickers to become a blaze, flames dancing above the other rooflines and licking for the sky. At the first scream of "Fire!" our guard leaps to his feet and reaches for his gun.

"Godspeed, partner," Boss says to him.

I realize what's 'bout to happen the same instant Hobbs and Diaz do. We go diving for shelter, flattening ourselves 'gainst the mesquite best we can as a shotgun discharges.

Splinters fly from the rocker. The guard goes tumbling back and hits the dirt, dead.

"Good to see you, Boss," Crawford says, appearing from the dark. He tucks his shotgun beneath his arm and darts for the guard. With a shove, the dead man's rolled over and Crawford fishes the keys from his belt.

He frees Boss, then Hobbs.

By now, lanterns are winking to life all through town. Shouts of concern fill the night.

"Faster!" Diaz urges.

But it's hard to work the key with such little light.

Across the way, the door to the deputy sheriff's house bursts open. He stumbles into the street wearing only his night things, but his arm's raised, and I don't got to see the pistol to know it's there.

A bullet screams our way, thankfully going wide.

Crawford turns away from Diaz's cuffs and fires back on the deputy. As they engage, shots ring and wood splinters. A chunk of the Jail Tree explodes near my ear. I curse and cower, yanking at my chains.

"Dammit, Murphy!" Diaz shouts. "Hold still."

He's got the keys, I realize. Crawford must've finished with Diaz's cuffs and passed 'em off before turning to face off with the deputy. If only he'd managed to get his hands on our effects too. There ain't much none of us can do to help him without our pieces.

Heat sears my neck. A bullet, just missing me. Thank God the boys set that fire farther up the street. It's keeping folk occupied, and the poor visibility down here by the Jail Tree is the only thing that's kept the deputy from shooting me dead. Granted, that same shoddy lighting's also keeping Crawford from hitting *him,* and keeping Diaz from fitting the key into my cuff locks. Don't help that our hands are damn near frozen, neither. December nights can get wickedly cold, and I reckon it's dipped near freezing in the past few hours.

The key finally slides home and clicks with a turn. I swivel my wrists in relief just as the gunfight dies. Looking 'cross the way, I find the damage. The deputy sheriff's lying in the middle of the street, crawling for his pistol, which he must have dropped when Crawford finally hit true.

"Horses're ready?" Boss shouts to Crawford.

"Along with all yer effects." He hands his pistol to Boss and with a pump of his shotgun yells, "Stay close."

We race up the street and toward the smoke. Already flames are flapping hungrily from the small wood-framed general store and reaching toward neighboring buildings. If'n folks don't act quick, the fire's gonna take the strip in a frenzy.

I yank my bandanna up over my nose and mouth. I feel naked without my pistol, and my muscles are stiff with cold, cramped from being chained to that blasted tree. I draw the knife from my boot, knowing right well it ain't gonna help me fend off bullets. Still, I need something in my grasp.

We race through a thick cloud of smoke, passing the fire with no real issue. For a moment I think we truly might just jog straight outta town, but then Crawford rounds a corner and pulls up short, swearing. "Jones was supposed to be here with the horses!"

There ain't nothing in the alley but a taut, empty clothesline.

"Musta been forced to move," Boss says. "Where's the fallback point?"

"The river. We gotta get to the river. Something musta gone wrong."

Boss looks 'bout ready to murder Crawford for his sloppiness, but there ain't time for it. He leads the way back onto the main drag and we sprint past Etter's, only to find ourselves the target of a couple of long rifles. Bullets chase us from the roof, and no matter how hard we run, they keep smacking the dirt behind us. One catches Crawford in the knee. He goes down hard. Boss yanks him back up, but Crawford's in bad shape, dragging us to a pace that's sure to get us all killed. We ain't gonna make it to the river. We ain't even gonna make it outta town.

Boss turns, shouldering his way into a boarding house. A man appears on the staircase landing, lantern held out to see what the fuss's over. He's young—maybe a few years younger than me. I watch his eyes go big with fear as he reaches for his waist, only to remember he's in his night things and don't got a pistol belt with him. He grabbed a lantern 'stead of his piece.

Boss's arm snaps up and he fires. The poor fella drops like a lead weight. He starts screaming and hollering in pain, and I feel that sharp sting of regret, that agonizing guilt. He weren't even armed. What was he gonna do, throw the lantern at us? It weren't a fair fight, and I just stood and let it happen.

Boss don't shoot him again. There ain't time to waste, and the poor kid'll be dead soon enough. Because I'm as awful as the rumors say, I don't do the merciful thing and finish the guy. I just run after Boss.

The hallway is long and narrow, lined with doors. Boss plows into the last room so hard, the window shutters on the opposite wall rattle and flap. A gust of cool December air hits my cheeks. The bedsheets are strewn about, but the room's empty. Boss jerks his head at the window, giving me a silent order. I'm to check, see if there's someone waiting outside.

I tuck my knife away, creep nearer, and venture a peek. The window opens onto an alley filled with goods, but it appears quiet. A lucky break. I throw a boot 'gainst the window ledge and heave myself out. Just before I hit the street, I catch movement across the way. Light glints off a long barrel.

"Shooter!" I yell to the others, but it ain't much of a warning. The marksman opens fire from where he's crouched behind several barrels. The wood 'round me goes popping and splintering. I flatten onto the dirt street.

"Murphy!" Boss shouts, waving wildly while Crawford sends shotgun rounds 'cross the way. "Murphy, get the hell outta there!"

He joins Crawford in his assault on the gunman, and I run like hell. Well, more like scuttle on all fours, staying low as I can and moving away from the gunfight till my back hits a wall. Feeling blind in the moonlight, I realize it ain't a wall, but a low ledge, maybe for keeping all the goods organized and in place. I haul myself up and over.

I land on my stomach—hard enough that the air blows outta my lungs. I heave and cough, glancing back the way I came. Boss and the others ain't following. They're trapped in the boarding house, maybe cornered. I need to go back for them and . . . do what? I don't got my belt. I ain't got a pistol to fire. I'm a dead man. Just like them.

"One went that way!" a man shouts. "Toward the stage stop."

I push to my feet and run. There's indeed a stage stop just ahead, with a coach parked out front and four horses already harnessed. Which don't make a lick of sense. No one goes leaving horses harnessed through the night.

But there's a tinge of color to the sky. It ain't the middle of the night like I thought it were, but rather much closer to dawn. This could be the very coach the deputy meant to escort us to Prescott in. Maybe the lawman even had the notion to depart early.

Gunfire rings back the way I came. I ain't gonna live through the morning, let alone the next ten minutes if'n I wait for my crew. And if I try to circle back and meet 'em, I'm just gonna end up shot or back in custody, with a noose in my future.

But the coach . . .

I look at it again, not quite believing my luck. Its curtains are drawn tight. The driver's box empty. And the reins are just dangling there, waiting to be took.

I scramble into the seat. The steeds spring to life at

the snap of the reins, and the coach lurches forward. I keep cracking the lines, urging the horses on, ignoring the hollering and shouting and gunfire that seems to be right on my heels. A couple of shots get fired my way. My experience driving a plow for the Lloyds is all that keeps me in control of the cumbersome coach, and I miraculously make it to the next cross street without a bullet in my back. Yanking on the reins hard, I turn north. Something thuds behind me—parcels and baggage falling off the rear boot, maybe. An empty stretch of pale dirt waits ahead, the last of Wickenburg's buildings fly by me in a blur, and then the coach is bouncing over the rugged terrain of the desert beyond.

If'n the Rose Riders manage to get outta town, they'll push hard a few miles, then rest.

And I ain't with 'em.

I ain't got a single way to even know where they're at.

And right then it hits me, like a bullet to the chest: I don't want to find 'em, and I don't have to.

I'm free.

Free.

The word's like a spike, a hammer, an echoing blast.

I do the math. These coaches can cover a solid five miles an hour, more even, in good conditions, which is 'bout the same as we ride any distance in the saddle. But if I run the horses ragged, Prescott could be in my grasp by late in the day. It'll be the last place Boss goes. He's sure to avoid setting foot where he's due for trial. While they're seeing to injuries and formulating a plan, I can outride 'em. Ditch the coach a few miles from the capital. Walk in not as Reece Murphy, Rose Kid and murderer and scum of the earth, but as any damn name I choose.

I can start again.

Jesus Christ, I'm free.

Getting arrested . . . damn near hanging . . . It's the best thing that's ever happened to me.

I slap the reins hard, guiding the team north and keeping within eyeshot of the Hassayampa. I'll slow in a few hours, maybe even give the team a rest 'round noon. But for now I'm putting as much distance between me and Wickenburg as possible. I'm still the only soul who can identify the cowboy Boss is after, and I ain't daft enough to think he won't come for me if he spots me 'long the horizon. And somehow I know he's gonna make it outta Wickenburg alive. That devil could crawl from the deepest pits of Hell itself.

The dry desert earth goes racing by. I keep my sights on the rutted trail of coaches that've traveled before me and pray I don't bust a wheel.

CHAPTER TEN

REECE

Hours later, the sun's peaked in the sky, but the temperature don't seem to be getting much warmer. I been gaining elevation most of the day, and still I'm sweating in the driver's box. The horses've slowed, too, their breathing growing labored.

I consider unhitching the team and riding one of the horses into Prescott, but I ain't a good bareback rider —'specially not for any long duration—and mountains loom to the north. I've crossed 'em a few times on those occasions Boss wanted to focus on the Atlantic Pacific for a change. It were a long, trying ride, even in the saddle. I'll stick with the coach.

Ahead, the pines are bright and lightly snow-dusted. The colorful sight is almost blinding after spending the last six months riding between Yuma and Tucson 'long the Southern Pacific. I'd been starting to think the whole world were nothing but shades of dirt.

I gaze back at the way I came and freeze. There's a speck of red in the distance, tailing me. But no, that can't be right. Not with the bullet Crawford took to the knee.

I shake my head, press my hand to my temple. When I look again, I can't make out nothing. No red, and rightfully so. If Crawford *were* following, he'd have that red where it belongs: *lining* his jacket so that he blends into the dirt and shrub.

I scan for a plume of dust, anything suggesting motion. Nothing.

Maybe the heat's getting to me. I've seen my pa before on the scorching desert plains. In the worst of the summer heat I'd sometimes look over my shoulder and catch him riding after me, a rifle aimed at my back. One time, when we were making for Bisbee in mid-July, we came out of a dry, parched valley, and at a crest in the land I saw all four of the Lloyds hanging from a mesquite tree. They rippled in the heat. When I blinked, they vanished.

Then again, it's December, nowhere near hot enough for that kinda mind trick.

I reckon I need water, then. Food. I ain't had neither since the sorry excuse of a meal (a scrap of stale bread and a sip of water) that were brought to me at the Jail Tree 'round dinnertime.

The Hassayampa's started to flow a bit here, prolly on account of snowmelt. It's as good a place as any to give the horses a rest.

I draw rein and stumble from the driver's box. When I get to the riverbank, I all but crumble to my knees and gulp down a few handfuls of water. It's cool and glorious.

My stomach growls in protest. I need more than just water.

I'm a good shot with a pistol—Boss made sure of that over the years—but there ain't nothing to shoot at. Even if there were, I don't got a weapon on me besides the knife. I return to the coach and search it, just in case it were loaded up with any food for the journey. What I find ain't impressive. The roof is empty, and the rear boot holds only one chest, filled with a blanket, some maps, and what looks like extra gear for the horses were one of their harnesses or reins to bust while on the move. If'n there were any other provisions aboard, they're now on Wickenburg's streets. I flew outta there like a gunshot, and I heard things go bouncing free. Foolish, really, to think I could shake the Riders so easy *and* have provisions waiting for me on a silver platter.

I pull Boss's kerchief from my pocket. It's got my blood on it from last night, and it still smells like his jacket, which makes a shudder creep down my spine. I take my hat off and rake my hands through my hair, use the kerchief to wipe sweat from my brow. Then I tuck it away and grab the coach's door handle. It's a fool's wish to think a chest of food might rest on the seats the posse intended us Rose Riders to fill, but I gotta be thorough.

I yank open the door.

It swings toward me.

And I swear.

The coach ain't empty. There's a body on the tiny strip of floor between the two benches.

It's the girl from the train. Charlotte, the deputy had called her.

At first I think she's dead. There's blood in her matted hair and a bit more dried between her brow and ear. Her body's at a weird angle, too, head near me by the door, arm pinned under her own weight, and one leg still up on the bench seat. But then I see the shallow rise and fall of her chest.

She's unconscious.

The goddamn, no-good, nearly-got-me-killed devil is just unconscious.

A pretty Colt pistol rests beside her face.

I grab it. Press the barrel to her skull. My finger rests 'gainst the hammer, but I don't cock it, don't reach for the trigger.

I ain't a virtuous man. I've watched plenty of women die at Boss's boys' hands. But I ain't never done the deed myself, and Boss ain't ever forced me to. For whatever reason, he were content with me watching the horror and saving my bullets for men.

I look at the girl, then the pistol in my hand, then the girl again.

Cursing, I withdraw the weapon and stuff it in the back of my waistband. I can't do it. Not when I'm finally free of the Riders and able to choose my own path.

She musta been on the run, maybe scrambled into the carriage for a place to hide. She's dressed, but barefoot, which makes me recall the empty bedroom at the boarding house, how the shutters banged as we barged in. She coulda been staying in that very room, mighta ran for cover soon as she heard Boss's shot in the foyer. All them things I heard go bumping when fleeing prolly weren't trunks falling to the road. It were her taking a tumble, hitting her head. That she's been out this long is troublesome. Could be she's close to death. Or dying. I look at the Hassayampa and consider dragging her from the coach and leaving her 'long the riverbed. But she don't even got shoes on. I reckon leaving a woman to starve ain't any better than shooting one in the skull. Maybe it's worse. It wouldn't be a quick death, the starving.

"Goddammit," I say, smacking the bench in front of me. The girl don't so much as stir.

"Goddammit," I say again. I stand there staring at her a minute, then finally draw my knife. It's a bowie, near identical to one Boss carries, with a smooth wood handle and simple guard. He gave me this blade when I'd been riding with him a little over a year, as a sixteenth birthday present. He'd berate me for not using it to slit the girl's throat, but I'm calling the shots now.

I shove the tip of the blade through one of the coach's leather curtains and start shredding it into strips. When I got myself a dozen to work with, I pat Charlotte down for other weapons and search the carriage, finding nothing but a half-filled journal sitting on one of the benches. I bind her ankles together, same with her wrists. My blue bandanna ends up serving as a gag.

I don't know what the hell I'm gonna do with her. Maybe

she'll stay out till Prescott. Maybe I can dump her near a doc's or something and her fate won't rot my conscience. *My conscience. Ha!* It's a miracle I even got one anymore.

When she's good and secure, I hop down from the coach step. After making sure the door is also tethered tight, the leather threaded through its window and the adjoining one, then knotted tight 'gainst the wooden framework, I head for the Hassayampa.

I wander the banks till I find a hearty prickly pear cactus. The pear-shaped fruit is long since gone, but with an extra strip of leather curtain wrapped 'round my hands, I cut off a few of the flat disks and take to stripping 'em of their skin and sharp spines. The plant were prolly ripe for eating a month or two back, so it ain't the most delicious or filling of meals, but it quiets my stomach some. Crouched low 'long the bank, I gather and skin a few more disks, then wrap 'em in another strip of leather for later.

Charlotte's still lost to the world when I return to the coach.

You should kill her, son, Boss whispers in the back of my head. *Before she gets you caught and hung. Or before word leaks of where yer at and I come to get you.*

I climb into the driver's seat and coax the team north. I wonder how far I gotta ride before I can get the bossman outta my head.

I hear another voice whispering, but this time it's my own. *You won't never be free of him, Reece. He's already a part of you. Yer already too much like him to turn yer life 'round.*

CHAPTER ELEVEN

CHARLOTTE

I rock like a babe in a cradle, my head heavy, my thoughts foggy and slow.

Forcing my eyes open, I find the sloped stagecoach roof overhead, and I remember . . .

I'd been awake, dressing for the trip to Prescott while people on the street shouted about fire. The devils were free of that tree. Just as I suspected, the plan was going south. As I grabbed my stockings, there'd been a gunshot in the foyer. Jake screaming.

I lunged for Father's pistol and my journal on the nightstand, stockings and boots forgotten. Then I was scrambling out the window. One step on the freezing boards of the porch outside, and a splinter lodged in my heel. Four paces, and my toes were already numb with cold.

I stumbled onto the main street and collided with a man Father's age. "They're in the boarding house!" I told him. Smoke clogged my nostrils, and gunshots echoed in the night.

He simply turned me around and sent me back the way I'd come. "The street ain't safe. Go this way. I'll take care of 'em." He cranked the lever on his rifle and squatted behind a barrel opposite my room. I ran on. Past the window I'd just climbed from, beyond the boarding house, over a low brick wall, until I found myself face to face with a plum-colored coach.

Dirt exploded near my feet, a bullet barely missing me. I dove forward, throwing the door open and scrambling inside. With a yank, the door was shut. With a tear, the leather curtains drawn tight. Putting the barrel of Father's pistol to the curtain, I moved it aside to get a look at the alley. A figure prowled the roof, no longer concerned with me on account of gunfire back at the boarding house.

I scooted across the bench seat to the opposite side of the coach, peered out that window. The stage stop waited, quiet, no threats to be seen. But before I could make a run for it, someone scrambled into the driver's box, rocking the coach. As I lunged for the door, the team lurched to life. I barely managed to get an arm out to brace against the frame and steady myself.

"Hey!" I shouted, banging on the roof. "Wait a minute!"

The coach turned sharply, and I flew toward the near side. My head struck the wooden frame of the window, and that's when the world went blurry.

I'd blinked, groaned, my arm being pinned beneath me. Everything felt heavy and wrong, but the sway of the coach on its leather thorough braces had been so welcoming. It whispered me to sleep.

And now it has coaxed me back awake.

My mouth is parched, and fabric sticks to my tongue. A bandanna. I'm gagged. My hands are bound in my lap, strips of leather tied so tightly, my skin has turned red. I reach up, bringing my hands over my head, but I can't unfasten the gag. It's secured tightly, and my bound hands are useless, trembling against my will.

"Hey!" I shout. "Untie me! Let me out of here!" But the words are muffled with the gag, barely comprehensible, and the coach goes lumbering on, bucking and rocking over ruts in the trail. I lunge toward the window. The curtain has been shredded, the coolness of late-afternoon air blowing through. Outside, the terrain is rugged and steep—saguaro cacti and dry, low shrubs.

"Hey!" I try again.

No answer. No stall in the horses' pace.

It dawns on me that whoever tied me may have sent the horses running, content to let them drag me into the mountains and to my death.

I scream louder. Pound on the coach innards with my elbow. Kick at the door. I continue yelling and hammering as loud as I can manage. It's draining me fast, but a passing party might hear me, and I can't miss such an opportunity.

Without warning, the horses suddenly stop. Weight lifts from the driver's box, causing the carriage to sway. Someone has been driving this coach all along. With me inside it. Someone bound me and gagged me and left me in here unconscious. Bleeding. Freezing. Someone did this to me. Someone with nothing to lose. A wanted man. A Rose Rider.

I should have fired Father's pistol as soon as the stage-coach lurched to life in Wickenburg. I should have aimed it at the driver's box and fired until every last chamber emptied. I scramble for it now, searching the bench seats and floor, but the pistol is gone.

A shadow passes by the window. I lean onto my back, and as soon as the door begins to open, I use both bound feet to kick it as hard as I can muster. It goes flying out-ward, catching my captor in the jaw. He stumbles back, cursing.

"Son of a . . . !"

"Help!" I shout at the heavens, only it comes out *Halp* because of the gag. *Halp,* as I crawl for the door, then freeze as I find myself staring down the barrel of Father's pistol. The devil has his Colt.

"Shut up!" he screams. I look beyond the barrel, into the eyes of the Rose Kid. His tan skin is red with rage, or maybe just windburnt with cold—narrow eyes, raw cheeks, mouth in a snarl. "I coulda shot you already, but I didn't! You want me to change my mind?"

His empty eyes blaze with a fierceness I know shouldn't be tested. He's a fuse already lit, a fire already burning. He will pull that trigger if he needs to. He will shoot me dead.

The Rose Kid climbs onto the coach step, blocking out

the light, filling the whole doorway. He's twice my size. I scurry away, my back striking the far wall.

"Don't you dare touch me," I say through the gag.

But he reaches out anyway, hooks a finger behind the gag, and pulls it from my mouth.

As soon as the bandanna falls onto my chest, I spit at him. Or rather, I try to. My mouth is too dry to work up any saliva, but he still flinches in anticipation.

"Get away." I mean to sound sure of myself, but my voice wavers. I've suddenly become as small as a mouse, prey cornered. I shake against my will.

The Rose Kid pulls a clean bandanna from his back pocket and moves to wipe my face. Like he's the good guy. Like he isn't the soulless monster who killed an entire family. Who hung two women. Who murdered a seven-year-old boy.

When his hand comes within range, I do all I can think of to keep him away—I snap at his fingers like a dog.

"Fine!" the Rose Kid snaps, snatching his hand back. "Ride with blood all over yerself. It don't matter to me." He steps from the coach without securing the gag. It hangs beneath my chin.

"Let me go!"

"I can't," he says.

"We're in the middle of the desert. I'm unarmed. I can't turn the Law on you. Just leave me and ride off."

"No."

I look at Father's Colt, stuffed into the waistband of the Rose Kid's pants. Like he owns it. Like it was always his. I think of my suitcase left behind in the Wickenburg boarding house. My pearl earrings and lined gloves and winter jacket. All things Father touched, all pieces of him, gone. And now his Colt, also lost to me. In the hands of this varmint.

"I want my pistol back," I say, staring at the piece.

The Rose Kid grunts out a laugh. "So you can shoot me with it? Nohow."

"Empty the chambers if you have to, but it's not yours."

"It's with me and staying there."

"Bastard."

"I been called far worse, miss," he says. "That ain't gonna make me give it back." And with that, he slams the door in my face.

CHAPTER TWELVE

REECE

I don't tell her it's true. That I'm a bastard born to a whore.

She weren't a whore when I were born, but she weren't married to Pa neither, and those very early years—the ones I were too young to remember—weren't half bad, according to Ma. It was when Pa turned to loving whiskey more than family that things got messy. Ma left with me in tow. She did all she could to keep a roof over our heads, and in the end, that meant being a painted dove.

I got a few fuzzy memories from the parlor house—learning to read and write in her drafty room, haircuts at the dry sink, sleeping curled up against her on a thin mattress. They're dreary moments to recall now, but I don't remember thinking 'em shameful or unfortunate back then.

Pa came for us one day, claiming a parlor were no place

to raise a child. He proposed a marriage, and Ma rejected him. He hadn't had the decency to marry her when he got her pregnant, and I reckon she simply saw the monster he was long before I ever did. She prolly figured a life of her own choosing were better than a life indebted to a man who were only gonna drink his weight in whiskey and throw fists into anything nearby. Problem was, the parlor owner weren't too keen on keeping children under his roof, and I'd outstayed my welcome. He tore me outta Ma's hands and sent me home with my father.

I were forbidden to see her, growing up. But I was allowed to write.

On the night I ran for La Paz, I went to the parlor first. I requested a room with my mother, slapped the coin down just so she could put a grown face to the signature I scrawled on so many letters. I told her I intended to come back once I had some money to my name. I'd give her as much as she needed, do whatever it took so she didn't have to live like this no more.

I ain't never forgotten her response. She was wearing some threadbare gown, shawl over her shoulders, hair half up while the rest tumbled down in an effort to hide a black eye. She looked me square in the face and said, "Nice to see you, Reece, baby. But you listen here: I don't need saving. I can take care of myself fine. Now go wherever yer getting, and fast, 'cus yer keeping me from earning good coin."

And look where I gotten to. Look at who I've become.

I pray she ain't never recognized my face on them wanted posters. She prolly always expected to be disappointed by me. I'm my father's son. I weren't never gonna make her proud. Hell, I'm the reason she still ain't safe. Boss's been holding her over my head since the first and only time I tried to run, threatening her life in exchange for my cooperation. It's why I ain't never run again till now, when I knew I could for sure get away.

"You'll hang for this," Charlotte says while I secure the door with the leather strip.

"I were already gonna hang. Now you want outta this coach? Sit there silent, or so help me . . ."

I leave it at that. I need her to believe that I'm capable of pointing her pistol at her chest and squeezing the trigger. Her fear will keep her quiet, and only that will keep me alive.

I climb into the driver's seat. With a flick of the reins, the horses lumber on, continuing the ascent into the mountains. The air's getting chilly, whisking the sweat from my skin and biting at my fingers. But at least Charlotte ain't screeching no more. In fact, she's so hushed, it's almost like she ain't even in there. Which makes me wonder if she's crying.

I squint at the trail ahead and tell myself I don't care.

Late in the afternoon the horses start lagging something serious.

I let 'em have a drink of water from my hat when we stopped 'long the Hassayampa, but it ain't just thirst slowing 'em now. We've gone some forty miles. That's 'round three times what they're used to. Stagecoach teams're changed often in order to keep the pace steady. I know it well 'cus some of the boys still talk 'bout the days they worked those lines, how they had to strike between switch stations.

Still, I keep the team going, their heads drooping low, and when the sky begins to darken, Prescott's within my grasp. I reckon it ain't but another ten miles or so, but I'm gonna have to camp in the mountains.

The Indian Wars raged through these parts till just recently, making the land a risk. Warrior tribes combing the mountains and the chance of military troops waiting 'round every bend. But just this summer, when Boss had us targeting the Southern Pacific, the mighty Geronimo surrendered. It were front-page news, big enough to make Diaz stifle his pride and ask me to read the story aloud. But even without the threat of Apache or military men, I ain't fond of quitting here. Coaches don't stop on the trail. They ride through the night and switch out horses at stage stops and get right back to driving. If'n anyone's to come this way, I ain't gonna look nothing but suspicious.

Still, waiting out the night sounds better than riding into Prescott now. It won't matter the threats I give or how tightly I secure the gag—so long as Charlotte is conscious when we ride in, I know she ain't gonna stay quiet. She'll scream her head off, wake even the heaviest sleeper. Plus, if my eyes ain't deceiving me, something's happening on the north side of town. Lanterns wink and bounce. Metal clangs and chimes.

Whatever the occasion, there's folk alert and mingling. They'll notice a coach entering Prescott—especially one that ain't running on a stage schedule and don't stop at the depot, neither.

I'll take my chances in daylight. There'll be more people coming and going, doing business. Might even be best to ride in alone. Leave Charlotte here. She could make the walk in all right, even barefoot. Course, then she might run right to the Law. I don't want to repeat Wickenburg all over again.

What the devil are you doing, son? Boss says. *She's gonna get you caught no matter how or when you enter town. Kill her and make a real run for it, or come home before I'm forced to come after you.*

I shiver and pull my jacket tight. I don't got gloves or nothing for my hands. There's my hat, at least, broad-brimmed and made of dark felt, with a high crown and Montana pinch. It's a beauty, but it ain't gonna do much in the fight 'gainst this cold desert night. The bandanna I usually wear high beneath my chin is still hanging beneath Charlotte's. I'm now wearing the extra from Boss —the one I tried to use to clean Charlotte up a bit. Her lip had split and I'd only wanted to scrub the dried blood from her mouth and chin.

She were so scared of me. I know that's a good thing, that it's what's keeping her compliant, but I hate it. The way she stared at me with such despisal and how her bound hands went clutching at the hem of her dress.

It made the Lloyd farm flash before my eyes. Bonnie, a year older than me, doing the same on the porch as

Crawford chased after her, laughing. I'd screamed for her to run, tried to push 'gainst Diaz, who were dragging me off the stoop, but I were just a scrawny kid then. No muscle or mass. I heard her the whole time Boss took his knife to my forearm. I still hear her, sometimes, in my sleep.

High-strung and jittery, I throw open the trunk on the coach's boot and pull out the blanket. 'Cus I'm curious and can't stand her silence no more, I peek at Charlotte through the slits in the carriage's shredded curtains. She's sitting on the bench, knotting strips of cloth together. It takes me a minute to realize they're torn from the hem of her undergarments.

"What'n the hell are you doing?"

Her gaze jerks up, and she tries to hide the bindings behind her back like I ain't already seen them. "Nothing!" she insists.

I move away from the window like I'm satisfied, but when I hear her return to her work, I peer through the window again. She's holding the cloth in front of her chin, sizing up its length.

There's a coldness to her expression, a vicious angle to her brows. It don't matter that her wrists are still tied or that I got the gun or that there's no way she'll be able to overpower me. I know what she's doing. She's making a rope that she aims to loop over my head and beneath my chin first chance she gets, pulling back as hard as she can muster.

I shoulda tied her damn hands behind her back.

She tightens another knot, unaware that I'm still

watching. I could haul open the door and snatch the cloth away. I could shred it to pieces before her eyes. I could do so many things, but I do nothing. She can go on sinking her hope into something impossible 'cus it's keeping her quiet. And right now, I need her quiet.

I climb back into my seat and eat a bit of prickly pear with the blanket draped over my shoulders, thinking 'bout how Charlotte's gonna get me caught. Or killed. Or leaking a trail plain enough for Boss and the others to come and get me. And then—for my ma's sake as much as my own—I'll have to cook up some story 'bout why I were racing north 'stead of trying to find 'em. So long as I'm alive, Luther Rose ain't gonna let me ride off into the sunset. Not till I've pointed a finger at that cowboy and Boss can hound some new bastard 'bout his brother's fate, working his way toward whoever done killed him.

Or *whatever* killed him.

Diaz claims it were a ghost.

I'd nearly laughed when he first told me such. We'd been at a saloon in Contention, celebrating a recent heist. I figured Diaz'd had one too many drinks, that his details weren't straight, but he swore it. Hobbs chimed in too, explaining that 'bout a decade back, Waylan Rose sent Boss and half the gang west to scout out the Southern Pacific's setup in Yuma. Trains were just starting to creep into the Territory back then, and Waylan knew it could serve the gang well. But while Luther were studying the rails, Waylan went chasing gold in the cursed depths of the Superstition Mountains, where him and his men got outmatched.

When his brother missed the rendezvous, Boss spent months chasing empty leads 'round Phoenix, then hit every hideout the gang had ever used—from a mountain pass up in southern Utah to the cabin in New Mexico where the gang originally formed. It weren't till nearly a year later that he returned to robbing and pillaging 'long the rails. It's all we been doing so long as I've been riding with 'em, and no one mentions Waylan's name if'n they can help it. No one mentions the coin neither, 'cept for Boss himself. He told me it were his brother's good-luck charm, that it never left his saddlebags. The cowboy done gave it to me either killed Waylan and took the coin as a prize or the coin's trail through owners will lead Boss to his brother's killer.

I used to think that only that coin would lead me to freedom, but if I play my cards right, if I run fast enough, I can cut free now.

After letting the horses graze a little, I hitch 'em up for the night. While climbing into the driver's box, I spot a fire in the distance, sparking and dancing, plus a flash of color. My heart kicks. It's that red coat again. I ain't been imagining it. The only reason I can think the lining's still facing out is 'cus Crawford don't know I'm running. He's likely trying to signal to me. *Hey Murphy, hold tight. It's just me, Crawford. See my coat? I ain't the Law. Slow up, partner.*

Like hell. Once the horses have a decent rest, I'm cracking the reins.

I settle in to sleep, but it ain't the restful kind. Sometime in the deepest part of the evening I wake outta discomfort. My left leg's fallen asleep and my neck's gone stiff, so I climb from the box to stretch. The fire ain't in the distance no more—it's gone out or been purposely smothered. The desert is quiet as can be, 'cept for Charlotte's fierce shivering.

When I peer into the coach, I find her curled up between the benches, her eyes pinched shut in a vain attempt to find sleep while her teeth knock. Each exhale leaves her lips as a visible puff of air.

"Hey," I say at a whisper.

She curls away from me, hugging herself tight.

I should let her freeze to death. It would make everything simpler.

Do it, Boss tells me.

And 'cus he says to, I don't.

I shrug outta my coat and shove it through the window, drop my last bit of prickly pear—my breakfast—on the bench, too. Then I return to the driver's box and hunker down beneath the wool blanket.

Charlotte's teeth go on chattering another minute or so. Then there's some shuffling and the sound of her eating like a heathen.

Last thing I wanted were to hang, and now here I am, actively keeping alive the thing that's sure to deliver my neck straight to a noose. I must be the world's worst outlaw or the Territory's biggest fool. Prolly both.

CHAPTER THIRTEEN

CHARLOTTE

The year of our Lord 1887 begins with a brilliant sunrise, a sharp bite to the air, and a stabbing in my side. Having slept at an awkward angle, one of my stays has popped through its lining and is now digging into my flesh. The pain is excruciating. I can feel the moisture just below my right breast, a warmth that is surely blood. The rest of my body is cramped with cold despite having the Rose Kid's jacket draped over my shoulders. I don't know why he gave it to me, why he hasn't shot me dead or left me along the side of the trail to rot.

I wiggle my fingers, trying to get feeling back into them, and my bladder tightens with every jolt of the coach.

"I need to use the necessary," I call out the window.

"Go in the coach," he says back.

"I'm not an animal."

"And I ain't a magician. There's no *necessary* for miles."

He's kept me alive, fed me, given me his coat. And yet he won't grant me the decency of relieving myself outside my cage.

"I can't feel my fingers or toes, and I'm also bleeding from my stays. I need to stand, lessen the pressure. *Please*."

To my surprise, the reins are tugged and the door yanked open. The Rose Kid snatches the undergarment rope I wasn't smart enough to hide from my lap, then grabs the leather at my wrists and pulls me forward. I spill from the carriage, the stay stabbing at me again, and his jacket falls from my shoulders. The Rose Kid unties my ankles before threading the makeshift rope between my bound wrists and tying it off tight.

"Come on," he says, tugging at the short leash.

My legs ache with relief. I haven't stood in more than a day, and it feels glorious. The pain in my side subsides too, the boning of the stays no longer prying as aggressively into my flesh while upright. I spin, taking in the desolate land, and my heart careens.

The frozen dirt trail we are following descends into Prescott.

The city is a familiar and beautiful sight, with its broad streets stretching around the central plaza. Since we moved to Yuma, the ponderosas in the plaza have been cut and a regal Victorian-style courthouse has been built. I can see its fine peak from here, bare elms at the edges of the fenced courtyard, and the businesses and homes lining the surrounding streets.

I don't know what the devil the Rose Kid expects to

find in the capital besides a jail cell or a noose, but the sight of the city wakes a flurry of hope in my chest. The rail gala is this morning, and if I can only get into town, everything will be fine. Mother will be there, and my cousin Paul. Even Uncle Gerald would be a fair sight given my circumstances.

"Behind that rock," the Rose Kid says, letting go of the leash. He jerks his chin at a crop of boulders beyond the rutted trail. "Go quick and then get yer ass back in the coach. I see you move a toe in a suspicious direction and I'll be forced to draw."

I do as he says, feeling his eyes on me as I move. The rock is not terribly large, but my bladder has reached a point where it's hard to care about decency. It's either this or soil the only bit of clothing I have.

When I'm through, I make my way back.

"Hurry up," he mutters as he gathers up the leash-rope.

"Just let me go!" I wail, struggling to keep his pace as he leads me toward the stagecoach. "I can walk into town. Just leave me here and run."

"Like you won't talk when you get there? Like you won't tell them I came through this way ahead of you. I can't have that. I can't have 'em knowing where I'm at."

He looks back at the trail when he says the last bit, not ahead. Almost as if he fears the Wickenburg lawmen more than those in Prescott.

His nose is raw and caked up, same as mine feels. Frozen moisture coats his stubbled jaw, and it glints in the early-morning light as he regards the trail we've already traveled. Maybe someone *is* chasing him. Deputy Montgomery, perhaps.

The Rose Kid plucks his coat from the dirt, shrugs it back on. "Can you ride bareback?"

"I've never tried."

"Then that's a no," he says, and I immediately regret my honesty. Had he been offering to unhitch the team and give me a steed?

"I can manage. I'll figure it out," I insist.

"Figuring it out ain't gonna result in a fast ride, Charlotte."

I freeze. He knows my name, likely overheard Deputy Montgomery saying it.

"Don't call me that."

"Call you what?"

"By my name."

"What am I supposed to call you?" he scoffs. "Miss Vaughn?"

"Call me nothing. Or call me *miss,* for all I care. Just don't act as though you know me, or as if you're not using me for your own means."

His eyes flash. "Listen, things would be a hell of a lot easier if you hadn't picked this damn coach as yer hiding place. But it is what it is, and now we're both in a bad place."

"*We're* in a bad place? I'm the one held hostage."

"I ain't got time for this, Char—Vaughn. We gotta keep moving."

"No, *you* have to keep moving. I'll stay right here, thank

you very much. Tie me to a tree." I tug at the ropes, walking for the nearest stubby shrub. "You can get a good, long lead and I can't run to alert anyone. I'll hitch a ride with whomever you're running from when they pass through."

"I can't do that."

"Why the blazes not?" I can hear my voice going high and panicked, feel the tears coming on. I'm being more than fair. There's no reason why he can't leave me. None. The first tear breaks free, smacks the frozen ground near my feet.

"Dammit, don't cry. Just . . . Come on, get in the coach."

"Just *leave me!*"

I'm sobbing now, completely against my will, everything that's transpired in the past two days catching up to me.

"I can't leave you 'cus it's them coming. The Rose Riders."

He's running from his own people, and he almost sounds afraid of them. I can't help it; a small laugh escapes my lips. My amusement only angers him further.

"You see this scar?" the Rose Kid snaps, rolling up his right sleeve and showing me his forearm. Half of a rose is carved into his skin. "Luther Rose did that. I been his prisoner same way you've been mine. Sometimes folk use others 'cus they need to, not 'cus they want to."

"You expect me to believe that Luther Rose has been using you?" I stare him straight in his rotten eyes. "I don't know what game you're playing, but I've read about you, Reece Murphy. You worked as a farmhand to get close to that family. Then you relieved them of their fortune, hung them from the rafters of the barn they let you sleep in, and joined the Rose Riders because no one else would have you. The papers say you are more vicious than Billy the Kid, that you earned your nickname at just fifteen."

"It ain't true," he says.

"You're not known as the Rose Kid? You didn't join the most vicious gang in the Territory after the slaughter of the Lloyds in eighty-three? You haven't been robbing trains since?"

"The details ain't right, though," he insists. "What happened at the Lloyds'—I didn't do that. Boss and his men did."

"And yet you still ride with them."

"I don't!" he shouts. "I'm here, ain't I?"

"With a girl bound and often gagged. You've changed your ways so."

"You ain't dead!"

"No," I murmur. "But *you* will be. You won't get away with this."

I have no way to see through the threat, no way to get out of my bindings. But they feel right, those words. I mean them.

He yanks the rope, and I stumble forward, cringing as the frozen earth bites at my palms and the stays stab at my flesh. I wrap my fingers around a loose stone in the trail, and as I crawl to my feet, I keep the rock cupped tightly, hidden from view.

"I got my reasons for doing what I do," the Rose Kid snarls, his dead eyes locked with mine. "I don't care if'n you understand, 'cus right now, alls you gotta know is one of Boss's men is on my tail and he will gladly kill you before taking me back to Boss. I gotta run to where they'll never find me, and if they do, I'm gonna need a damn compelling reason for why I'd done run."

He grabs me by the meaty part of my arms, pushes me toward the coach. My legs hit the step and I walk up it backwards, falling on my rump inside the carriage because I refuse to expose the rock in exchange for bracing my fall.

"So unless you know who killed Luther's brother," the Rose Kid continues, towering in the doorway, "you are absolutely worthless to me. Be happy I'm bothering to keep you alive. It ain't a kindness the rest of Boss's men will allow."

There is sincere worry in his voice as he looks back the way we've traveled. I don't believe that he is innocent of his crimes. What sort of man rides with men like those in Rose's gang for more than three years if he doesn't truly want to be there? Madmen. Monsters. Fools who wear a brand like cattle because maybe they don't know how to think for themselves.

But I do believe that the Rose Kid is running from them, to whatever end. He has indeed kept me breathing when others may have killed me or left me to freeze in the mountains, but only because I will serve as his armor. I will be his shield—quite literally—if folk confront him in Prescott. He will use my life to barter for his.

And so I will use my words to barter for my own.

I've heard enough rumors about Waylan Rose's death

to fill a novel, read enough speculation about his men's demise ten years past to make up my own account. And if an old schoolyard rumor will buy my freedom, well, I don't care quite so much about the facts.

I won't be a journalist today, I'll be a writer of fiction. I'll deal in whispers and sensations and legends.

"I know who killed him!" I blurt out, and the Rose Kid freezes, a hand on the door he intends to swing shut. "I know who killed your boss's brother."

CHAPTER FOURTEEN

REECE

I catch the door at the last second, keeping it from slamming shut.

"You *what?*"

"I know who killed Waylan Rose."

I reckon I must look shocked as all can be, 'cus she keeps on yammering.

"I've read an awful lot of literature on the topic. I want to be a journalist, so I've devoured just about every newspaper I could get my hands on. And when Waylan died, everyone reported that the gang was disbanded, that the plains would be safer. When the first accounts of robberies at the hands of a man claiming to be Waylan's half brother reached the paper, everyone panicked. Father was convinced the gang was back in full force, that they'd challenge his rail project in Prescott. There wasn't a day I spent as a child not hearing him bemoan and worry that—"

"Just skip to the part 'bout who did it," I snap.

Charlotte—no, I'm calling her Vaughn now—ain't dumb. After her stunt on the train and how she got us pinched in Wickenburg, that much is certain. But this is exactly what's troubling. She's smart enough to try to con me, and I ain't got time to waste. Crawford's on my tail. He must not've been hurt as bad as I thought, 'cus when I got the coach moving before dawn, there it were again—that red coat, bobbing in the distance. He's gaining on me. And while I could prolly manage the rest of the descent into Prescott bareback, Vaughn can't, and I ain't 'bout to leave her to a fate at Crawford's hands.

"Well, it's more of a theory," she says.

"A theory? I don't care 'bout theories. I care 'bout facts."

She shrugs. "Then I'll just keep this to myself."

I glance the way we come, then toward Prescott. *Chasing a theory* is still gonna sound better to Boss than *running*.

"Fine, what is it? Quickly."

"There was a Prescott homesteader who supposedly got himself killed by the Rose Riders. His daughter hired a gunslinger to get justice."

"What's the gunslinger's name?"

"I don't know. No one does."

It's all too convenient, another could-be and might-have, a trail like all the others Boss chased over the years. Chances are he's prolly even chased this one already.

"I was only six when this all happened," she continues, "but my father wasn't good at whispering when he discussed things with my mother. And his theories matched what some of the children said at school. You don't forget rumors like that."

"I think yer lying. About all of it."

"Suit yourself." She shrugs. "But it seems to me that a man seeking the truth would follow a lead to its end. What harm can it do to find the daughter and ask her yourself? The gunslinger she hired is the man your boss wants."

Goddammit, she's right. On the off chance she's telling the truth, well, I'd be a fool to keep running. I could get the gunslinger's name or, better yet, *him*. He could live right in town. I could have the prize in my grasp when Crawford catches me. My fleeing won't look suspicious if'n I have the killer. It'll look brave, daring, loyal. I do this one final job, and then I'll be free, truly. 'Cus I know sure as hell, they ain't gonna quit coming for me.

"The girl who hired the gunslinger—what's her name?"

"Thompson?" Vaughn says, only it comes out a question.

"You think, or you know?"

"I'm pretty certain."

"Where's she live?"

"If I tell you, you have to let me go."

"Yeah, yeah. You tell me where I can find the girl, and I'll let you go, but only if you give yer word you won't go

94

running to the Law." I spit in my hand and hold it out. She stares at my palm. I can almost hear the gears churning in her head. Is making a deal with the Rose Kid smart? *No.* Is she putting the Thompson girl in danger even if all I'm after is the hired man? *Prolly.* When a Rose Rider touches yer life, even with the slightest brush, it only leads to bad things.

"Do we have a deal or don't we?"

"All right," she says finally. She spits in her palm, and we shake.

"So where's she live?"

"Lived," she corrects. "She lived on Granite Creek, first homestead past Fort Whipple, big mesquite out front."

"*Lived!* You saying she's dead?"

"No. She moved, barely a month before we left for Yuma. Father said she was headed for Wickenburg."

I slam the coach door shut, fastening it in place.

"What are you doing?" Vaughn shouts. "We had a deal! You said I could go. "

"Yeah, but I never specified where or when. A ride to Wickenburg'll kill these poor horses, and besides, I think yer lying. I think you intend to alert folk in Prescott, and then I'll be caught between the capital and Wickenburg, lawmen bearing down on me from both directions."

Plus, heading directly into Crawford's arms, which ain't where I'm fond of being.

Vaughn appears at the window, color draining from her cheeks. "But you gave your word."

"And I'll honor it if *yer* word proves true. Yer either ly- ing, meaning you've already broken our deal and I don't got to do nothing, *or* you sit there quiet and patient while I ride into town and confirm yer story, and I'll let you go after that. Now, what's the Thompson girl's first name?"

"Funny," she says, "but I don't feel all that inclined to help you further. Perhaps you should have asked that before shutting me back in my cage."

"What's her name, Charlotte?"

"Don't call me that."

"What's her goddamn name?"

Silence.

I stare at the patterns painted on the stagecoach door. I consider kicking it and slapping it and cursing at the heavens, but there ain't time for tantrums. I climb back into the driver's box and, once again, flick the reins.

The horses wind outta the mountains, listless and weary.

Even from a distance, the city is bustling, perhaps on account of the new year. Folk on foot are congregating on a street running 'long the east side of the courtyard plaza. There's folk on horseback too, and in carriages. I swear I can make out uniforms, and the muzzles of long rifles glinting in the sun. The pounding of drums and the pomp of trumpets reaches me, even at a distance.

Whatever's happening, it's the perfect cover.

Word of the gang's escape from Wickenburg prolly ain't made it here yet, and with all the fanfare, no one's gonna notice one extra stagecoach rolling into town, not even one operating off the schedules and running a team that looks damn near beat.

Vaughn don't make a peep as we roll in. Maybe she were being honest after all and knows if she just stays quiet a bit longer, I'll be setting her loose. I turn a corner, staying a block west of the commotion so I can find a good spot to ditch the coach and carry on alone. A pair of young boys dart 'cross the street, startling the horses and nearly getting themselves trampled.

"Sorry, mister!" one of the kids shouts.

"Hold up!" I say, stopping the team. "What's the commotion for?"

"Don't you know? It's the Prescott and Arizona Central! It's finally here."

"They finished last night," his friend says, "and are gonna lay the final tie today, then drive the last spike while everyone's watching. Yer gonna miss the procession."

They race for a cross street.

"Hang on. You boys know the Thompson residence? Long Granite Creek?"

They look at each other and shake their heads. "No, sorry, mister. Don't know any—"

The door to the coach bursts open with a kick from Vaughn. She stumbles out, hands still bound, and hurls something my way. I duck instinctively, and a rock strikes my shoulder—jagged and sharp. Prolly she used it to saw at the leather strip on the door till it were frayed enough that a good kick sent it ripping. She goes tearing up the street, the undergarment rope trailing behind her like a stringy veil.

The two boys stare.

"My sister," I explain, cursing myself for not resecuring her ankles after letting her pee. "She ain't right in the head."

The boys shrug, seeming to buy it.

And that's when Vaughn decides to start shouting. "Help! It's the Rose Kid—Reece Murphy! The Rose Kid's in town!"

CHAPTER FIFTEEN

CHARLOTTE

I expect him to put a bullet in my back, but it never comes. I keep running as fast as my legs will carry me.

Over on Cortez Street, the procession has started, led by a band trumpeting out a fanfare. Loud, boisterous cheering joins in and happy salutes are fired, drowning out my cries for help. The crowd moves north, heading for the depot.

Glancing over my shoulder, I find the Rose Kid has urged the horses to action. They're tired, but they'll catch me. I cannot outrun a team of horses, even drained ones. I reach the southwest edge of the plaza and turn right, sprinting for the procession. I pause only to loop my hands over a picket of the plaza's iron fence, using the point as a wedge against my leather bindings. They've been secured with a simple square knot, not unlike the bow one puts in a shoelace, and once I push the picket point between the two crossed sections of leather and pull back, the knot gives. I wriggle my wrists back and forth, and then the binding falls away, the undergarment rope trailing with it.

I'm free.

I race on, the stays digging into my flesh with every stride.

"Help me," I gasp as I burst onto Cortez and enter the throng of citizens. "The Rose Kid. He's here. He's going to kill me."

I'm passed along like a leaf caught in a current, bumping from shoulder to shoulder as the happy townsfolk move north with the procession. My begging is but a whisper compared with the merry band and cheering. What appears to be a small militia of uniformed men from Fort Whipple fires off salutes, and I become just another boisterous face in the sea of winter jackets.

Desperate, I push through the crowd and stumble into the street, where a string of carriages bring up the rear of the parade. Men grin from drivers' seats, and townsfolk wave from the windows.

"Charlotte!" a voice snaps. "What in the blazes are you doing?"

I twist toward the voice, and there she is. Mother, sitting in one of the final carriages, her eyes wide with astonishment. She signals for Uncle Gerald's son, my cousin Paul, to slow the carriage. When the wheels creak to a halt, she throws open the door.

"Get in."

"Mother, listen. The Rose Kid. He's here. I need to find the sheriff and—"

"Charlotte Vaughn, get in the carriage this instant."

I glance toward the courthouse. The coach and the Kid are nowhere to be seen. Perhaps he gave up his pursuit in favor of running. The entire procession is focused on the depot at the end of Cortez, and he will likely be able to slip through town unnoticed.

I scramble into the warmth of Mother's carriage.

She stuffs her hand back in her muff and fixes her gaze on me firmly through the black veil that hangs over her eyes. Her hair is pinned back severely, her mourning obvious from head to toe: black wool dress, black winter cape, black boots. She does not have to say a single word for me to know she is furious.

"I'm so sorry, Mama. I know you told me to stay home, but I thought that if I secured a job with Mr. Marion's press, with *any* press, maybe I wouldn't be a hindrance and Uncle wouldn't be able to use me to pressure you into marriage. But then the train was robbed, and I—"

"Robbed?"

"It was the R-Rose Riders," I stammer, everything crashing into me with a force I have not yet felt. "The Law captured half the men in Wickenburg, too. They had them, on account of me, and the devils still broke loose. And I was caught in the stagecoach, and the Rose Kid trapped me, and I couldn't get away until—I need to find the sheriff. I made a mistake, Mama. I made a deal for freedom and told a story that was based in fact, and now I worry that another innocent soul will be in danger."

I collapse into her lap, draw one quavering breath after the next as she gathers me in her arms.

I never should have used the Thompson name in my story. I should have made something up. But I'd feared the Rose Kid might consider my words a farce, as he did, and then where would I have been?

But now he'll find her.

Her father truly *was* hanged, but according to anyone who remembers the unfortunate affair, the Thompson girl claimed there was no rose symbol on his person. She went to stay with a family friend for a few weeks and then returned to continue caring for her homestead alone. That's it. It was the minds of curious schoolchildren who jumped to the Rose Riders, who thought stories of revenge and gunslingers sounded thrilling. But there's no proof to any of it. And she never moved to Wickenburg, as far as I'm aware. I made that part up. I tried to send the Rose Kid where I knew he'd be trapped, and he didn't take the bait.

"Charlotte." Mother brushes tears from my cheeks. "Are you hurt?"

I look up at her. There is a sheen of water in her eyes. She's finally noticed that I'm without shoes and is staring at my bare feet.

Am I hurt? I am sore and cold and tired and hungry, and my chest throbs from the loose stay, but I know this is not the type of hurt she is implying. I shake my head.

"Good, good," she murmurs, patting the back of my hand.

"How did things go with Uncle?" I ask when I've composed myself.

"About as well as I thought they would. We discussed the will over a private dinner last night, and he was furious to learn he was left nothing. He took my purse and has had me under lock and key since. Paul's been assisting. As far as the boy's aware, I'm trying to keep his father from his fair share of the mine."

"He's despicable. Aunt Martha is surely tossing in her grave."

"She married your uncle for money, and now he's trying to force a marriage with me for the same reason. I can't say she'd judge him too harshly."

The carriage jostles to a halt. We've arrived at the depot. The crowd cheers and whistles outside, calling for the driving of the last spike.

"Let me slip out," I offer. "I'll find the sheriff, a lawyer —anyone who can help."

She shakes her head. "Everyone is preoccupied with the celebration, and sadly, Paul would drag you back to the carriage before you were within spitting range of a deputy." She leans in, so close the coarse fiber of her veil tickles my nose. "But I saw Mr. Douglas while we waited for the procession to start. Do you remember him? He was a good friend of your father's, an attorney. I asked him to stop by after the ceremony, help explain the will to Gerald. If we are patient, if we do not act rashly, this will all be over by late afternoon."

I marvel at her strength. How her chin is held high, how her voice does not quaver or tremble. Despite all that has befallen her, how our world has spilled its innards in the span of a few days, there is not a seed of doubt in her expression.

I do not know when my mother became so fierce. Perhaps she has been this woman all along and I just never bothered to see it.

I watch the ceremony from the carriage, leaning out one window while Mother leans out the other. She's given me her cape, which I've draped over my knees like a blanket, fingers and toes curling into the heavy material.

Though it is only midmorning, I wouldn't be surprised if the temperature crawls to above sixty later in the day. I can feel the sun on my cheeks. Its warmth is blissful after the long, hard night spent in the Rose Kid's coach. I try to remind myself that even if he seeks out the Thompson residence, no one is likely to be at home while the gala is held, as all of Prescott and even the surrounding mining and ranching communities seem to have packed into the streets. I can alert authorities after the gala, or even have Mr. Douglas alert them if Uncle refuses to let me visit the sheriff's at the close of the celebration.

Raucous cheering pulls me from my thoughts. The mayor has hammered a gilded spike into place, and two locomotives are chugging onto the site—the *F. A. Tritle* and the *Pueblo,* whistles screaming and bells ringing.

The militia fires off what must be a hundred-rifle salute, maybe more.

The shots echo, skirting over the valley and into the mountains, bouncing off Thumb Butte, which throws the sound back to us on the streets. These mountains have long since looked down on the city of Prescott, a place of great promise, of bustling lives. For twenty years the townsfolk have been discussing the possibility of a railroad, and now the Prescott and Arizona Central has finally reached the capital. It may have been built on a shoestring, but the people of the city are bursting with pride.

The engines hiss to a halt. As children climb onto them, cheering and waving, the first speaker ascends the grandstand and hushes the crowd. "This is a happy day," he exclaims, "which connects us by rail to the outside world. We have just reason to feel proud of this occasion, and the advantage which it will confer should be duly appreciated." He is followed by men of all walks — bankers, donors, esteemed townsfolk of Prescott and beyond, the commander of Fort Whipple, and even the railroad director himself. They all prophesy the same great future. Today marks a great epoch in the progress of Arizona, the brightest era ever inaugurated. We stand at the dawn of greatness, destined for prosperity and growth.

How I wish Father could have seen this.

When the speakers are finally finished, the platform clears, but the crowd does not. Cheering and merry chatter continue, but they fade, then become almost illusional as a figure moves into the frame of the carriage window. He blocks out the sun, and though he is wearing a dapper jacket over a fine suit, a silk scarf knotted at his throat, and a Homburg hat atop his head, there is no mistaking that I am still a prisoner, still trapped in a cage.

"Charlotte, my dear niece," Uncle Gerald says, smiling wickedly. "So nice of you to join us."

CHAPTER SIXTEEN

REECE

When Vaughn runs for the crowded street and the noise of the procession, I know instantly it's a lost cause. Too many people, too many guns, too many lawmen, and a whole goddamn militia. I don't stand a chance at catching her in the crowd she's racing toward, nor do I fancy getting myself snatched when I'm so close to freedom. So I let her run. I weren't never gonna shoot her to begin with, and by the time she gets someone's attention, pulls them away from the ruckus, I aim to be long gone.

The hell with her story and the gunslinger that mighta killed Boss's brother. The hell with all of it. I'm flying north.

I tug the reins, keeping the team on the west side of the courthouse plaza and moving at a fair clip, not fast enough to draw attention, but not exactly dawdling neither. I stare up at the courthouse. Even from the rear, it's intimidating, towering over most of the surrounding businesses and structures. It's square in shape, built with bricks and a roofline that boasts a tall steeple with a clock face on each side. I squint as I look into the sun. More than half past ten. The edges of the plaza are fenced off, and there's ample space for sprawling and strolling, plenty of room for townfolk to come and watch men like myself hang when we're found guilty of our crimes.

I'd be in that building right now if it weren't for Crawford springing me free. Crawford saved my hide, and now I'm running from him. It's easy to feel I owe the gang something when I ain't with 'em. When I don't got their dark deeds unfolding before my eyes. When I ain't subject to Boss's deceptions and threats.

Stop running, Murphy, I hear him say. *Come back, son. We're missing you.*

I do stop, but only to unhitch the team. Putting a palm to their flanks, I find the horse that's breathing easiest, then use the stagecoach wheel as a leg up so I can mount the steed. With a quick nudge of my heels, we're moving again.

A block east, the masses are crammed before a grandstand at the depot. Two trains come chugging in, pulled by screaming engines, and the crowd goes wild. Rifles salute. The whole valley seems to echo, and I thank the heavens for this tiny stroke of luck, 'cus no one looks my way as I pass by.

It don't take more than a few miles for me to realize I've made a mistake.

I ain't had nothing to eat since the prickly pear, and my stomach's grumbling something fierce, plus my throat's gone scratchy on account of not drinking much neither. Worse still, I'm so tired I can barely keep my balance on the steed. My thighs burn from the effort.

I ain't sure who's more beat—me or the horse.

I shoulda stolen a mare in town, stolen a bite to eat, too, but I were too fearful Vaughn's shouting might put men on my tail.

This is why I'm a burden, a hindrance, a heel. This is why I ain't a boss like Luther Rose.

The street that left the city has since turned into little more than a dusty trail cutting 'longside the creek. As I crest a small rise, the horse's head hanging low, a homestead comes into view. Plain house, barn set nearby, massive mesquite growing out front. I think it's the first since passing Fort Whipple, which means it matches Vaughn's story.

Take a peek, Murphy, Boss whispers in my ear. *What harm'll it do if'n this residence ain't that of the girl? At the very least, go steal yerself a strong mare from the barn and some bread from the kitchen, then move on. And if'n it's the right place . . . if'n she knows who killed my brother . . .*

I guide the horse from the trail and dismount. Walking slow, I approach the house. No one blows me to pieces. Nor does anyone come running when I put a toe to the door and push.

It swings in, creaking.

I draw Vaughn's Colt from my waistband and step over the threshold. There's hooks for coats immediately to the left, and some shelves holding books and photo albums. Opposite that is a modest kitchen, and straight ahead, two doors. I find a bedroom behind each, a half-finished cradle and wood shavings on the floor of the smaller. The whole place has fancy pine floorboards, but the kitchen hearth looks twice as weathered as the walls surrounding it. Coals from a morning fire are still putting off a bit of heat. I go 'bout scouring the cabinets, and sweet Lord, there's bread in the breadbox. I scoff some down like a heathen, find a pitcher half full with water. I drink feverishly, then roll up my sleeves and wash in the dry sink. When I'm somewhat clean and starting to feel a little ill from how quickly I ate, I glance out the front window. It opens onto a nice view of the creek and the plains, the newly laid rail a dark scar as it cuts south into Prescott. The happy rifle salutes must be over, 'cus the world is hushed. If'n I listen real hard, I think I can catch a bit of cheering, but it prolly ain't nothing but the wind.

It's almost eerie, how quiet it is here. I ain't that far from the city, but I'm very much alone.

Solitude, freedom—it's what I wanted since steering the coach outta Wickenburg, and now it suddenly feels like a curse. I need to keep things this way, but every single person I cross could be a threat—a bounty hunter, a rival. I don't know if I'm gonna be able to trust no one, least not for a few good years.

I wanna be Reece Murphy again. I wanna use my real name and have that be all right, but those cards ain't in my future. Reece Murphy *is* the Rose Kid. They're one and the same. I'm as vicious and unforgiving as Luther Rose, and at only half his age. That's the person the world has made me.

I told you yer making a mistake, son. Now come back to where you belong. I got yer horse waiting.

"Goddammit," I mutter, turning from the window. I pace the small kitchen for a few seconds, minutes, hours. I lose track of time trying to think up a plan. When I come outta a daze, none the wiser on where I should be heading, I find myself facing the wall of books. There's more of 'em than I've ever seen in one home before—several shelves' full. I run a finger over the spines. *Little Women, The Adventures of Huckleberry Finn, Moby-Dick, Around the World in Eighty Days, Pride and Prejudice* . . .

I freeze at the end of the row. Stare.

A wedding photograph is on display within a simple wooden frame. The folks who own this claim, prolly. The man's wearing a pair of Remingtons slung low on his hips, plus a fine suit and tie. He's got an arm 'round his woman, and he ain't on a horse or flicking me a coin, but there's no mistaking him. It's the cowboy. The very same who gave me that blasted coin. The stranger I ain't never been able to point out to Boss. Three years on the plains, in and out of every town under the sun, and here he is in this commonplace farmhouse, staring back at me from a wedding photo.

There's a creak on the stoop.

I spin. The woman from the picture is standing in the doorway, a Winchester rifle aimed at my head. Her dark eyes glare, focused on my face, then suddenly shine with recognition. She knows who I am. The dog at her heel —gray-muzzled and ancient—bares his teeth and snarls.

"You so much as blink too fast," the woman says, sharpening her aim, "and I will put a bullet between yer eyes."

I don't know if she's heard of the Rose Riders' escape from Wickenburg or if Vaughn managed to alert folk at the railroad gala. But I do know this: the lady with the rifle has recognized me, and if I don't wanna die, I'm gonna have to shoot a woman after all. Maybe I can get her in the leg or something—spare her the worst but buy myself a window to run.

It won't be an easy draw, not like pulling a piece from a holster. The Colt's tucked away in my waistband, and she's already got that rifle pointed at me, the butt of it pressed into her shoulder, the barrel aimed at my chest.

And then—right as I'm seriously considering snatching the Colt and trying my luck anyhow—I see her belly. It's big, bulging, full of life.

Goddammit, I can't do it. I don't got it in me. I think I really would rather die than draw on her.

"Yer kind deserves to rot in hell," she says, glaring at me fierce.

"You gonna be the one to send me there?" I half pray she does. Maybe it'd be better for this to all be over. To just quit running. To close my eyes and not have to live like this no more.

"What'n the hell is that?" She jerks her chin at my forearm. The rose scar's sitting there pretty, all clean of dirt and sweat from when I washed in her dry sink.

"You won't believe me," I say. "No one ever does."

Something flickers over her face—sympathy, maybe. But it's there and gone so fast, I'm certain I imagined it. Especially when she unloads a shot.

I flinch, but the lead flies past me, splintering the door of the bedroom to my rear.

She missed, but she coulda hit true. She's only standing a few feet away. I twist back toward her, and that's when the butt of her rifle comes flying at my face. There's a crack—my nose breaking—and the world goes dark.

CHAPTER SEVENTEEN

CHARLOTTE

I inform Uncle Gerald about the Rose Kid and my need to speak with the sheriff, but he is woefully unconcerned about a bloodthirsty criminal roaming Prescott's streets.

"I'd think something like that would be all over the wire," he says, "and we have pressing business to see to at the house."

Of course, lining his own pockets is more important to him than the well-being of the community.

We make haste for the family residence. It is an older property, built before the Victorian style of construction swept through Prescott—or rather, it *was*. When we pull up to the plot, the childhood home I remember is gone, replaced with a regal building that does not appear more than a few years old.

"What happened to—"

"Your uncle had it rebuilt," Mother supplies. "He said the place was drafty and dank, and if he was to oversee your father's affairs, he ought to do it from a proper headquarters."

"But Father spent nearly every night at the mine. There's no need for posh headquarters here."

Mother simply nods in agreement. It's only a half day's ride in the saddle to Jerome, the mining community that's home to the Gulch Mine and a few others. What Uncle Gerald is doing is preposterous. How he expects to maintain a rapport with the copper miners when he spends most of his time in Prescott escapes me. Theft and high grading stem from overworked and underappreciated miners, and Father at least recognized this.

"This must have cost a fortune," I say, peering at the steeply pitched roofline of the two-story house adorned with detailed trim work and bracketed eaves. A front porch with intricate spindles and columns frames a large bay window that overlooks the street. The only thing Uncle has saved is our old barn, which stands behind the new home looking dreary by comparison.

"Yes, Gerald certainly spends beyond his means," Mother says bitterly.

The door to the carriage opens, and Uncle Gerald escorts us inside. We are quickly ushered through the foyer, past the sitting room, and into the study. A fire is blazing in the hearth, and the curtains are drawn, so the room is quilted in shadow. Uncle's writing desk is littered with papers and ledgers, his glasses resting atop both.

Mother and I are instructed to sit in upholstered velvet

chairs facing the desk. I've no sooner leaned into the backrest when a knock sounds at the door and Mr. Douglas enters.

"Ah, Barty, thank you for joining us," Uncle says.

"Mr. Douglas," I blurt out, "I need to speak with the sheriff. It's of upmost importance that he knows—"

"Priorities first," Uncle barks out, shuffling through the papers on his desk until he finds what he's looking for and plucks it free. "The will," he says, passing it to Mr. Douglas, who reads it over carefully—once, twice—then turns to Uncle.

"It seems all is in order. A pen, Gerald?"

Uncle supplies one. Mr. Douglas signs the document. And the men shake.

"Mr. Douglas?" Mother says, raising a hand, but he is already shrugging on his jacket. "Mr. Douglas!"

"Nice to see you again, Lillian," he says, and strides from the office.

Mother and I stare at the door as it swings shut.

"I've had an attorney review the documents as you requested, Lillian," Uncle says, propping his elbows on the desk. "I hope you are pleased."

"What did he sign?" Mother asks.

"I have worked hard for my brother, and how does he repay me? By cutting me off, keeping me from inheriting what is rightfully mine." Uncle crosses his ankles and rubs his chin, as though we are merely discussing the fine winter weather or the merriment at the earlier gala. "So I've been forced to take matters into my own hands, find someone willing to overlook a few legalities. This is what my brother always failed to understand: everything is a business, and everyone is for sale."

Dread blooms in my stomach as I make sense of his words. Uncle paid Mr. Douglas to ignore the will. Why, I wouldn't be surprised if the paper they just signed is a contract between the two of them, an agreement where Mr. Douglas forgoes the proper execution of the will in exchange for . . . something from Uncle.

"You weren't owed any of it," I snap. "You never backed the Gulch Mine with investments, and you never did the real work, either. You swooped in when you saw Father was onto something, when the Territory's gold veins dried up and they turned to copper and silver instead. And then you sat behind a desk. You wrote numbers in ledgers while Father repaired smelters and stacked dynamite and ate alongside the miners in the chow house. And then when we moved, you hired new people to do those tasks and built this house to lounge in while other hard-working men saw to things in Jerome. How dare you insinuate that you are owed Father's hard-earned money."

"Are you quite finished?" Uncle says calmly.

"Charlotte, please," Mother warns. "Keep your tongue."

"Yes, listen to your mother, Charlotte. Better yet, listen to me, for I will be your father in due time."

Now it is Mother's turn to raise her voice. "Gerald, that will not happen, and you know it."

"I thought that might be your answer," Uncle says. "In which case, Charlotte"—he looks at me—"you will marry Paul."

"But he's my cousin!"

"A fine observation. And this will not be the first instance where such a marriage is arranged. It's about keeping assets in the right pockets. This is an agreeable match."

"But he's my cousin." I say again. "And I'm only sixteen. I'm too young to marry."

"You're too young to be a journalist also, nor are you suited to become one, ever." He folds his hands over his chest. "Your place is alongside my son, not taking an educated man's job by playing reporter."

I'm so livid I could scream. Instead, I say as evenly as I can manage, "I'm not marrying Paul. Now, if you'll excuse me, I must find the sheriff."

As I stand, Uncle Gerald draws a pistol from the folds of his jacket and aims it at Mother. Time seems to slow. The world narrows.

"I urge you to reconsider," he says.

"All right, yes," I say immediately. I don't need time to deliberate. There is only one answer. "I'll do it."

I feel as though I've been slapped in the face, as though the floor has given way beneath me. I always anticipated Uncle playing me against Mother. I don't know why I didn't consider that he might hold her hostage to control me. This is everything we sought to avoid. I should have stayed in Yuma as Mother demanded. If only I'd listened, this wouldn't be happening.

"Enough of this, Gerald," Mother snaps. "Charlotte has the world ahead of her, or as much as society will allow; don't steal that away. Let it be us instead."

"Mother, you can't."

"I can, and I will. Do not tell me what I'll do."

"So you accept?" Uncle Gerald says, smiling. Mother nods. "Splendid! I will make arrangements straightaway." He holsters his pistol.

Mother pushes out of her chair and heads for the hallway.

"Lillian?" Uncle Gerald calls after her. There is a formidable air of warning to his tone.

"I'm going to see Mr. Douglas, in regards to business matters," she says pointedly.

"You'll be interested to know that Mr. Douglas's business is now mine. I have arranged a deal with him. Fifteen percent stake in the Gulch Mine Company in exchange for his cooperation. You see, I have expressed concerns over your mental health, and he has garnered documentation reflecting such a diagnosis. Should you act rashly, say, by involving the sheriff in this matter, it would be a pity. I'd hate to be the one to alert authorities that your madness drove you to put a bullet in your own child."

For what feels like an eternity, Mother stands there, a palm on the office door, frozen like a statue, her eyes on me.

Finally, she blinks. Her face snaps up to address Uncle. "Thank you, Gerald," she says, "for illustrating so clearly why my husband was wise to never make you a partner in his endeavors. It pains me that I have to reward his astute observations by marrying you and allowing for what he sought to avoid. Now if you'll excuse me, I need fresh air. To clear my *troubled* head."

She pulls the door shut with more force than necessary. A painting on the wall shudders.

"The logic works multiple ways, Charlotte," Uncle says to me. "For instance, no one would be surprised to learn that your mother has brought a bullet to her own temple. So tread carefully. It would be a shame for you to lose both parents in such a short span of time."

His words are spoken like a Sunday sermon, vehement, indisputable. He means it. He will kill me, or her. It doesn't matter which, so long as he gets his way.

How foolish to believe that bad men would outwardly declare themselves as such. How painstakingly naive to think they would wear bandannas over their faces and ride only with equally vile creatures. Some bad men, it turns out, can wear smart business suits and fine silk scarves and be respected within the community. Some look like your uncle.

"I suggest you clean yourself up," he adds. "For all I know, insanity plagues the women of your family, and that disheveled, barefoot ensemble is not helping your case."

CHAPTER EIGHTEEN

REECE

I come to in the barn with a sharp headache. My nose is swollen, partially obscuring my vision, but it ain't too banged up to ignore the scent of hay and horse shit.

"Tell me how you got it."

I search out the voice. The pregnant woman's leaning into the wall 'cross the way, the barrel of her rifle resting 'gainst her shoulder. Outside the barn, the setting sun casts a blanket of twilight over her claim. I move to stand, only to find my ankles bound with rope. My wrists're secured, too.

"That scar," the woman continues, nodding at my arm. "Tell me."

"Why—you ain't certain you got the right guy? Don't wanna get shortchanged on the bounty, huh?"

"Boy, I don't got a need for money, but you sure as hell got a need for some sense. A person don't shoot you dead when they know you's wanted, and you refuse to answer their simple questions? You got a thirst for dyin'?"

"Some days."

She barks out a laugh, then puts a hand to her lower back to brace 'gainst the weight of her belly. The babe's gotta be coming soon. Maybe days off, or a couple weeks. Some mama she's gonna make. I've known her all of two minutes and am certain she don't got a nurturing bone in her body. Even now, her eyes are hooded, dark and uneasy, like she's bent on distrusting the whole damn world.

"I'd rather kill you than involve the Law," she tells me. "All the latter'll do is invite the rest of yer boys my way, and I ain't too keen on that."

"So crank that lever and be done with it. I know you figured me to be the Rose Kid by now."

"Yeah, I know who you are, Reece Murphy, that's true. I also know that Rose only puts that mark on his victims."

"Interesting theory."

"It ain't a theory. Rose put that carving in my father's forehead. He also did it to my husband's brother. He don't do that to folk he rides with. So I know you ain't a Rider by choice. At least you weren't originally."

"You know Luther Rose?" I say, doubtful.

"I knew Waylan. Like most folk, I didn't know there were another Rose waiting to take the reins till talk of train strikes started gracing the papers."

Her knowledge 'bout Waylan Rose . . . this claim that matches Vaughn's description . . . This woman's shaping up to be the very same from Vaughn's story.

"Say, yer name ain't Thompson, is it?"

"It's Colton," she says. "Now talk, before I kill you outta boredom."

She means it. She'll pull that trigger if'n I don't oblige. She ain't gonna believe a word I say, but I'm outta options.

"I did work on the Lloyds' farm," I say reluctantly. "That bit of the story's true. But the Rose Riders raided it one afternoon, and there weren't a thing I could do to stop it. I were fourteen at the time, 'bout three months from a birthday. Mr. Lloyd had sold a herd of cattle just that morning, and they took the cash before stringing up the whole family. I don't know if they got roses carved in 'em too. I was too busy trying to wrestle free of my own branding."

"And why'd Rose stop his work on yer arm? Why ain't you dead like the others?"

"He said he needed another man," I say. Despite all my yammering, I don't really wanna be shot, and that's exactly what's gonna happen if I mention the coin her husband gave me.

"That sounds like a lie. The Rose Riders don't take on just anyone."

"Well, they took on me, and at the time, I weren't complaining. It sounded a heck of a lot better than hanging."

"'Cus yer weak," she says. "Rose knew he'd be able to bend you to his will. And he were right, seeing as yer what now—eighteen, nineteen?—and still ain't made a break for it."

"Look, are you gonna shoot me or ain't ya? 'Cus I don't

particularly like getting lectured while bound and beaten. This ain't what I wanted! You think I asked for this to be my life? I didn't have a choice."

"Were you followed?" she says, like I ain't even had an outburst.

It ain't worth mentioning how Crawford'd been on my tail. All it'll do is put her on edge, make her trigger finger all the more eager to flex, and I'm sure I lost him in Prescott, besides.

"Not that I know of," I say.

She scoffs, shaking her head. "I swear, them lawboys are worthless."

"You sound like Vaughn."

"Who the hell is Vaughn?"

I open my mouth to answer, and pause.

Any other soul'd be lugging me to the sheriff right now. Most of 'em would shoot me first and deliver a corpse later. They'd take the bounty and revel in the praise they'd get from townfolk, the story in the papers painting them a hero. But this woman don't want none of it. 'Cus she don't want to be named, don't want to be known for her heroics.

Not when she hired a gunslinger to kill Waylan Rose and his boys. All this time I been thinking the cowboy would lead me to Waylan's killer, but he prolly *is* the killer. The cowboy could be the gunslinger and the Colton woman coulda married him. Her surname's changed with the exchange of wedding vows, but her past ain't.

This is the end of the puzzle, no matter how I look at it.

I almost wish Boss were here so I could point a finger,

say *Her husband's the one you want,* and then walk away. But Boss ain't here, and his boys ain't neither, and I'd rather keep it that way. This is valuable information, worth bartering were they to catch up with me. But right now I need this woman to cut me loose. I need to take a horse and keep on running.

And Vaughn—God bless her—is the way.

So I look back at the Colton woman and say, calm as anything, "Vaughn's a girl with ties in Prescott. She were hiding in the stagecoach I stole when fleeing Wickenburg."

The woman's face goes blank. "Where's she at now?"

"In the city, I reckon. She ran, and I let her go."

"And she knows you're the Rose Kid?"

I nod. "She knew I were headed this way, too. Chances are she's found a lawman by now. Hell, I'm half surprised they ain't shown up inquiring after me yet."

Panic flicks over the woman's features as she considers her options. She'd be best off letting me go and when the Law come knocking, telling them she ain't never seen me. It's obvious she don't wanna be the one to turn me in. She don't want that printed in the paper. That she's stayed hidden from Boss so long already is a small miracle.

"Why'd you keep the girl alive?" she asks. "You shoulda killed her. That's what yer kind do to folk that get in the way."

"Killing unarmed women ain't really my fancy."

She frowns, glances at her rifle, frowns deeper. Finally she says, "You coulda picked any godforsaken claim 'long this creek, but you picked mine, and now I got myself tangled in some Rose Rider mischief whether I asked for it or not. There'll be consequences if'n I turn you in. Same goes for if the Law comes investigating and finds you here."

"So why don't you just shoot me and get rid of my body?"

"'Cus I got a notion you ain't the monster yer pretending. I don't think yer good, neither, but I wouldn't feel right 'bout shooting you no more. Not after what I's learned."

Her eyes are fixed on my scarred forearm. Well, I'll be damned. She's got a nurturing bone after all.

"Then let me go," I offer.

"That would require me to trust you. And I don't. Plus, it ain't just me I gotta think on no more"—her hand moves to her belly—"so I'm gonna wait for Jesse to get home. We'll decide what to do together."

"Jesse. That yer husband?"

Her lips pinch tight. She's said more than she meant to.

She's right not to trust me. I got the name that will buy me freedom now. If'n I get outta this barn and Boss still somehow catches me, I'll gladly hand over the name Jesse Colton and the place he calls home, so I can walk free. Boss is a man of his word, and so long as he swears he won't lay a hand on the woman or her babe, the devil in me'll give her husband up.

It's like she said. I ain't a monster. But I ain't all that good neither.

Back up at the house, her dog starts barking, and not

in a friendly way. This is a guttural growl, capped with sharp *yips* like the ones he threw at me earlier.

"What the—" The woman grabs her rifle.

It could just be the sheriff, come calling on account of Vaughn's babbling, but I fear it might be worse.

Crawford.

I'd left my horse out front of the woman's house. The mare's prolly still standing there, seeing as she ain't with me in this barn. If'n Crawford carried on through Prescott, he could be stopping at every claim 'long this creek, searching high heaven for a sign of me.

"Wait!" I shout as the woman waddles outside. "It ain't safe."

It's dark now, the best sun lost till morning.

The dog goes on yapping.

"Yer gonna need me!"

But she keeps walking and don't look back.

CHAPTER NINETEEN

CHARLOTTE

I stand with my ear to the bedroom door Uncle has deemed my new cage. When I hear him enter the neighboring room and begin talking to Mother, I sneak out and pad for his office.

It's locked, but that's never stopped me from forcing my way into Father's office when I desired to read his correspondences with Uncle Gerald regarding one of my pieces for the *Courier*. I fish a pin from my hair and go to work on the lock. It clicks open a second later.

I rush to the desk only to find that Uncle has taken the will and contract with him, or perhaps stored them in the safe. He is not *that* dimwitted to leave them in the open, but ledgers are spread across the desk in plain view. I can't help but scan the earnings—those of the Gulf Mine in one ledger, then Uncle's personal finances in another. The numbers seem off. I run through the columns again, certain I've read things incorrectly in my haste. But no, the amount of copper that came in each week at the Gulch Mine in December is higher than the amount he's been shipping to Yuma, which in turn is sent to buyers by steamer. The difference is finding its way directly into Uncle's personal bank account. And it is no small sum.

I check the columns a third time, unable to believe it. When I flip back and check previous months, they all show the same trend.

Uncle has been stealing from Father—from our family. Stealing also from the buyers Father worked so hard to forge relationships with in California and along the Gulf. Stealing from the miners, even, to whom Father promised small bonuses on particularly profitable months. According to the ledgers, there were two months in the past six alone that should have yielded those miners extra earnings, but the profit went into Uncle's pocket instead.

I flip back to a year ago. This is where the trend starts, at least at an easily recognizable rate. Father's illness had grown exceptionally grave then. He was unable to have any involvement in the mine, and Uncle did his worst as Mother and I were distracted at Father's bedside and waiting for the inevitable.

I tear out the sheets from both ledgers for November and December of last year, knowing they're old and Uncle won't miss them. Folding the papers up, I tuck them into my journal and arrange the ledgers as I'd found them. Then I dart back to my room. When I hear Uncle leaving Mother's, I throw open the closet door and begin to plan.

It is not until twilight that I have a chance to speak with Mother alone.

I squeak my bedroom door open, tiptoe down the hall to hers. I knock. Her door opens a crack. "Charlotte," she breathes, and ushers me quickly inside before locking the door behind me.

"We have to leave," I say, swinging a makeshift bag onto the bed. It is actually more of a sack, thanks to the sheet I stripped from the mattress and the curtain ties I used to secure it. I stuffed it with anything from my bedroom that I deemed remotely useful: two candles and their gilded holders, matches, a wool blanket, a wooden bowl that had been holding potpourri, a steak knife I stole during dinner, and a bit of bread, also swiped from the table, wrapped in a napkin. My journal and the stolen ledger pages are tucked inside as well.

"And go where?" Mother asks. "We've no money, certainly no appropriate attire." Her eyes fall on the plain brown work dress I'm now wearing. It surely belonged to Aunt Martha before her passing and is too large for my frame, but it was the only woman's dress in my room's closet and much cleaner than my stained and sweaty mourning dress. I've an apron wrapped around my middle—for added warmth—and a robe over my shoulders, as any winter coats are sure to be in the hall closet and I won't be able to grab one and mosey out the door while waving to Uncle Gerald. Perhaps most important, I have shoes again—a pair of boots. Like the dress, they are a bit too large and sure to give me blisters, but I do not mention it. I need Mother agreeable, not armed with excuses for staying put.

"That doesn't matter. We have to go. Now, before things get worse. We could head to the mine, get help from the workers. He's been pocketing some of the profits," I explain, telling her quickly about the falsified ledgers. The shock that paints her expression informs me that this is a surprise to her too, that even though we've always known Uncle Gerald to be greedy and manipulative, she never once expected him capable of such flagrant fraud. "The miners will be up in arms," I continue. "They'll help us! Or we can write to your sister in Pittsburgh, Cousin Eliza. Write to an attorney in Yuma. *Anything.*"

"To what end, Charlotte? We cannot send any word until first light, and our chances of freezing with no place to stay during the night are too high."

"I didn't freeze in the Rose Kid's coach."

"A stagecoach still offers more protection than the streets."

There's a knock on the door. "Lillian?" calls Uncle Gerald.

I grab Mother's hands, desperate. "If we stay together, just get outside town, we can sell the candlesticks and purchase passage south. We only have to make it back to Yuma, and this will all be over."

The doorknob jiggles. "Lillian, unlock this door."

Mother thrusts open the window. "You go," she whispers, dragging me near it.

"But he'll kill you. He said as much."

"He wants the mine, which he'll only get by marrying me. Mr. Douglas is ignoring the will, but the words written within it are still true. A wedding ensures that the transfer of ownership of the mine won't look suspicious —not even to people your uncle hasn't bought."

"But after."

"I'll delay as long as possible then," she says. "Just go get help. People in town may be in his pocket, same goes for folk at the mine. There's no guarantee he hasn't paid off some of the employees for their silence. After all, look at what happened with Mr. Douglas. Find someone impartial, an outsider."

"Lillian!" Uncle Gerald roars from the hall, his fist pounding on the door.

"Go," Mother urges. "Please. I'll stall him, discuss wedding plans, whatever it takes to keep him from your room and give you time to disappear."

She grabs my sack and shoves it out the window. It drops to the ground with a heavy *thunk*. I glance at the door, which is trembling under Uncle's fist, and then at Mother, her eyes pleading with me.

I don't like it. Leaving without her was never part of my plan. But she does have a point. How far will we get, truly, if we flee together? Uncle will notice our absence the moment he breaks down her bedroom door, and then he'll start combing the streets, enlist the help of townsfolk and the Law. But if Mother can stall him, if I have time to slip off unbeknownst, I might have a shot.

I heave a leg over the windowsill.

"One moment, Gerald!" Mother shouts. "I'm not decent." She turns to me. "I love you, Charlotte."

I drop down to the ground, glance up at Mother. If I ignore the panic in her eyes, she looks almost like an angel, with her hair spilling over her shoulders, the lanterns illuminating the room behind her.

She slides the window closed and turns for the door without a backward glance.

"I love you, too," I whisper. Then I grab the sack, sling it over my shoulder, and run for the stable.

I steal one of Uncle's sorrels. No, I borrow it. I'll bring it back when I return with help.

I'm glad to have the cover of night in my favor. If someone were to recognize Uncle's mare, if I were to be deemed a horse thief . . . Men have hung for such crimes.

Is that all it takes? One misfortune in your life, one act done out of desperation, and suddenly you're a criminal?

I push the thought away and focus on the saddle. When the sorrel is ready, I scramble into the seat, not caring that my skirt is hiked up around my waist, that my bloomers are showing, or that the cold winter night is blowing straight through them. I urge the sorrel out of the stable, along the edge of Uncle's property, and into the street.

No more than two blocks from the house, I realize I haven't the slightest idea what I'm doing. Where am I supposed to go? I don't have the supplies to make a trip to Wickenburg, where I have an ally in Deputy Montgomery, or even to a neighboring mining community. And like Mother said, I can't trust anyone in Prescott.

I glance to the north. There's the Thompson girl's residence, but a few miles off. She lost her father to criminals. Surely she understands what it's like to be left powerless and alone, and she will not turn me in. And if she gives me the name of the man she hired . . .

That's the solution, I realize.

I need a gunslinger. Not to kill Uncle, but to scare him honest. I need someone dark and dangerous enough to make him listen. Someone Uncle believes will come back and finish the deed, as only a gunslinger can, if he reneges on his word.

I turn the sorrel north and flick the reins.

CHAPTER TWENTY

REECE

I wrestle 'gainst the ropes till I manage to kick off a boot. My bowie knife ain't inside. The Colton woman musta found it before securing me.

Every curse I know comes tumbling from my mouth as I go on struggling. I kick off my other boot, hoping in vain that I remembered wrong, that maybe I stashed the blade in the other shoe after cutting all those bindings from the coach curtain. But nothing. I'm bound, weaponless, helpless. This must be how Vaughn felt in the coach. It's goddamn awful.

I knock my boots aside in anger. Then pause.

The ropes 'round my ankles ain't nearly as tight without footwear. I wriggle, flexing my feet till I can slip free, then grab my boots and stuff my feet back in. The bindings on my wrists I can deal with later. Snatching up the rope I just freed from my feet, I tear outta the barn.

As I close in on the farmhouse, I can see the horse I rode bareback from Prescott still waiting out front. Two additional horses stand beside it. The lighting's too poor to make out their coats and identify them as belonging to the boys, so I creep closer, praying they belong to a pair of lawmen. That's when I catch sight of a figure standing at the foot of the porch. His back's to me, his focus keen on something in the house. His uneven hunch is immediately recognizable, one shoulder slouching more than the other. *Hobbs.*

He musta been on my tail, too, traveling with Crawford.

The Colton woman lets out a sharp cry from the house, and for a second, all I can envision is my ma pleading for mercy as well. The first and only time I tried to run from the gang, Boss sent Diaz to pay her a visit, and he took a finger from her like it were nothing but a coin. This is how Boss keeps me in line. It's how the Rose Riders keep *everyone* in line—threats and violence and fear. It's how they'll get whatever they want outta the Colton woman, and there ain't no denying that I'm the blasted reason these men are at her door.

I glance at the horses, the dark expanse of land to the north. If I run now, her blood will be on my hands.

I creep toward Hobbs, stealthy and painfully slow.

Inside, the dog's still growling, but not so loud that I ain't able to hear a second voice—Jones. "If he ain't here, why you got a problem with us searching yer place?"

The woman says something I can't make out, but the sound of him striking her—skin on skin—is clear.

Three more paces to Hobbs. Two more. One.

He hears the whoosh of my arms, but not soon enough to do nothing 'bout it. Hands still bound, I loop the rope from my ankles up and over his head, then pull back, dragging him away from the porch.

He grabs at the rope beneath his chin, choking and sputtering. I pull back harder, landing in the dirt and taking him down with me. With his back to my chest, I use the weight of my body to keep the rope taut. Hobbs's boots kick and dig in the dirt, searching for purchase, trying to roll us over. He's stronger than me on a good day, but we both been riding hard for a while, and I got the element of surprise. I can feel the fight leaving him, the kicks weaker, and then he finally goes still. His hands fall away from the rope.

I scramble from underneath his dead weight. When his head lolls to the side, his lifeless eyes bore into me, staring at the killer he never saw.

I bend and retrieve his six-shooter, check the chambers.

You best holster that, son, Boss growls in my ear. *You kill one of my men, and I might be able to forgive you. He were dumb to drop his guard like that, anyway. But you go killing a second, and I ain't gonna be able to turn a blind eye. You'll pay for it with yer own blood.*

I cock the hammer, step onto the porch.

A board creaks beneath my weight, and Jones freezes. "Thank God, Murphy," he says, his face bright with relief. "We were getting worried. Where's Hobbs?"

The Colton woman stares. She's figured it out, I can tell. She knows what I aim to do.

Her rifle's resting on the table—put there by Jones prol-ly—and she's sitting in a chair little more than an arm's length away, her dog tied to the table's leg and growling. Her hands ain't bound, nor is she secured to the chair, but I know plain as day why she didn't put up a fight. Even now, her palms are on her belly, like they alone can keep that second heart beating if'n hers stops.

Her cheek's bleeding. Jones is still holding the knife he used to slice her open.

I don't say a word, but Jones senses a shift in the air.

"Murphy?" he says, cautious.

He's standing a few paces from the Colton woman. I could get him without endangering her. I could shoot him dead right now.

And even still, I hesitate.

It's Jones. He's only three years older than me, the closest thing to a brother I ever had. We've watched each other's backs during jobs, joked in the saddle, talked 'bout what we'll do when we retire from robbing trains. He's the only guy who ever talked 'bout an *after*. I thought that meant we had something in common, that maybe he also dreamed of being a better person, that this was all just temporary, not the people we're destined to be. But he's got that knife in his hand, and the woman's just sitting there holding her belly as her cheek bleeds on his account, and I know I don't wanna share this with him. I don't wanna have a single thing in common. Not nothing. Ever.

"I'm sorry," I say.

This is what betrayal looks like. He knows what's

coming. God, he knows. It's written in his wide eyes and slack-jawed mouth. Then his lips harden into a line, his brows come down.

He stares at me and I stare back, and it lasts what feels like an hour.

Suddenly, quick as a rattler, he draws his pistol.

I fire mine.

Clark Jones don't even get a shot off. His head snaps back and he drops to the floor, the knife and pistol clattering from his hands. The Colton woman gapes at me like I'm a stranger. It's her expression—caught between gratitude and shock, admiration and horror—that causes it all to crash into me.

I shot him. Holy hell, I blew away Jones and I strangled Hobbs. I murdered them both. I'm not just the vile Rose Kid, I'm the coward that turned on his own.

It's fine, it's all right, I tell myself. *You had to do it. No one's gotta know. Not Boss. Not the others. They'll never find out.*

"Jones, what the devil're you shooting for?" a voice shouts from outside. *Diaz.* "He ain't in the barn. She could be telling the truth, and we need to—"

Diaz goes silent, and I know he's found Hobbs's body. He musta gone looking for me. Only reason I can think that I didn't cross his path is maybe he searched the rear of the house first, approached the barn from the rear too, and by the time he got there, I were already gone.

"Jones?" Diaz calls out. "You all right, partner?"

He moves into view cautiously, framed by the open farmhouse door. He's in the saddle, wearing Crawford's jacket, red side out. It's been *him* on my tail. Course it has. Diaz is our best tracker, knows which wheel ruts to follow on any stretch of overrun plain, can tell where a lead turned where all others went straight, leaves no stone unturned. Crawford's prolly still hurt and hanging back. He'd've lent Diaz the jacket as a sign, a signal that help was coming, that the plume of dust in my shadows was friend, not foe.

Diaz's shock that I've done those very friends in is etched on his face. He can't process it: the image of me standing over Jones's dead body, Hobbs strangled out in the frozen dirt. Me, alive. The woman, breathing. But two Rose Riders dead.

The Colton woman grabs her rifle from the table and sends a shot out the door, clipping Diaz in the arm. The blast jolts me to action, and I send my own shot after him, but he's already spurred the horse to life. He goes streaking into the dark evening, firing a couple times over his shoulder. He can't get away. He can't.

I lurch onto the porch, and the Colton woman joins me. We unload shot after shot, the dog snapping and snarling behind us till we finally click empty and there ain't no point reloading. Diaz is cloaked by darkness, near impossible to sight and slipping outta range. I lose the shape of him long before the pounding of hooves fades to the south.

He'll be back. When and with how many ain't certain, but he'll be back. The boys'll want justice, and there ain't no way I can talk myself outta this one.

I'm done for.

Boss is gonna kill me. Not even the name Jesse Colton's gonna save me no more. Boss'll take it if I offer it up, sure. He'll go avenge his brother's death, but he'll also finish the rose on my forearm and kill me in the most vicious manner he can dream up.

You'll pay for it with yer own blood.

"Why'd you lie for me?" I ask the Colton woman. She wipes the blood from her cheek.

"Why'd you kill yer own men?"

"I didn't have a choice."

"You did," she said. "We always got choices, and yers say you ain't one of 'em. Which is what I suspected the moment I saw the scar on your arm, mind you. That you didn't kill the Vaughn girl that got in your way confirmed it. So I made the choice to not hand you over to men yer clearly running from."

"Thank y—"

"Don't go saying that. I woulda given you up if I had to." She's holding her belly again. A thin line of red appears on her cheek. She grabs the corner of her apron and brings it to the cut, applying pressure.

"They'll be back," I say, glancing the way Diaz rode.

"And I need to not be here when that happens."

I think of the half-finished cradle and the wall of books and the husband that ain't even home.

"Mrs. Col—"

"Kate," she says. "Call me Kate."

"I'm sorry I brought this to yer door. Truly."

"Life don't care 'bout *sorry*s, kid. So make yerself useful and help me feed these bodies to the hogs."

We lug the men round the back side of the barn, where there's a sty for the pigs. Kate removes the rope from my wrists and hands me an ax, telling me that if she grows to distrust my motives even for a second, she will not hesitate to blow me away.

Then she picks up an ax of her own and goes to dismantling one of the corpses by the light of a lantern.

"Don't you wanna get the sheriff?" I ask, trying not to watch. "They'll take care of the bodies."

"They'll talk, and even if these boys' deaths ain't printed in the paper, word'll get 'round. It ain't gonna be nothing but a waste of time, besides. I want the bodies gone—want no evidence that they were ever here—and then I'm gonna get gone myself."

"And yer husband?"

"He ain't yer concern."

"Seeing as I got you into this mess, I kinda feel like he is."

She stops cold, the ax hanging from her hand. "We got by just fine before you brought the devil's army onto our claim. Now you gonna help or ain't ya?"

The boys don't deserve a proper burial, same as I don't. Hell, the fate she's giving 'em is kinder than being left for buzzards. Still, it makes me sick. I *am* weak, just like she said back in the barn.

"I'll move the bits," I say finally, grabbing a shovel.

I expect her to roll her eyes or give me cheek. Instead, she just says, "I reckon yer in a strange place, and I won't deny you a moment of remorse. It's the folk that don't feel the hard stuff—regret or guilt or doubt—that you's got to watch out for. They're the real demons. You remember that."

I don't know what she's playing at. Maybe she thinks I can be saved. Maybe she thinks I'm more good than bad 'cus I saved her. I got a feeling she would've grabbed her rifle and sent Jones and Hobbs to hell when the opportunity presented itself, with or without my aid. Still, she can go on thinking whatever. I owe her this much —moving the bodies and dealing with the pigs—but soon as it's finished, I'm taking one of the boys' saddled horses and riding off. I'm done. I bring bad fortune and loss wherever I go, curse whatever lives mine touch. I need to ride outta here and hole up somewhere no soul's gonna find me.

Just as we're finishing with the pigs, Kate's dog starts growling again. "What now?" she grumbles, and grabs the lantern. We hurry up the rise. As the house comes into view, so does a new mare, standing riderless just beyond the front stoop.

"Yer third?" she whispers to me.

"Don't think so. He were riding a buckskin, and he'd've returned with backup."

Still, I creep forward, cautious, Hobbs's pistol held out. Kate puts a finger to her lips as we step onto the porch. I motion to the door, touch my chest. It should be me. I should go first.

She nods.

The door's already open, a lantern Kate left in the kitchen illuminating the muddy stain on the floorboards where Jones bled out. I step forward, cross the threshold. And a pistol touches my temple.

CHAPTER TWENTY-ONE

CHARLOTTE

"Give me one good reason why I shouldn't do it," I say.

"Put the gun down," the Rose Kid says calmly, as though I can't see the red stain on the floor.

I never should have made a deal with him, dragged innocent folk into the matter. The Thompson girl is dead because of me. I gave the Rose Kid her name, and he came straight here. He got the name Luther Rose seeks and then killed her for good measure. That's her blood on the floor. This is *her* pistol in my hand, swiped from where she dropped it.

My trigger finger trembles. This wouldn't be in self-defense, like on the train. This would be me doing God's will, picking and choosing who dies, acting as judge and executioner. No soul should have so much power. Even if the bastard on the other end of the barrel is deserving of such a fate.

And he's so deserving.

No one would have to know.

No one but me.

"You don't got it in you, Vaughn," he says. "And that's a good thing. Don't do this. It ain't a line you wanna walk."

"You know nothing about me!" I shout, pushing the barrel into his skin. "How could you? You *killed* her."

"He didn't kill no one but the men that had it coming," says a voice from out on the porch. "Now put the damn pistol down. I ain't had the greatest night, and I don't got time to dispose of another body."

I lower the weapon as a woman pushes past the Rose Kid, bringing a lantern and rifle with her.

It's her—the Thompson girl.

She hasn't aged, which is impossible, so perhaps it is more that I have aged too, that the woman simply looks as she always has: a dozen or so years older than I am. Her dark hair is pinned back, showing the whole of her face, which is a map of seriousness. A fresh cut marks one of her cheeks, the dark pink line a contrast to her tawny beige skin. I once heard Mother say that women glow when pregnant, radiating warmth, but the Thompson girl—woman—is the opposite. From her stern eyes to her proud chin, she strikes me as someone not to be trifled with. Her expression is cold, her posture resolute. Perhaps the only soft thing about her is the swelling curve of her belly.

I look at the pistol in my hand. If what she says is true, it is not her gun, but that of a "man who had it coming." A man the Rose Kid apparently shot.

"I need to pack," the woman says, turning her back on me.

"Pack? No. I need to talk to you. I need to know where I can find the gunslinger you hired to avenge your father's death."

The woman pauses, her hands on the kitchen table. For a brief moment the house is unnaturally quiet. Then the woman straightens and marches into the bedroom with such conviction, I'm convinced her pause was nothing but the baby kicking, a fleeting twinge of pain. There's a small racket as she shuffles through things out of sight, but when she returns, it is not with the name written on a piece of paper for me. Nor is it a sketch or an address or anything of use.

She returns with a legless cradle in her arms, the bed filled with an assortment of oddities: a metal lunch pail, a bundle of clothes, what appears to be the grips of a pair of twin pistols. The woman plucks a single book from the bookshelf and tosses it in, along with a framed photo.

"Who did you hire?" I ask again.

"Can't help you there," she says plainly.

"But my life depends on it."

"Then I reckon you oughta move on to someone who can help."

This is not how I envisioned this conversation. I did not sneak out of Uncle Gerald's house and travel these five miles by night for nothing. It was no easy ride. The darkness was constant, leaving me to fret over the horse and the possibility of a lamed ankle with one careless step. And when a lone rider came tearing down the slope, riding for Prescott with the speed of a vengeance, I thought maybe Uncle was already onto me, that men were searching me out. The shrub I chose to hide behind was just barely off the trail, and while it sheltered me completely, it did not fully obscure the stolen horse. Luckily, the rider had stronger priorities, because his focus did not shift from the city in the distance.

"But you've been in my shoes. You know what it feels like to need help."

"I have made my own help, always," she says, "and I suggest you do the same."

I'm at a loss for words. I have yet to consider a situation where coming here does not yield the name of a hired gun. I imagined her handing it over quickly and letting me stay the night. What the devil am I going to do now?

"This one's good with a pistol," she continues, jerking her head at the Rose Kid. "Maybe he'll help you."

"Him?" I scoff. "He's the Rose Kid. You do know that, I hope?"

She nods, as though I've merely introduced her to the local clergyman.

"The Rose Kid," I say again. "Reece Murphy, murderer and thief, rides with Luther Rose and the band known as the Rose Riders. His head is worth five hundred dollars. He robbed a train I was riding three days ago and had me bound and gagged in a coach just earlier today."

"That all true?" she asks, looking toward the Kid.

He doesn't deny it.

"Mrs. Thompson, I beg of you—"

"There ain't no Thompson here," she says. "Now, I need to put the horses to the wagons and get moving."

"In the dead of the night?"

"Yes. Yer friend here—"

"He is *not* my friend."

"—only got two of his buddies. The third rode off, and he'll be back. I reckon they'll be just as keen to learn the name of that gunslinger yer after, and they'll gut me to get it, so you'll understand when I say I ain't got time to dally."

I gape at her, the situation gaining clarity. The blood on the floor. The man I saw racing for the city. Two "buddies" dead and a third riding for help. I glance at the Rose Kid.

He killed his own men. *Why?*

There was his story about the scar, his sincere fear when he mentioned that the Rose Riders were following our coach. Perhaps he truly is trying to make a run for it, only he's come for the gunslinger's name as insurance.

The woman sets her cradle on the front stoop and lumbers down the step. "Reece, help me with the horses, won't you?"

"You want *his* help? But he's the Rose Kid!"

"I ain't deaf. I heard you the first time. Don't change the fact that he's coming with."

"I am?" the Rose Kid says.

She looks him in the eye. "I'm grateful for what you did here, I am. But that don't mean I trust you, nor that you won't slink back to whoever can protect you best when the time comes."

"I ain't gonna slink to no one," he counters. "I wanna disappear."

"Wanting to disappear don't mean folk won't find you. So I can't have you seeing which way I ride off."

"I wouldn't tell 'em."

"I ain't so sure that's true."

"I'll help you with the horses," he says to her, "but I ain't coming with."

She points a finger, her eyes ablaze. "They will kill you for what you did here, and they won't do it kindly. If'n you survive the torture and die without giving me up, well, that's a small victory for yer black soul. But if'n you let slip *anything* of use, my family ain't in a good place."

"What family? Yer husband ain't even here!"

"Leaving you to run is a risk I can't take!" she shouts back. "So you will get in the wagon of yer own volition or I'll escort you aboard with a rifle to yer back. You hear me?"

She turns and heads for the barn, making her way down the slope with a speed and confidence that prove she's walked this path many a time, that even poor lighting is no obstacle.

The Rose Kid moves to follow her.

"Unbelievable," I mutter at his back. "No one's safe from you. Not even your own kind."

He looks over his shoulder. "If it makes any difference, one of 'em was the guy who shot the lawman you rode beside on the train."

"You didn't kill him because he murdered that lawman," I spit out. "And you didn't do it because he's wretched and vile and wicked. You killed him to protect yourself."

"It were a little of both. Plus, Kate was . . ." He makes a gesture at his stomach, illustrating the pregnancy. "Forget it."

He turns and follows the woman—Kate—toward the barn. I hate that his revelation *does* make a difference. I hate that I'm glad the bastard who shot that lawman is dead. I hate that it was at the Rose Kid's hands that he was avenged, not the Law's. But perhaps above all, I hate that all the Kid's told me is starting to seem possible.

He *must* be trying to escape the gang, or he wouldn't have shot two of his own crew. It's possible he has some semblance of a conscience after all, or it wouldn't have mattered to him that Kate had been in danger. Still, this is the Rose Kid, an outlaw twisted enough to have killed two of his own simply to earn another's trust. This could all be part of a greater plan, a calculated maneuver to lower Kate's guard. He is after the same thing I am, and though Kate will not divulge the gunslinger's name at present, she may, in due time, to someone she trusts.

There's a creak in the distance, and Kate's wagon rolls into view. She's got a lantern hanging from the driver's box, and in its soft orange glow I can make out her form at the reins, two horses leading the way. The Rose Kid sits in the back of the wagon. It isn't loaded up much. Either she's not going far or she's heading to a friend's. Maybe both.

Kate draws rein, bringing the wagon to a halt.

"Are you really in a bad place?" she asks me. "Sometimes

folk think they need a gunslinger when really they just need time to find peace with what's happened. Revenge ain't always the answer."

"This isn't revenge for the sake of spilling blood. This is a necessary retribution for greed, and a bullet would only be the final resort. My uncle is a crooked business-man, and he's trying to seize my father's fortune by forc-ing my mother's hand in marriage. And if not her hand, it will be mine. And if one of us does not oblige, the other will be killed in order—"

"All right, all right, I don't need the whole damn epic."

"Why don't you just run to the Law, Vaughn?" the Rose Kid says from the back of the wagon. He's leaning against the side rail, looking all too pleased about the turn of events: him, riding cozy. Me, out here, spooked, my world crumbling. "That's what you do best."

"He already has folk in his pocket, and I can't risk trust-ing the wrong person. I need a gunslinger. I need some-one who can scare him honest, and if that doesn't work, shoot and not miss."

"Ain't it interesting," he goes on, "how when the Law fails people, they always turn to the outlaws."

"A lone gunslinger isn't the same as a pillaging gang of thieves."

"Enough!" Kate barks. "Get in the wagon, girl. I'll tell you 'bout the gunslinger while we ride."

"What?" the Rose Kid and I say at the same time.

"You coming or ain't ya? I'm not asking twice."

I can't go home without endangering Mother or myself, and I have only days—weeks, at best—to relieve Uncle

Gerald of his grip on our family. If Kate will only reveal the gunslinger's name while in the wagon, I don't have a choice.

I will have to travel with the Rose Kid again. At least this time I'm in possession of a pistol.

CHAPTER TWENTY-TWO

CHARLOTTE

Before we leave, Kate takes the reins of the horses that must have belonged to the Rose Kid and the two men he shot and positions the steeds facing Prescott. Then she gives them each a swat on the rump. Two spring off, and the third trudges on, weary, but it's likely they'll all make it back to town.

I tether Uncle Gerald's horse to the rear of the wagon while Kate heads to the mesquite to hang a noose. I must look worried, because she says, "Don't put wrinkles in yer forehead. It ain't nothing but a signal. My husband'll know where I's gone once he sees it."

It's the grimmest signal I can think of. Why not hang a colorful scarf from the tree? A blanket? Leave a note? But maybe the point is to have something that doesn't look terribly out of place but is still visible from afar.

I climb into the wagon. The Rose Kid is sitting near the rear, so I move all the way up to the front, as close to the driver's box as possible.

"I ain't gonna bite, you know," he says.

"You haven't proven yourself terribly trustworthy, so I'll take precautions, thank you."

He lets out a small laugh, then mutters "Goddamn mess, this is" before leaning back to rest his head on the sideboard. The stars twinkle off his dark eyes. I search his waist, but where he'd previously kept Father's pistol tucked into his pants, an unfamiliar weapon is now stowed.

"Where's my Colt? I'll take it back now."

He ignores me.

"I'm willing to make a fair trade." I hold up the revolver I found on the farmhouse floor, dropped by one of his men.

"I don't got the Colt," he says finally. "Kate busted my nose and took it, plus my knife, when I first showed up. You gotta talk to her."

The thought of her cracking his nose gives me some glib satisfaction. It's quiet a moment, him staring at the stars with a peacefulness about him that seems wrong, given that he's just killed two of his own men. No one should feel so indifferent to such a crime—not even if that someone *is* trying to escape a bad situation and *might* be more innocent than the papers claim.

"I won't let you have it—the name of the gunslinger," I tell him.

He makes no response.

"That's what you're after, and surely you don't have it, else you'd have simply given it to your boys earlier rather than gun them down."

"Maybe I gunned 'em down 'cus it's like I told you: I'm getting out. I'm leaving my past behind."

"I don't think it works like that. Our pasts define us."

"Horseshit."

"You mean to say our pasts have no bearing on our present, who we are now?"

"I'm saying just 'cus someone makes a mistake in their past don't mean they're always gonna go on making that same mistake forever and ever. Folks can change."

"Change, sure. But you're running. You can't do certain things and then pretend they never happened."

"I can try."

And this is why I find it so hard to buy the stories he's telling. He runs and runs, not caring who he hurts in the process or how those around him are affected as he achieves his end. That does not strike me as someone innocent. It only strikes me as cowardice.

The dog—which Kate called Mutt—leaps into the back of the wagon and curls up beside the Kid. Kate climbs into the driver's box next, which is no easy ascent with that belly. Truly, one of us should be driving, but she's refused to say where we're going or even in which direction we'll head.

The bed of the wagon is filled with her gear, from the half-finished cradle to crates of chickens. Three pigs and one cow will follow on foot. She better hope the Rose Riders are nowhere nearby, because this caravan of ours will stick out like a sore thumb, and make poor time, too.

"Blindfold yerselves," she says, tossing a pair of handkerchiefs at me and the Kid.

"You ain't serious," he says.

Kate cocks the hammer of her pistol and stares impatiently.

"All right, all right." The Rose Kid holds up his hands. He must be used to being threatened, or perhaps this doesn't feel like much of a threat to him at all, because he puts the blindfold on without any additional fuss.

Reluctantly, I do the same, tying the kerchief off behind my head.

"Good," Kate grunts. "Take 'em off before I tell you, and you'll find yerself dumped from the wagon and left to starve."

The reins snap, and the hitched horses surge forward.

The Rose Kid falls asleep almost immediately. Or at least I think he does. His breathing seems to change—grow shallower—but the creaking of the wagon makes it difficult to be sure.

I wait a while longer and then lean toward Kate. "Is he asleep?"

There's a creak from the driver's box and then her response. "Looks like it."

"He's after the same name I am. You know that, right?"

She grunts. "I been waiting for this moment a whole decade. It were only a matter of time before a Rider finally stumbled onto my claim."

I frown, confused.

"So you wanna know 'bout that gunslinger I hired, huh?"

"Please," I say.

"Went by Nate."

"Nate who?"

"Never caught a last name."

"Where can I find him?"

"You can't. Gunslinger died 'bout ten years ago, shortly after finishing my job."

"So what am I supposed to do now?" The only light I can make out through the blindfold is that of the lantern Kate has in the driver's box. The wagon was facing east when I climbed into it, but I haven't felt anything that suggests we've crossed the rail, and if we'd gone south, into Prescott, there'd be more light and sounds. We must be headed north or west, where there is nothing but mountains, but even if I leapt from the wagon this instant, pulled off my blindfold, and mounted the sorrel, I'd have no idea how to get home.

"This was what you wanted," I say, realizing far too late the con she's pulled on me. "I'm nothing but a liability to you, and you didn't want to leave me behind. What if I talked? I could put others on your trail. So you promised me a name, knowing it would do me no good, and then you gave it once you had me trapped."

"Let me assure you, while I hate extra fleas on my hide, I didn't try to trap you nowhere. I'm doing you a favor. We women have to look out for each other. No one else will."

"But—"

"But those devils'll return to my farmhouse, end of story. You couldn't stay there, and you couldn't go home 'cus of yer uncle neither, so I said what I needed to get you in this wagon. The least you could do is thank me, seeing as I'm saving yer life."

"But not my mother's. She'll be dead as soon as my uncle marries her if I don't do something."

"So figure something out," she says. "Get Reece to do the job, like I suggested earlier. He's good with a pistol and sure don't seem to care 'bout killing folk."

"That's the problem. I don't want to kill Uncle if I don't have to, and besides, the Rose Kid is the *last* person I'd ever trust for help."

"If'n he's so vile, just make sure the Law's there to arrest him when it's said and done."

I frown. "I thought he helped you, that you're bringing him along because he saved your life and now you're paying him back."

"I'm keeping him with me 'cus it's best to have yer enemies under yer nose than frolicking 'round in valleys you can't see. A Rose Rider is a Rose Rider is a Rose Rider. Soon as you drop yer guard, they tear yer damn throat out—and whistle while doing it."

CHAPTER TWENTY-THREE

REECE

I hear every last word.

They think I'm sleeping, but I woke when the wagon bucked over a rut in the trail. I'd nearly grumbled 'bout it, too, only the words leaving Kate's mouth made me pause.

Nate.

I sit there, still as a statue, eyes still closed behind my blindfold because I don't dare move. In order to hear each other over the creak of the axles and the plod of the steeds, the women ain't able to whisper, and I can just barely make out the rest of the conversation.

She never got a last name.

She's heard the gunslinger's dead.

Lies, all of it. She's protecting her husband still, turning eyes away from her family. If I had any qualms 'bout the theory, they vanish as Kate keeps yammering.

She ain't helping me, she's using me. She reckons I

should be Vaughn's hired gun and suggests turning me in when the deed's finished. 'Parently only her family and Vaughn deserve happiness and safety.

I told you ya can't outrun this, Boss says. *I told you yer stained black. You don't deserve happiness. You don't even deserve a quick and painless death.*

Well, I know one thing for certain. If Kate and Vaughn don't got no regard for my well-being, I sure don't got none for theirs. Once we get to wherever we're going, I'm cutting free, slipping off when Kate's not watching. And I know she'll be watching. *Keep yer enemies near,* and all that.

I'm used to double-crossing, backstabbing, dark-as-the-night bastards. This is my game the women are playing, the ploy I been training at for the past few years.

I'll get my way when the time comes.

I settle back to sleep a bit more. I guess Kate's right after all. A Rose Rider is a Rose Rider is a Rose Rider. I ain't gonna lose at my own game.

She stops the wagon sometime in the night.

It don't matter how well one knows a trail. Starlight, a weak moon, and a lone lantern ain't much to go by. We sleep huddled under blankets.

The next time I wake, it's to Kate saying, "You can take those blindfolds off now." I yank mine free and crane my neck 'round, trying to get a hold on my surroundings. We ain't on the plains no more, and though the trees and brush seem to be cleared wide enough for the wagon, there ain't any tracks in the thin layer of snow we're crossing. This ain't a well-traveled trail. Pines line it, and based on the low position of the early-morning light filtering between limbs and trunks, I figure we're moving northwest. I turn to the south, hoping to spot Thumb Butte or *some* familiar landmark, and see only more forest. We coulda traveled five miles since leaving Kate's place or three times that. I dozed too often, and Kate's stopping the wagon in the middle of the night for a rest only confused me more.

Vaughn said she grew up in these parts, but she don't appear any more aware of our surroundings. Soon as her blindfold comes off, she's gawking, head swiveling like an owl.

We pass through a corridor of pines that lean in slightly, crowding the trail. Then, like a train shooting through a tunnel, the wagon emerges into a clearing. Kate pulls the reins and climbs from the driver's box. I just stare.

Here, in the middle of the mountains, somewhere outside Prescott, is a haven.

The clearing is covered in a dusting of snow, with dry, brittle-brown grass poking through. At the rear of the clearing is a steep incline, and just before that is a house. It's built in almost the exact likeness of the one we just left, from the paned windows and plain shutters with crosses cut in 'em to the weathered, unadorned wood siding. There ain't a porch here, but the home overlooks a decent tank of water. Prolly there's a dam somewhere on the small stream that feeds it, allowing the tank to hold water long after the stream quits running. The pigs go lumbering for it, slipping in the slush and flopping into the mud like it's the finest goose-down bed in the Territory.

Set on the far edge of the clearing is a stable that don't look big enough to house all the livestock we got. Behind it—just like behind the house—the land goes steep. It's like the whole clearing is hugged from the rear, protected, its only point of entry being the trail we just took.

"Well, don't go sitting there all dumbstruck and wide-eyed," Kate snaps. "Help with the unloading."

We start with the goods that need to get moved into the house: the half-finished cradle and the stuff it's holding, the few blankets Kate brought with her. I'm wondering if she plans on wearing the clothes on her back for the rest of her life, when I step into the house and realize how grossly I've underestimated her.

This ain't just some building in a clearing. This is a hideout—and a fully furnished one at that.

The place is covered in a thin layer of dust, but the kitchen cabinets are stocked with cans of condensed milk and beans, bags of coffee, and strips of dried meat. There's a root cellar, filled with pickled vegetables and jams and a small mountain of potatoes. I peek into the bedrooms—two again, just like her place 'long the creek—and find made beds, extra blankets, dressers stuffed with clothes. This is a second home, ready to be lived in, its contents looking new and untouched.

It's like Kate has been waiting for this moment her whole life, like she knew her deal with the gunslinger might return to haunt her, that someone might come riding onto her claim demanding vengeance. She built this place ages ago and has been prepared to run ever since.

"How in the hell did you finance this?" I ask, setting the half-finished cradle on the kitchen table. "Hauling all the wood in, building here? There ain't exactly conveniences nearby."

"There ain't conveniences nearby for a reason," she says, scowling, "and how I financed it ain't yer business. Now I gotta beat some rugs and do an ungodly amount of dusting. See to the animals, will ya?"

Her confidence that I won't go running is damn infuriating, but I reckon it's founded. Just 'cus I figure Prescott sits somewhere south of here don't mean I'll find it with ease. Hell, I'm just as likely to get lost among the pines than to saunter into the city. Plus, wearing that blindfold means I don't got a clue if the trail splits or which way to travel if it does, and last thing I wanna do, even if I miraculously find my way outta the mountains, is run into Diaz or Boss.

Best to wait it out a few days. I got Ma to think on, after all, and I know Boss won't kill her so long as I'm free. That threat only worked to keep me reined in, loyal to the gang. But if he gets me back . . .

"I'll help with the dusting," Vaughn says.

"You'll help with the animals," Kate counters.

"I will not help him"—she glances my way—"with anything."

"You *will*, 'cus you got things to discuss, plus someone's gotta keep an eye on him."

Vaughn actually laughs. "You can't keep an eye on a Rose Rider, least of all the Rose Kid. Accompanying him to the stable is the most foolish thing I could possibly do. He could shoot—"

"I'm not gonna—"

"No shooting!" Kate snaps, cutting us both off. "Not now, not so long as we're here. It's too easy for gunfire to carry off them mountains."

"So civilization's near after all," I say, hopeful.

"Just 'cus a place ain't easy to find, don't mean it's invisible. Nor that yer boss ain't gonna find us if we go 'bout firing bullets like men cleaning house at poker. We trap and snare for food. Nothing gets shot. If'n I hear a bullet go off, it better mean we's been found out and yer firing at the enemy."

"So we're just expected to get along?" Vaughn asks, motioning at herself and me. "You want me to pretend like he isn't the killer we know he is? I'm not doing anything with him!"

"You will, 'cus you ain't got another option. It's this or I shoot you both right now."

"I thought there weren't to be shooting," I say.

No one smiles. Shame. It were a decent joke.

"Let me clarify," Kate says, slow, glowering at both of us. "There'll be no shooting unless we're found out *or* 'cus I'm shooting yous."

Vaughn looks terrified, but I see it for the bluff it is. Kate wouldn't've saved my hide yesterday only to blow me away today.

"I'm not comfortable with this," Vaughn says.

"I ain't gonna touch you," I tell her. "Hell, I won't even look at you, if that makes it better."

"It doesn't."

"Aw, the hell with this," I say. "I don't need it. I'll deal with the animals alone."

I turn 'round and shove out the door.

I see what Kate's doing. She hopes I'll take Vaughn's offer. She wants to send us both out on horseback to see to Vaughn's uncle in town, then not be able to find our way back. Or maybe we get lost in the mountains and starve to death. Either way, she's free from the Rose Riders and safe at her hideaway, only our fate won't rot her conscience too much 'cus she did her best to give us a fair shake at things.

Well, I ain't falling for it.

This ain't a bad setup—the house and the stable and the reservoir tank. I could hole up here a few months, carry on once the Riders've quit searching for me and the papers believe me to be dead.

I unhitch the wagon from the two quarters that pulled it. The bay is agreeable, but the palomino nips at me like I ain't doing things quick enough, her silver mane flouncing. Figures Kate'd have a horse as ornery as herself.

I grab the leads and walk the horses in a wide arc, turning for the stable. Vaughn's standing but a few paces off, blocking my way. Jones's pistol is clutched in her hand.

"I don't care what Kate says about firing bullets. If you lay a finger on me, I *will* shoot you."

"Fair enough," I say.

Vaughn frowns. I don't think she expected that answer.

I know what she anticipates from a person like me, but it ain't like I'm gonna hurt her. Not now or ever. There's some lines I just ain't gonna cross, and if I don't stay honest to 'em, then I really am gonna end up just like Boss and the boys.

Vaughn don't seem to believe any of it, not no matter what I say, so maybe this is the way I start trying to communicate. Maybe 'stead of telling her the truth, I just let her discover it.

"I'm gonna walk in front of you now," I say, nodding toward the stable. "That all right?"

She nods.

"You could bring the other horse."

She glances at her sorrel, tethered to the rear of the wagon.

"Or you can just follow with the pistol. Don't matter much to me."

She stands there as I walk past, staring like I done shucked my clothing and started dancing naked in the snow.

CHAPTER TWENTY-FOUR

CHARLOTTE

Despite his promises and the I-mean-you-no-harm act, I'm not comfortable being alone with the Rose Kid. But seeing as Kate all but chased me from the house, I'm left with no choice but to help with the animals. I try rounding up the pigs, but they'll have none of it. They find the mud most inviting, and after I slip in the freezing muck on account of my too-big boots, I give up on the creatures and head to the wagon instead. Seeing to the sorrel will bring me near the Kid, but the chickens . . . I lug three crates from the wagon bed and bring them to the coop.

As I set them free, the chickens squawk and ruffle their feathers. I imagine Kate intends to gather their eggs, but depending on how long she remains in these mountains, a couple of the birds will likely become food, too. I hope

I'm long gone before it comes to that. I've wasted too much time already, on account of Kate's trickery, and I suppose it would be foolish to not even consider the role the Rose Kid could play in liberating our family from Uncle Gerald's grasp.

I grab the pistol from where I left it on a fence post. It was used to do unspeakable things, and I hate the way it feels in my hand, but until I'm able to speak to Kate and request a trade for Father's Colt, I refuse to approach the Rose Kid unarmed.

I find him at the stable, moving the palomino into the final stall.

"What in the hell happened to you?" he asks, gaze locked on the muddied state of my dress.

"I fell."

He raises his brows. His lips don't curl into a smile, but I can spot the amusement in his eyes.

"Trying to get the pigs to the sty," I explain, not sure why I'm defending myself. I could not care less what he thinks.

"Them hogs don't need to be penned up till later. Let 'em have their mud bath."

"I did. They're still down at . . . Never mind that, I have a proposition for you."

"Ain't interested." He turns his attention to the horse.

"But I didn't even make it yet!"

"Don't care." He picks up a brush and begins grooming the palomino's coat. "Still ain't interested."

"Allow me to propose it, at least."

"It's yer breath to waste."

"All right. My uncle is a bad man, and my mother and I will not live freely until he is relieved of his position."

"All the fancy speech in the world don't make the deed less vile," he says as he moves the brush in long, smooth strokes.

"How is it vile? I simply need someone to scare him honest, convince him to abandon his cause or face disastrous consequences."

"And if he don't listen, what might those consequences be, exactly? A bullet?" He glances at me over his shoulder. "That's a thing yer comfortable with, admit it. You'd be fine with someone murdering yer uncle."

"That's not true! I only want—"

He gives me a look so condescending that the words die in my mouth.

I cross my arms. "Will you or won't you take the job?"

"So you can turn me in before his body's even cold? No, thanks."

"I wouldn't turn you in."

"If you say so, Vaughn."

All I hear is, *You're a bad liar, Vaughn.*

The Rose Kid continues to tend to the horse's coat. He's good with the animal, deliberate with his strokes. When he spreads a blanket over the steed's back, he calls her *girl* and runs a palm down her neck several times. It is almost as if he has forgotten my presence.

"Look, you're the Rose Kid. For what reason would you not do this? I can pay you, once it's done."

"I got no reason to do this for you, coin or not."

"Then what do you aim to do instead, live here forever? You think Kate's going to provide a permanent room for you once her baby arrives? Or her husband returns? You can't run from your past. Do this, and I'll tell your story, let the Territory know how you changed your ways."

He turns to face me. "If the world does not believe my own words, why would they believe yers?"

"For one, because I am not an outlaw. Second, because I am a reporter with the *Morning Courier.*"

"In the coach, you said you were aspiring."

"I haven't had my big break yet." A truth. "But I can print your tale."

"Right." He scoffs. "'Cus all printed word is true. 'Cus the tales they wrote 'bout me years earlier and've been telling ever since can be washed away with a single article."

I can see the doubt in his eyes, but also the hope: that I could really offer such a solution. Wipe his slate clean. Give him a fresh horizon.

"You really write for the paper?" he prods. His sleeves are rolled up to the elbow, and I can make out that half-finished rose scar on his arm.

If everything he's told me is true, his predicament is far from favorable. But the Rose Kid has also done horrid things to save himself, to secure a future, so I cannot be faulted for telling a small lie for the same reasons. To save Mother, to secure *our* future . . .

"Yes," I answer before I lose my nerve. "I write for the paper."

A pause.

"Let me think on it," he says finally.

I don't have the luxury of time, but I know better than to push my luck.

Father always said a person can fight only one battle at a time, and though I wish to see all the Rose Riders hung for their crimes, my largest quarrel is with Uncle. I could live with watching the Rose Kid ride for the horizon if he takes my deal. Because as wicked as he may be, I do believe him when he says he wants to start again.

If I write anything on his actions, I surely will not paint him a hero. He just needs to believe I will. So if the Rose Kid threatens Uncle Gerald, convinces him to see reason, then I will do him this one decency: I will not have the Law there, waiting to arrest him. I will let him keep running from his past. He best hope he can run faster than his demons.

The day is long and fruitless.

I help Kate finish up the dusting; then we inventory the root cellar, Mutt rubbing against our legs as we count jars. Kate is stocked well enough to eat comfortably through the winter.

Here in the mountains, shadows begin to stretch earlier than I am used to. As the sun sinks from view, Kate scrubs potatoes in the dry sink and passes them to me. I quarter them for boiling, trying to ignore the pain in my heels, where the boots have rubbed and chafed.

"I'd like my pistol back," I tell her as I add newly cut

pieces to the pot. "The Colt—the weapon you took off the Rose Kid."

"That's yers? Big gun for a little lady." She gives me a sly smile, as if perhaps this isn't a bad thing.

"It belonged to my father."

She nods as though she understands, when she can't, not truly. She lost her father too, but years ago, and suddenly. She didn't see the suffering drawn out, didn't watch him change from a vibrant, energetic man to a weakened, frail thing that couldn't leave his bed. The sweaty brow. The heavy eyelids. The blood-soaked handkerchief that constantly remained in his grip. He wasn't himself by the end. My father died long before he took his last breath, and that was the hardest thing to witness.

I think maybe I should tell Kate this. I haven't said it to anyone, and maybe it would be good to get it out, to throw the words into the open instead of letting them fester inside. But when I raise my head to say something, Kate has disappeared into her bedroom.

She returns with Father's pistol and lays it on the table. Seeing it makes me feel better *and* worse. Better, because it's as if I've been reunited with a piece of him. Worse, because it reminds me of all the things I was forced to leave behind in that Wickenburg boarding house.

"A trade?" I put the pistol I found on the floor of her Prescott home down beside Father's.

"Keep it," she says. "I got a pair of twin Colts myself, and I ain't been able to carry 'em proper in months."

She's too big for a belt, and even if she managed to fasten one below her belly, I imagine its lowered position would change her draw. Her rifle, however, has barely left her side since I've met her. During the wagon ride here, it sat in the driver's box. Now it's propped against the kitchen table, even though there are pegs for it above the door.

"How much longer?" I ask, nodding at her belly.

"A week or so, according to the midwife, and hopefully not a day longer. I'm ready. Lord, am I ready."

"My mother said she cried with joy the first time she looked down and could see her feet again after my birth."

Kate barks out a laugh. It's the most unladylike laugh my ears have ever witnessed, but she does not seem embarrassed by it. It makes me want to live so freely, to throw my head back rather than merely smiling, to guffaw instead of giggle.

"What will you do if your husband is not back before the baby comes?"

"What do you mean?"

"There's no midwife here."

"Women pushed out babies in covered wagons bucking over the plains. I sure as hell can push one out in the comfort of a bed, with or without help around."

Her confidence is endearing. I do not mention the stories Mother has told me, where complications keep the baby from coming, where the mother sometimes perishes with the child.

"Besides, what do I got to worry about?" Kate continues. "I got two extra sets of hands 'round now."

I freeze up. "I'm no midwife. My mother is, and I know a little from her, but not enough to be truly helpful."

"Blood bothers you?"

"Not during a birth. It's more that . . . things can get complicated. I won't know what to do in that instance."

"We'll get Reece to assist you."

"He won't know either," I argue. "Besides, why do you trust him?"

"I don't trust no one but Jesse," she says. "Not fully, at least."

"Why do you trust him partially, then?"

"Charlotte, no one's all good or all bad. That ain't how humans work. Hear me on this, and trust me when I say that Reece Murphy is as solid a mix as they come."

Just last night she was arguing that a Rose Rider is a Rose Rider and that I should turn him over to the Law if he agreed to see to my uncle. How could someone deserving of a jail cell be a solid mixture of good and bad? I must appear confused because Kate adds, "He ran from the gang earlier this week. He shot two of his own just yesterday."

That she is defending him makes me furious.

"What was he doing the past three years?" I argue. "Where were his principles then?"

"Ask me," the Rose Kid says from the doorway. I don't know how he appeared there so quietly, only that he's heard everything.

"Go on, ask," he says again.

I return my attention to the knife. I bring the blade

down, halving a potato, then again, cutting it into quarters.

"Yeah, that's right about what I figured," the Rose Kid says, and moves to the dry sink to wash.

Before Kate can even propose sleeping arrangements for the evening, I demand to room with her.

"I'm not staying with him," I say plainly, as if the Rose Kid is not even present, when in fact he's sitting right there on the other side of the table. Full of food, his face and limbs clean from the quick wash he'd splashed on himself before dinner, he appears almost civilized. His hat hangs down his back, its string pressed against his throat. If I look at him only from the chin up—chapped lips, freckles on his tawny nose, brownish-blond hair that curls behind his ears—he's almost unrecognizable as the boy from the train. But he's still wearing that blue shirt, stained with sweat, and the jacket I used as a blanket at night in the coach.

"Thanks for dinner," he says. "I reckon I'll get a little shuteye now." He leaves his knife and pistol on the table before excusing himself.

When the door to the second bedroom clicks shut, I turn to Kate. "You should lock him in there for the night."

"If he wanted us dead, he'd've seen to it already. Besides, he left his effects." She pops a potato in her mouth and motions at the weapons with her fork.

"That doesn't mean . . . What if . . ."

"Christ, Charlotte. I said I didn't think he were all bad, not that I wouldn't shoot him square between the eyes if he proves me a liar."

CHAPTER TWENTY-FIVE

REECE

For someone living on limited quantities of damn near everything, Kate Colton makes a strong coffee. Maybe she figures some things are worth having proper or not at all.

After a breakfast of grits and flapjacks, I offer to do a little hunting. "Snares and traps only, of course. I know you don't want us firing shots."

Vaughn glares at me like I intend to run off. She ain't completely wrong. I aim to hike to a vantage point and have a decent look at our surroundings so that if I ever *do* get a chance to run, I know which direction I should head off in. Seems to me like instead of judging, Vaughn should be doing the same.

Ill-tempered as Kate may be, she's got a soft spot for her animals, 'cus she agrees it makes sense to trap what we can before we resort to slaughtering the hogs. If'n she didn't intend to eat the damn things, I don't know why she had 'em make the trek. All they've done is lay down prints. Granted, it did manage to flurry again last night, which mighta helped fill in some of the tracks and wheel ruts. By the time Diaz comes back with Boss and the rest of the gang, there might not be much left to follow.

"You got anything I can use—wire or rope?"

"Check the stable," she says. "Jesse thought of everything, so I reckon there's something useful there."

"When's he supposed to be back, anyway?" Vaughn asks.

"Always hard to say. Jesse don't know how to turn down Benny, and Benny's real good at roping him for another job. But last Jesse wrote, he said end of January."

"He keen enough to know if he's being followed?" I ask.

Vaughn shoots a look that suggests I'm being insensitive, but it's more than fair to assume one of Boss's boys'll be watching the Prescott house.

"Jesse's smart," Kate says.

'Cept for when he gave me that blasted coin.

As though she can hear my thoughts, Kate adds, "Most of the time."

I've barely made it off the porch when Vaughn comes nipping at my heels.

"Hold up! I'd like to talk to you about yesterday."

"I told you I'm still considering it."

"Not the offer," she says. "When I challenged your

principles the last few years, you said *ask me*. Well, I'm asking now."

I pause beside the first of the stable's stalls. The sorrel flicks her tail.

"I done bad things, Vaughn. I ain't participated in the worst of it, but I don't exactly think standing by doing nothing excuses a man of his crimes. So the truth of it is, I ain't had a ton of principles, but this ain't what I ever wanted, neither. I did try to run once, just weeks after Boss branded my arm and dragged me into the gang. I weren't about to try again."

"What happened?"

"Why do you care?"

"If I end up writing that piece on you for the paper, I can't very well do it without knowing the facts."

She's wearing a beige dress she musta borrowed from Kate, 'cus it's clean and a bit too big in length. A blanket's draped over her shoulders to shield from the morning's bite, and with her head cocked to the side and her hair spilling everywhere, she plays sincere mighty well. But I get the feeling she's also playing me. Like she's cutting me open just to watch me bleed, not so she can stitch me back up. Hell, I could see her writing the story for her career's benefit and still turning me in to the Law.

'Gainst my better judgment, I fold. For once I got someone standing 'round long enough to hear my side of things, and maybe just talking will do me wonders. It sure seems to help sinners at confession.

"Boss asked 'bout my family a lot in the first days I rode with him," I begin. "He wanted to know my history.

No detail were too small. I told him everything 'cus I were scared of what might happen if I didn't, and when I tried to run that first and only time, I realized I shoulda lied. At least a little."

"What do you mean?"

"We were down near Yuma." She bristles at the mention of her home. "Most of the guys were seeing ladies, and Boss had bought me one. I snuck out the gal's window, certain that were the best time to flee 'cus the boys'd all be preoccupied. I didn't count on one of the whores snitching to Boss. I didn't make it more than three miles north before he caught up with me. He beat me real good. I still got this lump on my nose where it ain't healed right." I go to point it out, only to remember that my nose is still swollen from where Kate cracked me with her rifle.

"So you took a beating," Vaughn says, shrugging, as if she's taken one herself and knows how it feels to have Luther Rose towering over you, kicking relentlessly, driving his fists into every bit of soft flesh he can find. "You didn't try again?"

"I planned to, but Diaz disappeared that day and rejoined us a week or two later. When I asked him where he'd been, he told me Boss sent him to visit my mother. She's a painted dove in La Paz."

Vaughn's gone pale at this point. "He killed her?"

"Nah. You can't kill someone yer using to keep another person in line. You should know that, what with the way yer uncle's playing you and yer ma 'gainst each other."

I walk to the far end of stable, where the only empty stall is filled with farming gear. Kneeling, I dig 'round in a crate, looking for something I can use to set a snare or trap. Vaughn's dress swooshes behind me. She's followed.

"What happened?" Her tone's demanding, but a little concerned, too.

"Diaz saw my ma, then cut off her little finger."

"Maybe he lied."

"He gave it to me, wrapped in a handkerchief. Said if I tried to run again, Boss planned to send someone else and they'd take two fingers. The next time, it would be three. And so on."

I glance at Vaughn. Her hand's pressed to her mouth.

"I guess there was no way of knowing if that finger were truly hers, but it weren't a gamble I were willing to make. So I stayed put till Wickenburg. It wasn't worth running till I knew—without a doubt—that I'd be able to get away. Now, so long as I keep hidden, my ma should be safe. I know Boss. He ain't gonna harm her if'n I'm gone. It's if he catches me that things'll get ugly."

"Jesus Christ," she mutters. "I'm sorry."

"Look, I ain't sharing this for yer pity. I told you 'cus you asked, and 'cus you need to stay away from me. Find someone else to take care of yer uncle. Trust me, I ain't worth it. Every life mine touches ends up cursed. I'm gonna lie low a few weeks and then get outta the Territory, go somewhere they won't find me."

"So that's it. You're turning down my offer? You're going to leave me to deal with my uncle myself?"

"*Yer* uncle, *yer* problem. I got enough of my own."

"Unbelievable," she says.

I grab a length of rope and leap to my feet. "And what, yer some kind of saint? Yer the one trying to hire the Rose Kid to threaten yer own family! Even murder on yer behalf if it comes to that. Maybe it's time you dirty yer own hands. Go kill him yerself, Vaughn. But don't you dare try to make me feel guilty 'bout not helping. I struggle to wake up every goddamn day. I hate who I am. Hate it. So I sure as hell ain't gonna let some spoiled, judging, pretentious, holier-than-thou city gal make me feel worse than I already do."

I storm off before she throws more insults in my face. I knew I shouldn't've told Vaughn 'bout my ma. Just like I shouldn't've told Boss 'bout her, neither.

Secrets are like bullets. Ditto the dark, personal stuff. Folks say they'll take 'em off yer hands, share the burden, but really they just load 'em into their own weapons so they can use 'em against you later.

I set one trap where it makes sense—'long the trickling stream that feeds the tank of water. Then I turn my back on the hideout and take to climbing the craggy mound of rock at its rear.

Only shrubs seem to have found purchase here, but a few are sturdy enough to use as leverage while climbing. By the time I work my way to what can be called the summit, a good chunk of time's passed and the sun is high in the sky. To the north and west there ain't nothing but more forest—ponderosas and other greenery dusted with snow. But to the east the land becomes a low swatch of dusty yellow—Chino Valley, perhaps—and to the south I finally spot something I recognize. Thumb Butte. I reckon it's five miles off as the crow flies, but it could be twice that trying to navigate on foot or by horseback. Least I know where Prescott is now, and if I wanna try disappearing into Utah, I'm best heading east till I stumble into Chino Valley, then heading north with the P&AC line. Maybe I can even scrape together enough coin to ride the rail right outta the Territory. I can see the irony: escaping Boss by relying on the thing he always robs.

I don't know where I'll get the money, 'less I steal it from Kate, and truth be told, I don't feel right about that. Maybe I can work for her a few weeks and she'll pay me for my labor. It's a long shot—she's already risked her neck hiding me from the boys back at her place and letting me tag 'long to this hideout when anyone else woulda shot me dead. Sure, she don't trust me fully. But I can't rightly blame her. I don't trust me fully neither.

There's the slightest breeze at this height, and it whisks away the sweat I worked up during the climb. I glance to the southwest, as if merely staring in the direction of La Paz could somehow reveal Ma to me. I wonder what she's doing right now, if she begrudges me as much as she does my father.

I sit at the summit a minute longer, letting the afternoon sun warm my face as I memorize my surroundings.

CHAPTER TWENTY-SIX

CHARLOTTE

I cannot sleep.

The Rose Kid left his pistol and knife on the table again. Kate calls it considerate. I find it confusing.

Say everything he claims is true: he is a young man in a poor situation, forced into his current station, held hostage by men who threaten his own life and that of his mother. Wouldn't anybody in such a position want to remain armed? Should his demons come calling, not having a weapon at his side may spell his demise.

Earlier in the evening, when Kate and I retired to bed, she mentioned that when she first stood face to face with the Kid, he'd all but begged her to shoot him. "Part of him wants to die," she said, "but a bigger part wants to live. Folks always underestimate how far they'll go—what they're willing to do—just to keep breathing."

Kate is sleeping deeply for once. Her breathing is low

and silent, almost peaceful. Mutt, too, is curled up at the foot of the bed, and it is a shame I am not taking advantage of the quiet. Instead, I stare at the ceiling, overwhelmed by the enormity of what awaits me in Prescott. I cannot stall another day. If the Rose Kid refuses to help me, I will have to do as Kate says and make my own help. Mother does not have days to waste, and I know all too well that someone like Nellie Bly would not sit still, worrying. She was just sixteen, same as I am now, when her first printed piece appeared in the *Dispatch,* and yet here I lie, staring at a ceiling while the story of a lifetime unfolds around me and I do nothing to document it.

Reece Murphy: the infamous Rose Kid who may not be as vile as the Territory has portrayed him, but is instead merely a boy forced to ride with the most wicked men in Arizona—a boy surrounded by demons, who finally raised his pistol to strike down two of his own while chasing freedom.

It's the type of story a journalist dreams of.

I should write it. I will write it, as soon as I'm home. *Home*.

Just like that, the fluster and itch to move a pen over paper vanishes. How can I be thinking of something so self-serving when Uncle Gerald sits in that home right now, holding my mother prisoner? The guilt becomes nearly unbearable, drowning out my thoughts, Kate's low exhales, everything, until the world falls completely silent. So silent that the snap of a twig in the distance renders me a statue.

I clench the blanket beneath my chin, certain I imagined it. But now I hear nothing, and the quiet itself is unsettling. There's too much of it. It's as if even the night creatures have been spooked.

I sit up.

"Kate?" I whisper, touching her shoulder. She exhales low. "Kate?" She's had such trouble sleeping that I can't bear to wake her for what is likely just my nerves getting the best of me.

I slip from the bed. The wooden floorboards are cold beneath my feet, and I move slowly, taking care so they do not creak under my weight.

Kate's Winchester rests against the wall. I grab it and step into the kitchen. The soft glow of embers still pulses in the fireplace. It will have to be enough to see by, because I don't dare light a lantern.

I pause near the window that overlooks the tank and peer through a cross porthole cut in the shutter, but nothing seems odd. Moonlight winks off the water. The evening is calm.

And then . . . movement.

Beyond the tank, at the start of the path that leads into the woods, is a lone rider. Saddled. Moving ever so slowly toward the house. My heart beats wildly.

His steed is dark, nearly as inky black as the night. Something glints in the man's hand. A pistol.

I swallow, wiping my sweaty palms on the nightdress I borrowed from Kate. Trying to ignore the frantic hammering of my heart, I slide the window open as quietly as possible, then bring the rifle up and aim through the shutter. Ever so carefully, I crank the lever.

The noise it produces is like cannon fire in the still night. The man's horse flinches, and his gun comes up.

I don't let him get off a shot.

I shoot first.

I've never fired a rifle before, but I've heard they are far easier to aim than six-shooters, that the long barrel allows for accuracy and precision. So when my target goes flying off his horse, I think I've hit him. It's when he scrambles to his feet that I realize his horse has bucked him in a panic; as he tugs the reins to steady the steed, I realize he is not hurt in the slightest.

The door bangs open behind me, and Kate stumbles from the bedroom, Mutt on her heels. The Rose Kid's door blows open next.

"They're here?" he gasps, snatching his effects from the table. "They found us?"

Kate grabs her rifle from me and cranks the lever. She takes aim as if it is her nature, as though the Winchester is an extension of her limbs. Her eyes narrow with focus, her finger quivers as it reaches for the trigger. But then her gaze jerks up, and she pulls the barrel from the window port.

"Don't shoot!" she shouts, lunging at Reece. He's at the second window, pistol also aimed. She knocks his weapon aside, then throws open the door.

"Kate!" he shouts after her.

But she's already running, her feet moving faster than

I ever imagined she could with that giant belly. She stumbles once but remains upright, her hands clutching the skirt of her nightgown as she flies.

"Jesse!"

The man's running now, too, the horse forgotten.

"Kate? Kate!"

They collide beside the reservoir, and for a moment I cannot tell where she ends and he begins. In the darkness, they are a single unit, their hands tangled in each other's hair, their fronts pressed together, their voices a jumble of relieved gasps. When they finally break apart, they stand there staring at each other and I'm struck through with a feeling of awe. At how the world can be falling apart and yet, somehow, there are moments like this. Moments that are nothing but good and whole and warm, where all the darkness in the world seems distant, as if it cannot touch us, or at least as if it cannot touch the likes of them.

"Thank God you missed," Kate says to me.

"Had it been trouble, missing ain't an option." The Rose Kid glances my way. "I'll teach you the rifle come first light. You should know how to shoot it."

We're all sitting around the table, the lanterns lit now that we've established there is no threat. Jesse Colton clenches a cup of hot tea, but his eyes never leave Kate. They're golden in color, a contrast to the rest of him. Dark hair is visible now that he's removed his hat, frost from the cold clings to his equally dark beard, and his skin is still tanned from the summer months.

"You weren't supposed to be back for weeks," Kate says.

"Benny postponed the last job on account of the northern territories getting slammed. They ain't seen a break in snow since November, and he told the buyer it was either get the beef to Colorado come spring or get the whole herd killed on the plains now." Jesse takes a quick sip of the tea and looks back at Kate, serious. "I know I agreed to this plan ages ago, but when I cleared the rise and saw that noose swinging, I damn near fell from the saddle. I ain't never been so scared in my whole life. The house was completely ransacked. Hoofprints everywhere out front, blood on the kitchen floor. I'm sorry I came creeping up in the night, but I thought maybe you were brought here 'gainst yer will. Or worse, you were already gone and they hung the noose to lead me into a trap. There was just so much blood, Kate. What the hell happened?"

"They found us," she says, plain as day.

"How many?"

"Three. One got away. That's why I had to leave. You weren't followed?"

"Nah. I watched the house a bit before I went for a closer look. How the devil did they find us? We ain't had a slip. We been doing the same thing for ten years."

" 'Parently Luther Rose's been looking for his brother's killer for ages, and Reece followed a rumor to me."

"Reece?" He follows Kate's gaze across the table. She'd forgone formal introductions in the panic, and Jesse now acknowledges our presence for the first time. He squints as he takes in the Rose Kid, and the moment he puts it all together, his eyes somehow manage to go even narrower.

Jesse lurches to his feet, drawing a Remington from his belt. The Rose Kid jumps up too, his chair toppling back as he draws his pistol.

"I know who you are," Jesse Colton says, his eyes burning with hatred. "Yer the Rose Kid."

"Jesse, can we talk for a minute?" Kate urges.

"Christ, Kate. Tell me you didn't know this when you spared him."

"In private," she snarls.

"Tell me you didn't—"

"Now!"

She steps around the table and moves between the guns. Jesse lowers his weapon immediately. The Rose Kid pulls his back too.

Kate pushes the door to the bedroom open, and Jesse, grumbling, stalks inside.

CHAPTER TWENTY-SEVEN

REECE

"We been through this a million times," Jesse hollers from the bedroom, so loud it ain't hard to hear him through the thin door. "Our shadows come riding back into our lives, and we shoot 'em in the skull. We shoot 'em and don't hesitate!"

"I know what we discussed," Kate says, dry.

"Then why the hell is that bit of scum standing in what's supposed to be our haven?"

"'Cus he killed two Rose Riders," she snaps. "I were in a pinch, and he killed 'em both. Prolly woulda got the third, too, but I took a bad shot and the bastard got away."

There's a pause as Jesse works over this new information. I don't got nothing but a view of the door's rugged wood grain, and yet I can picture him on the other side. Besides a beard he's got that he didn't have when I met him three years earlier, he ain't changed much. Only reason I can think he didn't recognize me straightaway is that three years changes a kid more than it changes a man. I've filled out since that day at the Lloyds', gained a few inches, have the makings of a stubbled beard myself, since I ain't shaved since before that botched train job.

"He's still the Rose Kid," Jesse says after a pause. "You can't trust him, not no matter who he put a bullet in."

"He's got the mark on his forearm, Jesse. A half-finished rose. Same as my father and yer brother."

"'Cept it ain't the same! Will had a *finished* rose, and he's dead, Kate. Dead! Same with yer father. That rose carving don't mean nothing if'n it's only half finished and the bastard wearing it is still riding with the gang."

"He ain't, though. That's what I'm saying. I think the Kid's been in a bad place these past few years, and he finally got a chance to run. That he ain't harmed me or Charlotte, 'specially when he's had plenty of time to do so, only proves it further."

"Charlotte were . . ."

"In the coach he stole from Wickenburg," Kate finishes. "She came to me looking for the name of my gunslinger."

"Did you tell her?"

"Course not."

Charlotte frowns beside me, confused. I can't believe she actually bought that lie 'bout Nate.

"You shoulda left 'em behind," Jesse says.

"And let 'em watch which way I rode out? Leave 'em to go 'bout their days with that knowledge, when we know damn well them Rose Riders don't let nothing rest?

They'd fish it outta the kids. They'd catch 'em and get that info, and then where would we be?"

"Then you shoulda—"

"No, Jesse. I shouldn't've. And you know it. It's easy to say that, but you wouldn't've been able to do it neither."

"To protect us, I could've."

"They're kids, dammit! They're even younger than we were when we got in our mess, and at least we counted on each other. But they got no one."

Vaughn flinches beside me, like the reality of the situation is hitting her at long last. I'd argue we ain't kids and haven't been for quite some while, but Jesse's implication that Kate woulda been better off killing us strikes fear.

It's funny. I thought Kate were the one without a nurturing bone, and now here she is, proving she'll make a fine ma, protecting the needy and all that. It's Jesse Colton I gotta worry about. I'd've pegged him a trusting, jovial fella based on his demeanor that day on the Lloyds' farm.

"And who did that family have to count on?" he continues. "I were there barely a week before the massacre. I say we shoot the Kid and be done with it, then bring the girl to town tomorrow. Hell, she can collect the Kid's bounty if she fancies it, but I want 'em both gone. They ain't nothing but complications, and we've always been fine on our own."

"Aw, horseshit, Jesse! I can recall a time you'd be dead had I not brought a 'complication' into our circle. Now do you trust me or don't you?"

There's a long pause.

"I trust you."

"Then promise me you'll be civil. We can figure a way outta this. Together."

"How?" he asks. "Have 'em live here forever? 'Cus that's the only solution that guarantees us safety, and I ain't fond of it."

"Everyone's got something they want above all else. I reckon the Kid's and ours align."

"Yer saying he wants free of the gang? He wants 'em disbanded?"

"Disbanded ain't the half of it. Wrongs don't disappear when people split. The only way he's gonna be truly free of his past is if they're all dead."

"Same goes for us."

"That's what I'm saying. We got the same wants, us and the Kid. If'n we strike the right deal, everyone'll part ways happy."

"So it's time we finally use it?" Jesse asks.

"I reckon so."

I'm guessing *it* is some coin I ain't seen, but it don't matter. I ain't taking their money. I ain't taking nothing that forces me to face down the rest of the Rose Riders. Call me a coward and a snake and a good-for-nothing yellow-bellied bastard, but I ain't drawing on Luther Rose for all the money in the world.

"Vaughn," I say, turning away from the door. "Lemme teach you that rifle."

"But Kate forbade shooting."

"We'll stick to form, then, and aiming."

Dawn's soft light is just beginning to spread over the land outside. It ain't much to see by, but if Vaughn's got the best ears among us and is gonna hear threats while we sleep, it's damn important she gets the basics learned.

Her eyes dart to the bedroom door, as if to say, *You don't want to listen to this?*

But I've heard plenty. The Coltons ain't been careful to keep their voices down, which means none of it's a secret or words they won't repeat to our faces when the time comes for 'em to play their cards. I gotta step away and figure what card I aim to play back.

"You wanna learn or not?" I ask.

"I do."

"All right, then. Outside."

"Right here. The butt's gotta be firm 'gainst yer shoulder pocket." I illustrate on myself, pressing my fingers into the depression below my collarbone. "The recoil's gonna hurt worse if you hold it loose. Also, quit lowering yer sight to the barrel. Remember what I said? You bring the barrel up to *yer* line of sight. Yer shooting the rifle, the rifle ain't shooting you."

She nods and tries again.

We been practicing like this for the last half hour or so, Vaughn bringing the stock up to her shoulder and the barrel to her sights, then lowering it. Over and over again with the emptied Winchester, only it ain't getting any more natural. We're gonna be out here all day. She's overthinking everything 'stead of letting her body learn the motion and just . . . *move.*

"Yer thinking too much."

"How else am I to do it?" she huffs. "There are a lot of steps."

"You gotta trust yerself a little. Have some faith in yer own limbs."

Vaughn lowers the Winchester and glares at me, peeved. This tough talk—the same way Boss helped me perfect my own aim—ain't helping with her.

"When you write," I say, searching for an example she can relate to, "do you sit there laboring over every last word?"

"Sometimes," she admits.

"And that works?"

"No, not typically. Sometimes I take twenty minutes to craft a single sentence, and then it won't even be a good sentence, at that. But other days I let myself make mistakes. I write and write and worry about making it shine later."

"Then look at this the same way. You can focus on each step so precisely that it's all a waste. Or you can just trust yer hands to do it right."

"That is the worst analogy I've ever heard. Writing and shooting have nothing in common."

I motion at the bucket I placed a few paces off to serve as a target. "Just aim again. And for the love of God, quit thinking so hard."

"I'm *trying*."

"Try harder."

"But that requires thinking."

I throw a hand up. "God Almighty, I can't win."

Her lips pinch into—I'll be damned—a smile. I ain't

seen such an expression since she pointed a finger at our crew in that Wickenburg saloon and got me tied to the Jail Tree, but that smile was vengeful. This one's different . . . pure and loose. It makes her whole face light up. I ain't never looked at her proper, I realize, and now the looking's making my stomach pinch up funny.

There's a creak behind us, and Kate waddles off the front stoop, her hand supporting her belly. "I'll do the teaching from here."

"You just remember everything I taught you so far," I say to Vaughn. "I ain't a bad teacher. I know what I'm talking 'bout."

"Jesse wanted to talk to you," Kate says by way of a dismissal. "Inside."

Swell. The man who aimed to shoot me just earlier wants to see me alone.

Kate turns her attention to Vaughn and starts her lesson. "It's all in yer head, see? You gotta be quicker than quick. Ace-high. The best."

What a load of horseshit. It's 'bout getting *outside* yer head, living free of yer own constraints. Lord help us if trouble comes calling and Vaughn is the only one to hear it ride in.

Jesse Colton is leaning 'gainst the frame of the open bedroom door when I step into the house. He's got his arms folded and one boot crossed over the other. It's a relaxed position, but one that drips confidence.

I've learned there are two types of men that project this look. Cocky ones that're bluffing, or men that are cocky for just cause—men that've earned their scars and drawn their own on others and looked death square in the eye but still managed to walk away smirking.

I get the feeling Jesse's the latter.

"Kate says you got her outta a bind. I owe you my thanks." He extends an open palm.

I ain't buying it. Just earlier, I heard him arguing that Kate shoulda shot me, and now he wants to make amends? I don't trust him, but I realize he ain't exactly going nowhere, and the longer I stand here denying him my hand, the more suspicious of me he'll get.

So I reach out.

His grip is firm—more a clench than a shake—and our hands bob just once before Jesse yanks me nearer. With his free hand he grabs the cuff of my sleeve and rips it back, exposing the rose scar. As he takes in the puckered flesh on my forearm, his jaw tightens.

"Did you kill that family?" he asks.

"No."

"Why not?"

"Why *not?*" I echo. "Why would I? Why would anyone? They were good people, the Lloyds. I worked for 'em and ate with 'em and slept under their roof. No one deserves what they got."

Jesse's brows rise a fraction, but he drops my arm. "Kate said Rose brought you into the gang 'cus he needed an extra, but I think that's a lie."

There's a pair of twin Remingtons on his hips, just as

there'd been the day I first met him. I'm bigger than I were then, fuller and taller, and still, Jesse Colton makes me feel small. His palm rests 'gainst the grip of one of the pistols. He's waiting for an explanation, and I fear that if I answer wrong, the words may be my last.

But God, am I sick of lying.

Plus, I've a notion Jesse already knows. He's quick to doubt, and I reckon he's already figured it's the coin that brought me here. He made a mistake. After killing Waylan Rose, he never shoulda emptied the man's pockets and saddlebags. He just shoulda walked away.

"You were at the Lloyds' 'bout a week before their deaths," I say to him. "You gave me a gold piece in exchange for tending to yer horse."

"I remember."

"Boss was halfway through with the scar when he found it."

"And why's that matter?" Jesse asks. His face is calm as can be, his eyes stuck in that narrow, unflinching glare. He's playing out a bluff, still trying to pretend he's not the gunslinger who done killed Waylan Rose.

"You tell me," I challenge.

"I remember what I gave you, not 'cus it were important, but 'cus its value were questionable. A standard three-dollar coin, but with the three filed off plus some more gold shaved from the edges. Desperate men do that sometimes, shave a bit of the gold for their own pocket and then attempt to use the coin at its face value. Dumb to file off the number, though. No merchant's gonna miss that. So I gave the piece to you. Figured you could melt it down, find a use for it."

"Boss said it were his brother's coin," I explain, "that he carried it everywhere. He looked 'bout ready to kill me, but I told him it were given to me by a cowboy."

Jesse pales. "And?"

"And when he asked me if I could recognize the fella, I said yes."

Jesse grabs the front of my shirt and shoves me into the wall. I cough out all my air.

"I *knew* you killed Waylan Rose," I say, gasping. "Yer the gunslinger."

"You shut up," Jesse snarls. "You don't know nothing. *Nothing.*"

I jerk my chin at his hands, still tangled in the front of my shirt. "Quite the reaction if'n yer innocent."

"You just told me that yer boss thinks I killed his brother, which puts me and my family on his kill list. How else am I supposed to act?"

"For one," I say, shoving him hard, "you can go back to thanking me for helping Kate."

He steps away, running a hand through his dark hair. When he turns back to me, he spits out, "If'n you aimed to run from them after Wickenburg, what in the devil were you doing at our house to begin with?"

Only a fool would answer that question.

"You knew the bastards were on yer tail," Jesse says, thinking aloud. "You worried you weren't gonna cut loose after all, and you wanted information that could buy yer way back in. So you somehow figured out where I lived and paid a visit."

"But I didn't do nothing with that knowledge. I changed my mind, killed those guys when they did catch up with me."

"Didn't do nothing?" Jesse roars. "Look around you, boy. We had to flee our home. We got a cross on our backs now, just like you." He turns away, then toward me, then away. His right hand's curled into a fist by his thigh.

"You gonna get this over with?" I say. "Finish *thanking* me?"

He notices I'm looking at his fist and shakes it out. Then he steps real close, a finger held an inch from my nose. "I can be grateful for what you did for Kate and hate you at the same time. 'Cus you ain't kept no one safe, not truly. You wanna right wrongs, Reece Murphy, then yer gonna have to face yer demons. We all are."

He stomps out, leaving me standing there perfectly still, unharmed, un-struck.

When Boss makes threats, I always feel 'em. He punctuates his screams with fists and boots, and the following morning, bruises always remind me of his fury. Same was true with my pa.

This, somehow, is nearly as bad. Jesse Colton's barely laid a finger on me, and yet I feel every last word of his speech. Those words hit real deep, in a place that don't bruise but is just as tender.

I slide to the floor, my face in my palms.

Vaughn's been right. There's no running from this. If'n I want a new future, I'm gonna have to earn it.

CHAPTER TWENTY-EIGHT

REECE

Kate and Jesse spend the rest of the morning whispering to each other outta my earshot, eyes consistently flicking my way. If they think I ain't aware they're talking 'bout me, they're mad. When Jesse finally disappears to check the traps I set 'long the creek yesterday, it's a relief.

Late in the afternoon, Vaughn works on her aim again while I stand in the doorway and Kate watches from the stoop.

"I don't like having an audience," Vaughn complains.

"Too bad," Kate says. "It ain't likely to be a relaxing moment next time you gotta use that thing, so you might as well practice in similar circumstances. Now, let's get to it." She's set up additional targets—her Stetson hat a few paces to the left of the bucket and a saddle from the stables a few paces to the right—and starts calling out "hat" or "bucket" or "saddle."

I gotta admit—Vaughn's improving. Her form is better, her aiming quick. Ain't I a fine teacher.

"I don't see what help I'll be if I never practice with ammunition," she says.

"The last step is squeezing the trigger," I call from the doorway. "Yer learning everything up to that, and if you can't do those first steps sure and true, the trigger and bullet ain't gonna matter. Besides, you know how to shoot a pistol. You understand enough."

Vaughn rests the rifle against her shoulder, frowning. "If you both expect me to live in this charming residence for the duration of my life, sighting a bucket until I've developed the Territory's best aim, you are sorely mistaken."

"There're worse ways to pass time," I joke.

"I can't sit around anymore," she goes on. "I need to do something. I don't care what it is, but I can't waste a moment long—"

"Look here, Charlotte," Kate interrupts. "I know plenty 'bout acting without thinking. Hell, I could write a damn book 'bout it. The first lesson'd be that it's a trail blazed with misfortune and bad luck. You might get what yer after, but that don't mean there ain't gonna be consequences."

"Is there something you aim to confess," Charlotte counters, "or do you typically speak in riddles?"

Kate is quiet a moment, then says, "I done some bad things in my life. Good, undeserving folk have died on account of my actions. Like Jesse's brother, Will. He's dead 'cus my youth—Jesse's too—were founded on acting before thinking. That we didn't intend for it to happen don't excuse the fact that it did. And it's worth noting that justice don't always make a person sleep better at night. Not in the slightest."

Vaughn's listening, but she's not hearing, 'cus her frown's only getting deeper.

The sound of Jesse's boots crunching on the hard earth sneaks up on us. He appears round the side of the house.

"What'd I miss?" he asks.

"Only me preaching on deaf ears," Kate says. "Come on. It's time for dinner."

Vaughn spends the meal fuming, her eyes latched on to her plate, chewing 'bout as gracefully as a bull.

"Did I tell you I picked up the post in Prescott on my way through the other day?" Jesse says to Kate. "Sarah wrote. 'Parently our guest"—his eyes flick my way—"and his friends stormed her place when fleeing Wickenburg. They nearly got Jake. He took a shot to the right side, just above his heart."

Vaughn's gaze snaps up for the first time since we started eating. "But he's all right? The boy?"

"Yeah, he'll be outta work awhile, but he's healing fine. How do you know Jake?"

"I stayed at the boarding house a night. He showed me to my room. He's your . . ."

"Nephew. My sister's son. After I got married, I left the family ranch to her. Her drunk of a husband ran it into the ground a few years later, and she left him. Took Jake and moved to the city proper. They been running the boarding house ever since."

"I'm glad he'll heal," I say. "Boss took an unfair shot. The boy weren't even armed."

"That sincere?" Jesse says, angling toward me. " 'Cus I can't figure why yer still calling Rose 'Boss' if you ain't riding with him no more."

I swallow a bite of food, the truth too painful to utter. 'Cus I'm scared of Boss still. 'Cus calling him anything else would mean I've broken ties and moved on. 'Cus declaring my independence would as good as damn my mother were Boss to ever get his hands on me again.

"Jesse, please," Kate says.

"I can't be mad?" he continues. "Jake wouldn't be hurt right now if it weren't for the Rose Riders."

"Same could be said if you never sold the ranch. Or our lives never crossed."

"That's different."

"I know. But Jake's gonna be fine, and it ain't worth getting all riled over something already done happened. We gotta think ahead."

"Ahead," Vaughn says. "I like that. Since the Kid refuses to accept my offer, I'd like to discuss when I can go to town to find a gunslinger."

Kate wipes her mouth with a napkin, sets it down on the table. "I reckon you won't mind giving us a moment of privacy first? Me and Jesse and Reece?"

Vaughn's frown is back quicker than a snake oil salesman whipping out his wares. She glances 'round the table, pausing on me. I shrug. She overheard the Coltons' talk earlier, and she's gotta know that anything they propose ain't something I had a hand in. Still, this ain't the response she's looking for, 'cus she gives a mountainous sigh, tosses down her napkin, and stands up so quickly her chair skids back. Then she grabs a jacket from the hooks by the door and stomps outside.

The door slaps 'gainst the frame.

"She didn't have to vacate the damn house," Jesse says.

"Let her cool off," Kate says, then turns toward me. "I'm just gonna cut right to it: Jesse and I been talking, and we're willing to pay you five hundred if you see to the rest of yer buddies. Double that if'n you bring us proof the job's done. Payment'll be made in solid gold ore."

"Gold ore?" I laugh. "Why're you living in some drafty, isolated home if you got that much gold to yer name?"

"We don't like to touch it if we don't have to. It ain't worth the trouble."

"Yer lying," I say. "You don't got that money."

"What folk you know that got two residences fully stocked at all times if'n they don't got at least a little extra coin?" Jesse questions.

All right, then. I reckon he's got a point. How they financed this home were one of the first things to cross my mind when we entered the clearing.

"Fine, you got *some* money. But running cattle?" I glance at Jesse. "Fetching eggs from a coop and eating flapjacks every morning?" A nod at Kate. "This ain't how a couple with a thousand dollars to spare passes their days."

"Will you do it or won't ya?" Kate asks.

"And remember," Jesse says, staring me down, "if'n you wanna make things right, you gotta face yer demons."

And I do, I do. It's like what Vaughn was hinting at the other day—it ain't just about what I think or feel, it's how I show that in actions. But money is what drives men like Boss, and I can't let it drive me. 'Specially not when Ma's life'll be on the line if'n I mess up.

"If I do it," I say after a moment, "it's gotta be 'cus I *want* to, not 'cus I'm being paid."

"Fine, do it for no money at all," Jesse says. "Hell, I'll help ya, even. I gotta face my own demons, too."

"And what demons do you got?"

Jesse sets down his utensils, then looks me dead in the eye and says, "I killed yer boss's brother."

Well, there it is. The confession I been waiting for.

"Jesse!" Kate lurches upright.

"Nah, it's all right, Kate," he says, waving a hand to settle her. "The Kid's figured it out already. He's suspected it since he first wandered onto our Prescott claim."

Kate glances between the two of us, her eyes glossy and on the verge of terrified tears. Somehow she don't loosen a single one as Jesse goes on to spill what is surely their most valued secret: How Kate hired him, the son of an old family friend, to see to her father's killer. How Jesse did just that and took all the money off Waylan Rose's body when it was done, including a heap of gold and a mysterious three-dollar coin he didn't even discover among all the gold till months later. He passed that blasted coin on to me, and it cursed me just as it's now come back to curse him.

"This is why I need to make sure them Riders ain't a threat no more," Jesse says. "Luther ain't gonna quit seeking vengeance. Not ever. And me and Kate ain't gonna rest easy till he's gone, and all his boys with him. Same could be said of the rails they terrorize and all the poor souls they strike down in the process."

I thumb my lip. "I thought you didn't trust me."

"I trust that we got the same enemy, and that's a mighty fine ground for a partnership. Plus Charlotte said Luther's been using yer ma to keep you in line. I know you ain't gonna go rogue with that hanging over yer head."

"And when it's all said and done, how do I know you ain't gonna put a bullet in my back?"

"All any man's got is his word, and that's all I can offer, seeing as you don't want the gold. So what do you say, Reece?" Jesse Colton holds out his hand, reaching 'cross this table that divides us like a river, two souls on opposite shores thinking maybe we can meet in the middle.

I reckon we can, maybe even have to.

Hiding forever ain't an option for me, and finishing the gang ain't a thing I can do on my own. But with the help of a retired gunslinger? With careful planning and the right approach?

I thrust my hand out and shake with Jesse Colton.

CHAPTER TWENTY-NINE

CHARLOTTE

The Rose Kid finds me in the stables, brushing down the sorrel to keep some warmth in my hands. I hadn't realized how bitterly cold it was before storming outside, and then once I'd crossed the clearing, my pride kept me from returning to the house.

"Everyone's getting ready for bed," he says, his breath visible in the cold. "Now that Jesse's back—"

"I'll stay out here."

"It's freezing."

"I don't care."

"Well, I do." His brow wrinkles. "I'll manage here fine. You should take the bed."

It is not a large stable. The stalls are narrow, and the only one not housing a horse is full of farming gear—buckets and hoes, shovels and saddle stands. There's a wind tonight, too, strong enough that it cuts through my jacket. It even chased off the owl that had been singing a sad song from somewhere among the pines earlier. An evening spent out here will be a harsh, uncomfortable one, even bundled under blankets.

I think of the Rose Kid's effects sitting on the kitchen table these past nights while Kate and I slept with a weapon within reach. He has not acted suspiciously. He's stayed in his room every evening and done no one harm. My treatment in the stagecoach has become the exception, his actions suggesting that the person I faced on those barren Arizona plains is not truly him.

"If it's too cold for me," I say finally, "I don't see why you should have to suffer it either. One of us can take the mattress in the bedroom, the other the floor."

"Fair enough."

"What happened inside?"

"Dinner," he says.

"You know damn well I'm talking about the conversation I wasn't allowed to be present for."

"Jesus, Vaughn," he says, laughing. "Few days with the likes of me and yer already cursing like an outlaw."

"We are nothing alike, and you'd do well to remember it. Now, what did they want to discuss?"

He shrugs. "Taking care of the Rose Riders. Jesse were the gunslinger Kate hired to avenge her father. He admitted it."

So that tale Kate fed me about "Nate" was nothing but a lie. She never wanted to help me. She just wanted to protect her own hide.

"Jesse's gonna help me see to the boys," the Kid goes

on. "None of us got much of a future till they're in the ground, so we'll come up with a plan and then go after 'em."

"So that's it?" I throw the coarse-bristled brush into a bucket in the corner. "I'm stuck a prisoner here while everyone sees after their own needs? Why the devil wasn't I allowed to be present for that conversation?"

"Prolly 'cus they figured you'd react something like this." He makes a flippant gesture at my person.

"They still should have had the decency to say it to my face, to admit that my dilemma means nothing to them."

The Rose Kid frowns. "Jesse and Kate'll be dead if the Riders find 'em. Same goes for me or my ma. But what's the worse that happens if'n you don't get a gunslinger? Yer ma holds on to her family fortune and marries a businessman! What an awful fate."

My blood nearly boils. "You do know how one consummates a marriage, I presume? That she'd be forced to . . . She'd have to . . ."

The Rose Kid's brow wrinkles uncomfortably, and I surmise he hadn't considered how a man takes his bride to bed following a wedding, regardless of whether the bride desires to be there.

"And that's assuming he doesn't kill her following the marriage," I go on. "He doesn't want to share the wealth, my uncle. He wants to assume it and possess it fully in time. So pardon me for being concerned about an imminent threat in my life. My mother is already at risk, while you and the Coltons will only be in danger if you actively go looking for a fight and manage to get caught.

But please, tell me again how I am overreacting. Tell me again that my troubles are meaningless!"

He stands there, quiet, the weak moonlight catching his swollen nose as he diverts his eyes.

I shove past him and head for the house.

After confronting Kate about the "Nate" lie ("I said what I had to") and asking Jesse if he will serve as my gunslinger before tracking the Riders ("I ain't a gunslinger no more, and never really was one to begin with"), I retire for the evening, livid and fuming.

Too worked up to sleep, I scribble in my journal by light of the lantern, and by the time the Rose Kid reappears, I've already claimed the bed.

"I'm sorry for what I said 'bout the marriage. I hadn't thought of it that way."

I glance up from my work, but that's the only indication I give him that I've heard his apology. Perhaps it is petty of me, but emotionally, it's all I can offer.

He grabs the pillow and spare blanket I left at the foot of the bed and goes about setting up his own bed on the floor. When he lies down, he disappears from view and is so blessedly quiet, it's almost as if I'm alone again.

"So what's yer story?" he asks suddenly from the floor. "You know, besides the horrid uncle and all."

"I don't have a story," I say dryly, although perhaps I should have said *I don't want to talk.*

"No story! Yer a writer, ain't you? Yer type can pull a story outta a pile of cow chips."

I roll my eyes—not that he can see it from his bed—and continue to draft in my journal. I'm summarizing what I witnessed of the P&AC gala, which is pointless, as the affair has surely been covered by now, but it's keeping my mind busy and my anger somewhat quelled.

He pushes up onto his elbows, bringing his face into view. "Why you wanna be a journalist, Vaughn? They don't even print the facts, them reporters. You might as well just write novels."

That does it. I snap my journal closed around my pencil, marking my place. "That folks can print lies in the paper, and those words are then read as fact, is precisely what makes responsible journalism so important! One could argue it is the most important form of writing, and I'd have thought you'd agree. If all you say about your history is true, the papers have misrepresented you countless times."

"That a family trade, reporting? I got your relatives to thank for it?"

"No. My mother is a midwife and my father was a businessman."

"Was?"

"He passed last week."

The color drains from his face. "Oh."

"I don't want to talk about this. Honestly, I don't want to talk at all." I place my journal on the nightstand and my sleeve pulls up with the motion, revealing the still-chafed skin from when I'd been bound in the stagecoach.

"I'm sorry 'bout that," the Rose Kid says, his eyes lingering on my wrist.

"Sorry enough to help me with my uncle?"

He blows out a sigh. "It's possible yer uncle ain't gonna fold from a simple threat," he says. "It could take more —possibly a bullet—and I ain't the one to do it. I got a few killings left in me, only they're already saved for Boss and his boys. That's it. I gotta draw my line in the sand. You get that—right, Vaughn? You understand?"

He meets my gaze and holds it. There is sincerity in his eyes. I myself have preached about the necessity of change, insisted that he couldn't run from his past forever, yet this answer infuriates, because I *do* understand. I see his argument, and even still, I'm left confused. The Rose Kid was supposed to have no morals. He was supposed to be easy to hate.

I roll away, putting my back to him.

The room is swallowed in darkness a moment later when he douses the lantern.

There is no denying it: I am on my own. I cannot count on him or Kate or Jesse, so I will find my own gunslinger. Tomorrow at dawn, before anyone wakes, I'm leaving.

CHAPTER THIRTY

CHARLOTTE

I wind out of the mountains come early morning. The trail did not diverge, and for that I am grateful, because it was rather faded and difficult to follow to begin with and the weak light of early dawn certainly didn't help. As I nudge the sorrel out of the tree cover, the land bucks and heaves, unfolding toward a valley. It is a clear day, with good visibility, and I can see the railway in the distance, like a line of charcoal drawn across the dust-colored earth. The P&AC runs north to south, and based on the position of the sun, I'm well aware of my location. This must be Chino Valley before me. I'll find Prescott to the south.

Even on the horse, it takes a little while to pick my way down the shrub- and cacti-strewn slope, and when I finally reach the tracks, I gaze back up the hill. The trail to the Coltons' is just barely visible, a faint white scratch among the trees. It could be nothing but washout from rain or snowmelt. No one would expect a homestead here. There is nothing to be seen for miles.

I pause to make a small marker of stones beside one of the rail ties. If all goes well in town, I will not be returning to the Coltons', but nothing has unfolded as I've imagined thus far, and it seems prudent to take precautions.

A wind sweeps across the valley, tugging at my jacket, urging me on.

I turn the sorrel north and heel her. As we fly, I picture the P&AC rails plans I've seen spread over Father's desk. Seventy-three miles of standard gauge line, starting up north at the Seligman depot along the Atlantic Pacific and cutting south into Prescott. If I've determined my position correctly, it will not be a short ride to Banghart's, but it remains too risky to search for a gunslinger in the capital.

The tracks blur to my right.

The valley stretches out ahead.

And I fly like a bullet out of a barrel, following the rails straight and true.

Banghart's is smaller than I expected. The depot and hotel are easily the most prominent buildings, and the street is eerily quiet despite it being around noontime. The town—if it can even be called that—barely appears populated.

I visit the small general store and approach the clerk.

"I'm looking for a hired gun," I say, cutting straight to the point. "Are there any men in town looking for work?"

The clerk squints at me, then glances outside, past my sorrel at the hitching post and toward the building across the way.

"You could try Parker at the hotel. He's always looking to take on odd jobs. Tell him Norman sent you."

The hotel is not a grand establishment, but for the likes of the town, I'm rather impressed. The construction is well kept up and the carpet in the foyer is vibrant and clean, putting the one in the Wickenburg boarding house to shame.

"I'm looking for Parker," I announce to an elderly woman reading the paper behind the front desk.

"'Bout?"

"A job. Norman sent me."

She looks up from her reading, and her eyes crinkle at the corners as she finds the pistol belt slung at my hips. It's cinched down to the tightest buckle hole and still sags a bit, but I'd borrowed it from the Coltons nonetheless. It was hanging with their coats—perhaps the very belt Kate said she can no longer easily wear while pregnant —and it seemed a more convenient way to carry Father's Colt than the bedsheet sack I'd fashioned before leaving Prescott.

"Parker deals with some unsavory types and asks everyone to leave their effects with me," the woman says.

I don't like it, but I'm desperate. I unlatch the belt and place it on her desk.

"You can wait in his office—first door on the left." She motions down the hall. "And make sure to close the door to keep the heat in. I'll go find Parker."

The office is windowless but cozy. A fire crackles behind a simple writing desk, and the dark green walls are covered in framed newspaper clippings. I shut the door as instructed and examine a few of the pieces. Parker is a bounty hunter, according to the stories. The most recent pictures show an elderly man—perhaps nearing seventy —but his experience can't be ignored. There are at least a dozen outlaws whose capture he has immortalized on his wall.

I can barely believe my luck. I'm desperate enough to hire just about anyone claiming skill with a pistol, and here I've found a bona fide bounty hunter. That's sure to strike fear in Uncle Gerald, have him see reason. If Parker agrees to the task, he could be in Prescott by tonight, Uncle Gerald singing a new tune by morning.

I move along the wall, reading piece after piece. Just beside the door, I catch voices in the hall.

"A girl?" a man says. "That ain't my typical client. Think it could be Gerald's niece?"

I freeze, my heart thrumming in my chest.

"Maybe," replies the woman I spoke with earlier. "Go on and question her."

"Word is she ain't quite right in the head, that she'll likely give false names and make up some story. Gerald said getting kidnapped by the Rose Kid rattled her something fierce."

"Then don't bother interrogating. Just take her to Prescott and turn her over to her uncle. If it's a mistake, you let her go then."

"The money *is* good."

"Damn right, it's good. Even after giving Norman his ten percent for sending her our way. I'll get the horses ready."

One set of footsteps fades out, leaving the foyer, and the other gets louder as it moves down the hall.

I back away from the door, reaching for the Colt, only to remember I left it with the woman. The footsteps stop outside the door. I fly to the desk, my hands scattering papers and inkwells. The doorknob turns. My fingers close over the column of a wrought iron candlestick.

Parker grabs my shoulder, and I spin, swinging in defense.

He jerks his head away, trying to dodge the blow, and the candlestick connects with his temple. There's a sickening, dull *thunk,* and he falls to the floor like a lead cannonball.

Then comes the blood, pooling beneath his head.

There's too much of it.

The candlestick slips from my fingers and clatters to the floor. Bile scratches my throat. I stumble away, still staring at Parker as I wipe my mouth.

His chest isn't moving. His eyes aren't blinking. The blood seeps toward me, traveling along the grooves between the floorboards.

"Parker?" comes the woman's voice.

I race from the office, where I collide with the woman,

knocking her off her feet. Then I'm sprinting down the hallway, slowing only to grab the Colt from where it still sits on the desk, spilling into the midafternoon sun. I dart for the sorrel, my heels aching as the fresh blisters there burst. I've no sooner untangled the mare's reins from the hitching post and stepped into the saddle than the woman hobbles into the street, yelling, "She killed Parker! She murdered him!" A pistol flashes in her hand.

I heel the horse and fly out of Banghart's. When the first bullet screams, the sorrel nearly bucks me. My thighs and torso ache in protest as I use every muscle to stay in the saddle. With a firm hand on the reins, I manage to keep the mare headed straight, and after five additional shots miss me, there's a brief lull. I glance over my shoulder.

Banghart's is shrinking in the distance, and no one is following me.

Even still, I ride as hard and fast as I can manage, my heart never slowing its frantic beating in my chest. Shadows begin to stretch across the plains. The sun starts to sink toward the craggy land to my right. When I think I'm nearing the turnoff point, I slow and search along the rail until I spot my tiny marker.

I dismount to kick it over, scattering the stones. Then I'm back on the sorrel, turning her west and ascending the hill that leads to that faded, godforsaken trail I had no intention of traveling again.

CHAPTER THIRTY-ONE

REECE

As dusk falls, the sound of approaching hooves startles the lot of us.

Kate's just starting dinner and I'm stoking the fire, so it's Jesse who grabs the Winchester and darts to the window, expecting the worst.

"It's just Charlotte," he says, sounding 'bout as puzzled as I feel.

It were a surprise to all of us when we woke to find Vaughn gone, but we all understood. Kate was even a little relieved. "Let her go home. She ain't gonna find her way back, nor will she wanna." And that's why Vaughn's reappearance don't make a lick of sense.

I set the poker aside and push to my feet, following the Coltons out the door.

Vaughn draws rein near the stable and swings off the sorrel. I take one look at her and know something's wrong. She's wearing the same spooked look she had on for most of the time in the stagecoach, and her hands are trembling.

"We didn't think you'd be coming back," Jesse calls, 'parently unable to see the tension in her shoulders.

"Something's wrong," I say, shoving past them and jogging into the clearing. Vaughn's wearing the beige dress borrrowed from Kate, and there's blood on the skirt—dark, as though the material were dragged through a river of it—plus a spattering on her front.

"Oh my God. What happened?"

"I went to B-Banghart's," she says, her lip trembling 'bout as bad as her hands. "My uncle has a b-bounty on me. He's said I'm not right in the head after being kidnapped by you and that he just wants me home."

"You were recognized?"

She nods. "I thought I was hiring a gunslinger, but he was a bounty hunter, and instead of proposing a job for him, I had to . . ." She puts her hand to her mouth. There's water building in her eyes, but she blinks it back. "I didn't mean to kill him. I only meant to knock him out, but there was so much blood . . ."

"Were there witnesses?" Kate asks.

"A woman at the hotel," Vaughn says. "I wasn't followed."

"If'n yer uncle's bounty mentioned that I kidnapped you," I say, thinking out loud, "it won't matter that I let you go, that you came to Kate on yer own or went to Banghart's solo, neither. The Rose Riders'll hear yer name and my name and assume I'm holed up near Banghart's too."

"Jesus Christ, this ain't what we needed," Jesse says. "They'll come searching. They'll be crawling the valley."

Vaughn starts scrubbing at the blood on her skirt, not bothering to look at him.

"We were supposed to take care of them boys on our own terms, but now we gotta do it while they're looking for us!"

She scrubs harder.

"You might as well've advertised the whole thing!"

She works the material so hard, her hand blurs.

"Whitewashed a building and painted WE'RE HERE! Sent a telegraph saying—"

"Can you not do that?" I snap at Jesse. "Not now."

His mouth hangs open, mid-sentence.

"It's already done," I insist. "And a lecture ain't gonna change what happened."

Kate gives Jesse a knowing look, as if to say *I'm with Reece on this one*. Then she squeezes Vaughn's shoulder reassuringly. "I'll boil some water for tea," she says, and waddles for the house.

It's quiet for a moment, the clearing silent 'cept for the grunting of the pigs over by the tank.

"I'm sorry," Jesse finally says to Vaughn. "It's just—it ain't what we needed. More folk looking for us."

"Lord Almighty, I get it!" Vaughn erupts. "I messed everything up! I get it, I get it, I get it!" She jogs away from us, heading for the tank.

"You shoulda stopped at *sorry*," I tell Jesse.

"Kate says I never know when to bite my tongue."

"She ain't wrong."

224

He runs a hand through his hair, frowning, then grabs the sorrel by the reins and leads her to the stable. I grab a blanket from one of the stalls before darting after Vaughn. She's dropped to her knees in the shallow tank, scrubbing at the hem of her dress while she shivers.

"Get out before you damn near freeze," I tell her.

She turns and finds me standing there, blanket tucked under my arm. Her fingers are raw from the scrubbing, knuckles blue with cold. It's like me talking 'bout the temperature makes her finally feel it, 'cus she scrambles from the tank. She flops to a seat in the mud and I drop the blanket over her shoulders.

"You had to," I say.

She grunts but keeps staring at the water. "Is that how you deal with it? You tell yourself you had no choice and that soothes your conscience?"

I find a rock in the mud and sit beside her. "The first time's the hardest," I admit. "You'll have nightmares, prolly. I couldn't sleep for weeks after mine."

"How'd it happen?"

"You don't care."

"I do, or I wouldn't have asked."

I knead my hands together, not sure I want to reopen those wounds. They're hard enough to think on, but it ain't like I've ever been able to talk 'bout them neither. Riding with the gang made sure of that. But maybe that's how healing works. Maybe sometimes you gotta bleed out the poison in order to recover strong.

"'Bout a week after I started riding with the boys," I begin, "we were identified while passing through a town.

A deputy rounded up a small posse to come after us, but they never stood a chance. Boss waited till that posse entered a dry arroyo, and then he had us open fire from our perch farther up the gully. When he noticed I weren't shooting, he told the other boys to stop. There were only one posseman still standing by then. I reckon he were 'bout the age I am now."

I press my thumb into the palm of my shooting hand, staring at the thin scar there.

"And?" Vaughn prompts.

"The fella knew he was beat. He threw his gun up to us and told us to ride off. Boss picked up the man's weapon and told me to execute him. 'I ain't shooting an unarmed man,' I said. Boss kicked me in the back, and I went tumbling into the gully, splitting my palm open on rocks as I tried to slow my fall. When I came to a stop, I were 'bout a few dozen paces from the posseman.

"Boss checked the fella's pistol and snapped the chamber shut. 'He's armed now,' he said, and threw the pistol back down to the posseman. It landed near his feet. That fella looked at me and the gun and me again. He knew Boss weren't gonna let him walk home. I reckon he figured it better to die fighting than to just roll over and take it. So he dove for the gun and I made my decision as his barrel leveled with my chest. I shot him."

"You had to," she says, same as I told her.

I turn toward her. "You know what happened next, Vaughn? Boss came sauntering down into the gully. He plucked the pistol from the dead guy and showed me that the chamber were empty all along. He'd emptied it before tossing it over. Boss clapped me on the shoulder, smiled, and said, 'Guess you shoot unarmed men after all, Murphy. Yer one of us now.'"

"You didn't know. You didn't have a choice," she says.

"Ain't there always a choice?"

"But Rose tricked you. If the gun had been loaded and you didn't shoot, where would you be?"

"Dead," I say. "But like you, I did what I had to in the moment, and it's haunted me ever since. That's our punishment. We gotta live with the things we done."

She looks right at me, and it ain't like the glares I've been given so far. This look ain't hateful or vengeful or full of spite. It ain't judgmental neither. No, this is warm, something akin to understanding.

"Reece . . ." she says slowly.

I shoot to my feet.

She keeps looking at me, and I think there's gonna be more, but that's it. Just my name. Not the Rose Kid, but *Reece*. It leaves me feeling like I been knocked from the saddle.

"You should change out of them wet clothes," I say. "Before you get ill." I head for the house, not once looking back.

CHAPTER THIRTY-TWO

CHARLOTTE

Dinner is a stew of potatoes and rabbit (pulled from one of the snares), plus freshly baked bread. It is warm and surely flavorful, but I barely notice.

I can't stop picturing Parker's face as I struck him with the candlestick—his eyes wide with shock, his mouth caught in a perfect *O*.

You had to, Reece said.

I refuse to believe it. I understand what he meant, can follow every point he made, yet it still doesn't seem fair. Parker was my enemy for that one moment at the hotel, but that does not mean he was a bad person. In fact, the clippings on his wall suggested he was a very *good* person—an old man nearing retirement who had delivered many an outlaw to the Law. Uncle Gerald can be quite persuasive, and as far as Parker was aware, he was doing us both a favor. I was just a confused, ill-minded young woman, terrorized by the Rose Kid, whose doting uncle longed to see her safely home. Parker was only trying to do what he deemed right. And I killed him for it.

"You understand, right, Charlotte?"

"What?" I glance up from the stew.

"It ain't safe for you to leave again," Kate says. "Not after what happened at Banghart's. Word of that man's death's only gonna bring more bounty hunters to the area, and you'd do best to lie low a little while."

I touch my brow, feeling dizzy. She's right—I know she is. I can't very well help Mother if I end up thrown in jail or charged with murder, but Mother doesn't have days to waste. I could doom her by sitting still.

"At least one good thing's come of all this," Reece says. "The Rose Riders'll make their way to Banghart's."

"I already said that ain't nothing but trouble," Jesse argues. "They'll be looking for this clearing, searching us out."

"That's why I'm gonna go to them."

"They'll kill you," Kate says. "And if they don't give you the bullet, they'll give it to that ma of yers."

"Not if I give 'em what they want."

The room seems to ripple with tension, everyone at the table suddenly very still.

"I will shoot you myself before I let you give us up to Rose," Jesse snarls.

"Yer misunderstanding," Reece says. "See, I been thinking . . . Say I go for a ride 'long the rail, and when they show up, I tell 'em I've been looking for 'em. That I got an in with the man Boss wants dead—the gunslinger done killed his brother. They'll wanna come straight here, but

I'll say yer holed up strong. Too many guns. A path that bottlenecks. I'll suggest they get on a southbound train from Seligman instead and I'll be sure to get the man on-board. They'll think I'm turning you over, Jesse, when really, you and me'll be waiting to pick 'em off one by one."

"Why bother waiting for the train?" Jesse argues. "I'll follow when you try to meet 'em. Stay hidden in the trees and take 'em out while yer proposing the train setup."

Reece shakes his head. "You'll barely get one shot off before Boss realizes I've conned him and shoots me dead. And that's even assuming there's tree cover where we end up meeting. Or that the whole gang's together. Last thing I want is to be making the deal with Boss and one the other Riders finds you camping out in the shrub. Once they see I ain't loyal, it'll be over. The train job's the way, and I can pull it off if you let me set it up alone."

"There's just one problem with that," Kate says. "Remember yer buddy that got away back in Prescott, the one you and me shot at from the porch? He already knows you ain't loyal."

A smile spreads over Reece's lips. "Nah. He *thinks* I ain't loyal. He didn't see me kill no one, and his back were turned and fleeing by the time I joined you firing from the porch. It all happened so fast. All I gotta do is plant a seed of doubt, make Diaz reconsider what he saw, and Boss'll believe me."

It all seems too easy, but the Coltons are seriously considering it. As I swallow another spoonful of stew, they exchange meaningful glances, unspoken words passing between them.

Reece glances around at us, resolute. "Look, Luther Rose don't want to think I defected. He wants to believe I'm loyal. If'n I give him the right story, he'll accept it and fall right into our plan. His bloodlust is blinding him, his need for revenge making him sloppy."

"That I can believe," Kate says.

"But what if he doesn't buy it?" I argue. "What if Rose doesn't wait to hear your story and shoots you before you even get a word out? Folks entering the lions' den rarely emerge unscathed."

His smile flattens into a thin grimace. "I thought 'bout that too, Vaughn, but it's a risk worth taking. Even when I consider all the ways it can go wrong, it still feels like the right course." He glances my way, his eyes hollow. "I gotta do this. For myself, for the Coltons"—he glances at them—"for all the Territory. This is how I make up for the bad I done. This is how I set things right."

The Coltons nod in agreement and start discussing how Reece should wait a day before wandering the plains. The Rose Riders will surely hear about my incident with Parker, but it may take a little time for word to travel and for the gang to make it this far north.

And all the while I remain silent, thinking how grossly I have misunderstood the boy sitting beside me. He is not an innocent man, true. His hands are not free of blood, but neither are mine as of today. The lifelessness in his eyes no longer scares me. It is not an indicator of him lacking a soul, but rather the very real proof that he has one—one that's seen and done evil and struggles to make amends with that every single day.

Outside, I'd called him by his name for reasons I was not entirely sure of. I think maybe I just wanted to hear myself say it. But now I know the truth. He's not really the Rose Kid. Perhaps he never was. He's just a kid, just Reece Murphy. It's that simple, and that complex.

I have terrible dreams, as he predicted. Mostly of Parker not dying, but crawling his way across the office floor after me, blood dripping into his eyes, a hand clawing at my skirt.

The third time I wake, I am sweating, a gasp still on my lips. Reece does not stir from his spot on the floor.

I abandon the bed and wander into the kitchen, where I find Kate awake too, reading a book by the soft glow of the fire. She must have roused it, as it is not coals, but a nest of flickering tongues.

"Can't sleep?" she asks, but I can tell she knows precisely why. I imagine she is no stranger to the kind of nightmares that follow dark deeds.

I nod.

"Me either." She bobs her chin at her belly. "Figure I might as well enjoy myself if the little pest won't let me sleep."

"What are you reading?"

"A favorite." She holds it up, and I catch the foiled title —*Little Women*— glittering in the firelight. "I think I done read it a hundred times now. You wanna turn?" She holds it out.

"Oh, no, I couldn't."

"There's others," she says, signaling at the shelf behind me. I turn and find many of the books previously shelved in her Prescott home. "Jesse brought 'em," she explains.

I run a finger over the spines, considering my options.

"Yer daddy helped build the train, didn't he?" Kate asks.

"He funded a lot of it, yes."

"Try *Around the World in Eighty Days*. It's got trains and then some."

I lift it from the shelf and sit with her, reading. The protagonist, Mr. Phileas Fogg, strikes me as eccentric to the point of insufferableness, but his adventures are compelling enough and his passion admirable, and I find myself turning the pages in a bit of a trance. It is Kate who pulls me from my daze.

"Charlotte! Oh, Charlotte, feel this." She grabs my hand and presses it to her belly. The life inside her rolls beneath my palm, then jabs at me with what can only be a limb. Kate smiles wide, the firelight gleaming off her teeth.

I pull my hand back. "What happens if Reece can't make contact with the Rose Riders, Kate? Do you intend to hide here forever? Don't you want your normal life back?"

"There's no *normal*," she says. "Not for me. It ain't been normal since my pa died, and even when he were 'round, I ain't sure it was normal then, neither. We were always hiding."

"From who—the gang?"

She presses her lips together, sighs through her nose. "We're all running from something," she says finally. "Even you. Yer running, ain't you?"

"I suppose."

"Right. So you can either be scared yer whole life or you can try to enjoy it. I suggest the latter. Otherwise yer gonna blink and find yerself old and weary, taking yer last breath and regretting that you passed yer years tense and worrisome." She sets her book on the table. "What is it you really wanna do, Charlotte? Start now. Don't wait for *this*" — she motions at the room — "to pass, 'cus there ain't a guarantee it will."

She retires to the bedroom before I can tell her that what I really need is a hired gun to threaten Uncle Gerald. But after today, I know I need to lie low. I can't help Mother — can't save us both — if I get myself caught, so I take Kate's advice in the sense that I turn to my ambitions for a distraction. I retrieve my journal from the bedroom and write by the light of the fire. I write as though I am already the journalist I dream of being, and I make note of everything worth reporting. Reece's hollow eyes and crippling guilt. Kate's bulging belly and Jesse's history with Waylan Rose. Uncle Gerald's greed and extortion and illegal bookkeeping. I record it all, right down to what I can recall of the weather (frost-dusted mornings and crisp, arid days) and the landscape (ponderosa pines in the mountains and a valley lined with rails).

When my lids begin to droop, I pad to bed, my brain too busy sifting through narrative details to dwell on the thing that kept me from sleeping in the first place.

CHAPTER THIRTY-THREE

REECE

Come morning, Kate starts suffering what Vaughn calls false labors. Basically, her body's practicing for what's to come. Vaughn's ma being a midwife and Vaughn herself knowing a bit 'bout birthing might come in handy, seeing as the Coltons are far from their Prescott claim, and Kate's midwife ain't gonna be here when they need her most. Vaughn insists she don't know how to deliver no child, but seeing as she knows what false labors are, Jesse and me remain convinced she'll be a heck of a lot more help than the two of us.

Vaughn starts doing a lot of Kate's chores so the woman can rest—from milking the cows to gathering the eggs to churning the milk so there's butter for later in the week. It's keeping her busy, and I'm grateful 'cus she called me by my name yesterday—my real name—and I ain't sure what to make of it. Maybe it was outta guilt, or a slip in the wake of shock from what happened with Parker. Prolly it is for any reason but the thing I keep hoping: that she's seen I'm something more complicated and human than the monster stories have made of me.

I throw my attention into checking the snares that afternoon, happy for a distraction. I aim to ride for the rails early tomorrow. I weren't lying when I told the Coltons I could do this, nor when I claimed it were the best course. But that don't mean it's gonna be easy, and the waiting is damn near killing me. The snares yield two hares, but I'm still anxious and jittery as I hike back.

In the clearing, Vaughn's hauling a bucket of water from the tank. She straightens, waving when she sees me approaching, her other hand shielding her eyes from the sun as she smiles. My stomach twists like a wrung-out dishtowel, and I duck inside without waving back.

The Coltons and Vaughn spend dinner assaulting me with questions, pretending to be Boss and seeing how quickly and convincingly I can spit out a response. It ain't doing nothing but making me overthink things, and I don't wanna rehearse this. I gotta sound sure and honest tomorrow. Confident. I retire to bed early, and when they utter protests at my back, I close the bedroom door decidedly.

I don't hear Vaughn come in later, and 'bout an hour before dawn, when I wake, she's still sleeping.

I creep out to the stables and saddle Kate's horse, Silver—the palomino that tried to nip my fingers the day we arrived at this clearing. Kate said she's a good steed, will follow my lead once saddled. I cinch the billet strap and mount the mare.

It's a cold morning. Clouds are hanging thick and heavy in the sky, threatening snow, and a sharp wind bites at the back of my neck. I flip up my jacket collar. From a towering pine, a horned owl hoots eerily, watching me move through the trees.

When I meander outta the worst of the mountains, the sun's just beginning to crest the distant horizon. I scan 'long the valley, but there ain't a sign of no one nearby. It's good news for me. I wanna be wandering the rail, with no hint at where I done come from, by the time Boss shows up. *If* he shows up.

You better bet I'm coming, he whispers. *Did ya ever truly think I'd let you go?*

I look over my shoulder, tense in the saddle. I ain't heard him in so long, and now ain't the moment I want him back in my head. I heel Silver and fly into the valley. I keep her going at a good clip and don't see a soul the whole way to Banghart's, where I linger on the outskirts of town, worried 'bout the wrong type of folk recognizing me and alerting the Law. I chew on a bit of jerky I brought in Silver's saddlebags, drink some water.

Maybe they ain't gonna show.

Maybe the talk of Vaughn's mishap with the bounty hunter never reached 'em.

I glance at the sun, high in the sky. If'n the gang ain't here, I gotta get moving. Last thing I want is to be navigating the mountains back to the Coltons' at dark.

Grabbing Silver's reins, I turn her 'round, and once again, we're riding hard.

'Bout a mile or two from town I get an uneasy feeling someone's watching me.

Ahead, the land is flat as far as I can see, and ash white beneath the winter sun 'cept for a small smudge of black beside the tracks. It's moving. A man on horseback.

The skin on the back of my neck bristles. I glance over my shoulder, and my heart damn near drops to my feet.

Three more men have appeared 'bout a half mile behind me, too far off to recognize. But then one of 'em raises a hand to his mouth, whistling, and I know it ain't the Law that's done surrounded me in this pinch. It's them—the Rose Riders. Maybe they been holed up in Banghart's, snooping 'round for word of me. Maybe they been camping out here on the plains. It don't matter 'cus they've found me, and while this were exactly what I were planning on—hoping for, even—that whistle strikes fear.

The three horses behind me surge to life. They gain on me easy 'cus I've brought Silver to a trot so's to make it clear that I ain't meaning to run.

I recognize 'em as they close in. Diaz at my rear. Crawford to the left and Barrera to the right. They all got the reins in one hand and a drawn pistol in the other, their mouths curled into snarls. To the south, the dark figure is taking shape—Luther Rose, waiting atop his horse, a hand resting on the butt of his pistol.

"Boss!" I call out, the other boys closing in on me. "Thank God. I been looking for you guys all week and—"

Hands clench the front of my jacket and things tip sidewise as I'm dragged from Silver. I hit the hard plains, gasping, and find Diaz towering over me. He strips my pistol from my belt and tosses it aside.

"Diaz," I begin, hands held in surrender, but he just cracks me between the eyes with a fist. The world goes starry and crisscrossed as he throttles me again and again and again. I sputter, gulp down air, but Diaz goes right on attacking. Fists and boots, no regard for where he hits. The fleshier, the better. I curl—the only defense I got—but my face is already wet with blood, and Diaz shows no signs of stopping. Things go fuzzy. Darkness tugs at the corner of my vision.

"That's enough!" Boss shouts. "I wanna talk to a man, not a corpse. Bring him over."

Diaz hauls me to my feet. "There's a special place in Hell for traitors," he says, and spits in my face.

I don't even feel the saliva connect with my skin. My whole body's on fire, and I can barely keep my head up. I count to ten to keep from fainting, stumbling over my feet as Diaz drags me toward Boss.

With a shove, I fall to all fours before his horse. I don't got the energy to stand or look at him, so I stay there on the ground. A crunch of hard earth tells me he's dismounted.

"Leave us," he says.

"But Boss—" Diaz argues.

"I said fall back!"

He does.

A moment later, my chin is pushed up by a pistol and I find myself staring into Luther Rose's eyes. They're blue-green, like a reservoir reflecting the sky, cold as frozen ice.

"Sit up, Murphy," he says.

My head spins and my stomach aches. My right eye is all but useless, prolly swollen shut.

"Drink." Boss presses his canteen into my hands.

Half the water ends up on my shirt, so I reckon my lips are split and butchered, too.

"Apologies 'bout the treatment, but it ain't easy to swallow that you been looking for us." He takes the canteen back. "In fact, it looks much more like you been trying to run. First from Wickenburg, then Prescott, and now right here, too, just miles from where that Vaughn girl done bashed in some poor bloke's head."

"No, I been playing it smart," I insist. " 'Cus I found him, Boss—the cowboy you been after, the one that gave me yer brother's coin. I found him."

His brows peak with interest.

"I had to run from Wickenburg—I were surrounded, unarmed—but then I picked up a lead on the cowboy and followed it to Prescott. I figured I could get the cowboy first and then come find you. But he weren't home and his wife got the jump on me, tied me up in her barn. I think she aimed to turn me in for the bounty, but the boys showed up and—"

"You decided to kill Jones and Hobbs instead," Boss growls.

"No, that were—"

"Don't lie to me, Murphy! Diaz said you did it!"

"Diaz don't know nothing," I snap. "The woman killed 'em. I heard hollering, and by the time I got free of my ties in the barn and made it to the house, Jones and Hobbs were already dead. Diaz showed up a moment later, and the woman fired on him quicker than I could get a word out. He rode off, thinking I were his enemy. I went 'bout earning the woman's trust, then her husband's. They don't got a slightest idea 'bout my true intentions."

Boss's brow furrows as he works this over. "I only need the cowboy. Why didn't you kill the woman from the get-go?"

"I figured it'd be easier to earn her husband's trust if'n it looked like I helped her," I grit out. "And besides, she were pregnant."

"You always were soft," Boss says, "but that ain't a fault. Not really. You gotta have a conscience to run an outfit like this, and you could make a fine boss someday."

I barely contain a laugh. "A conscience? You kill women and children!"

"I ain't never killed a woman," he snarls, "nor a child. And I ain't never forced you to, neither!"

I open my mouth to argue only to realize he ain't wrong. In all the time I've ridden with him, I ain't never seen Luther Rose fire on no one but a grown man. He lets the others see to the women and children. He watches, like that ain't a crime in itself. Like he's somehow nobler for refraining.

"I argued with my brother on this constantly," Boss

continues. "I said it weren't necessary, all the innocent slaughters, but he said it keeps yer boys' bloodlust satisfied, controlled. The real villains are the ones beneath the fella in charge. You see what I'm saying, Murphy? We ain't that unalike, you and me. We both recognize evil, and you gotta have that vision to be a bossman. You gotta know the difference between good and bad so you can keep yer boys in line, know what's worth pardoning them for and what earns them a swift shot between the eyes."

I can barely believe what I'm hearing.

Luther Rose puts his hands on my shoulder. "I wanna pardon you, Murphy. And knowing you found the cowboy—that all this time you been trying to find me to hand him over—I can. Let's gut that pig so you can come home and take over for me someday. Yer the only one of my boys left that's got the disposition for it. What do you say, son?"

The way he says *son* is like the sweetest song. His hand's on my shoulder, warm and strong, and he's looking at me like there's something in me worth loving. Like he's proud of me. Like I'm a thing worth standing by. He'll clean me up and see to my injuries and make sure I'm cared for. I know it. He'll be my father if I let him.

But I ain't never gonna forget that those warm, strong hands are the same set that carved a rose into my forearm, beat me countless times over, and stood by while innocent folk died on his watch.

"I ain't yer son," I say, "and I don't wanna be, neither. I want out."

He frowns. "That's a shame to hear, son, truly. There's

lots I could teach you. But I'm a man of my word, and you claim you've found the cowboy. So lead me to him, and our deal's done. I'll have my revenge and you'll have yer freedom."

It's so damn hard to not smile. Even with my pulse throbbing in my ears and my body aching and beaten, I wanna grin ear to ear. I stifle the urge, keep my face serious.

"I can't bring you to him," I say. "He's holed up in a clearing, but the only way is in bottlenecks. Someone's always on watch, and they'd pick you off one at a time before you even got within fifty yards of the house."

This ain't true, of course, but he's got no way of knowing it.

"So . . ." Boss prompts.

"I'll bring him to you instead."

It don't matter that this is the plan. Boss's smile is wicked, and I feel like a rat, a bastard, a bit of slime on the side of a creek bed. 'Cus even with the best intentions, this could go wrong. Even with all the planning in the world, I could be damning Jesse Colton. This could end with him dead.

"When?" Boss asks.

"Sunday. Get on the southbound train at Seligman. I'll make sure the cowboy gets onboard before Prescott. Bring Diaz and the others, too, for backup. I'll meet you in the dining car."

Boss considers this a moment, his eyes firm on my bloody face. I reckon he wanted to take care of this first thing tomorrow, but he thinks I'm truly on his side, and he knows I can't show up beat this bad and demand that Jesse take a trip with me on the rail. It won't look nothing but suspicious.

"Fine, Sunday," Boss says finally. "But first, gimme the bastard's name. I ain't letting you ride off without any collateral."

I'd hoped to avoid this, and I know the Coltons had, too. But we all knew that gaining Boss's trust'd be easiest if I give him the name. And besides, Diaz knows which claim belongs to the Coltons back in Prescott. All the gang's gotta do is ask 'round a little and they'd figure out exactly what I'm 'bout to give up.

"The man you want's called Jesse Colton."

"Jesse Colton," Boss repeats, the corner of his mouth pulling into a smile. Then he leans in real close, every feature on his face going hard and fiery, and says, "If you cross me, Murphy, yer ma will pay for it tenfold. Do you hear me? If you don't bring me Jesse Colton on Sunday, she will lose a finger. And for each day that follows that I don't have my revenge, she'll lose another. When she's outta fingers, she'll lose toes. And when she's outta those, she'll earn herself some pretty scars. I hear folk don't like to pay for cut-up whores, and it'd be a pity if she can't earn a living."

His eyes dance as he makes this threat, the murderous bastard who swears he does no ill 'gainst women or children. But I can't show that I'm scared, can't give away that I'm upset. I gotta look like this ain't a concern in the slightest.

"I'll bring you Jesse Colton come Sunday," I tell him.

We stare at each other a moment, like two gunslingers ready to pull. Then he leans forward, ever so slowly, and offers me his gloved hand.

I shake it. Knowing right well I don't got honorable intentions, I shake that bastard's hand. 'Cus I ain't lied. I'll bring him Jesse Colton. Just not for the reason Boss hopes.

He straightens and waves the boys over. They gather round, looking at me like a pack of hungry coyotes. When Boss tells 'em they'll ride out first, Diaz explodes.

"You trust this rat?" he roars.

"I trust," Boss says calmly, "that he's got a plan with the best chance of success."

"The bastard killed Hobbs and Jones!" Diaz continues. "He's a backstabbing, no-good coward, and he's gonna stab us in the back 'gain now!"

"Murphy said the lady killed Hobbs and Jones."

"The woman weren't even armed."

"You were so frazzled, you don't remember what you seen!" I snap. "Who shot at you, Diaz, me or her?"

"She did," he admits. "She fired on me right through the doorway."

"Think it's possible you remembered things wrong? That maybe she were armed all along and it was *me* that needed help, only you rode off and left me to rot?"

His frown deepens. It were dark that night, and everything happened so fast. There's a crease in his forehead, and I know that if I press him more, he'll break.

"Well?" I bark.

"If'n that's all true, tell me why yer still alive, Murphy.

If'n she killed two of our boys and shot at me, why ain't you dead?"

"'Cus I'm sharper than you, Diaz. I played her like a fiddle, made her sympathize with me, pretended to be a victim. I got close to her so once her husband showed up —the cowboy Boss's been after all these years—I could turn him over. And look what I got for it!" I motion at my bloodstained jacket. "A beating for being loyal."

"I still got a bad feeling 'bout this, Boss," Diaz says, shaking his head. "Murphy ain't never been one of us, not really. We can't trust him."

"Aw, lighten up, Diaz," Crawford says, all his weight held on his good leg. "Kid's got a right solid plan, and if it don't pan out, his ma gets a knife. You think he wants things to go south?"

Boss nods in agreement, then grabs me at the wrist and pulls me to my feet. Every muscle in my body protests, bruised and weary.

"See you Sunday, son." The other boys don't seem to catch it, but his voice trails up at the end just slightly, like he's asking a question.

"See you Sunday," I echo.

That's all he wants to hear, 'cus he mounts his horse and heads north. The others follow suit. It begins to snow, and I blink fat flakes from my eyes as I watch the gang grow smaller. They disappear 'long the horizon, and I keep watching to make sure they don't come back.

I used to think Luther Rose didn't have no foible, but he does. Despite the legends and stories and infamous tales, he's human. He's got a weakness, and it's me. I'm the son he never had, but he ain't my boss no more, and I will be his undoing.

I smile, and it hurts like hell.

CHAPTER THIRTY-FOUR

CHARLOTTE

It is snowing heavily when Reece finally returns.

He appears on the trail leading to the clearing, and at first he is nothing but a dark smudge among a storm of snowflakes. When I see him slumped forward in the saddle with his oversize hat angled aggressively against the weather, my initial reaction is relief. Dusk is approaching, and we've been worried for a solid hour. He'd been gone longer than expected. But as Reece draws nearer, that relief dissolves into terror, for what little I can see of his face is revealed to be covered with blood.

"Reece!" I shout to the Coltons. "Something's happened to Reece."

I'm out the door before Kate has wrestled herself to her feet or Jesse has straightened from where he's stooped to tend to the fire. Mutt chases at my heels, then easily pulls ahead, kicking up snow.

Already an inch has covered the ground, blanketing the clearing and coating the tree limbs with white. Only the tank remains naked, its unfrozen surface reflecting the gray sky overhead.

I skid to a stop before Silver and tug at her reins. Reece takes this as a sign that I mean to help him down, which I do, but he leans forward too quickly, slipping from the saddle, and all but dives onto my shoulder. I do my best to slow his fall, but he still topples headfirst into the snow, graceless, limp.

I roll him over, and my hand flies to my mouth, smothering a gasp.

He found the Rose Riders all right, or rather, they found him. One of Reece's eyes is swollen clear shut, and his nose—which was still recovering from when Kate cracked him with the rifle a few days ago—is broken once more. Blood coats his mouth, chin, and the bandanna around his neck. His jacket is stained with it too, and I'm sure that beneath all those layers of clothing he is covered in bruises. It's a miracle he even made it back to the clearing, that he didn't fall from the saddle miles earlier.

"Christ," I mutter.

"It's a sin to take the Lord's name in vain, Vaughn," he grits out. "Don't tell me I done had a bad influence on you."

He has to be clever about everything. Even now.

"You haven't seen yourself. You'd be swearing too."

"Made it all this way in a snowstorm," he counters. "Can't look that bad."

"Smart-aleck."

He smiles and cringes just as fast, but not before I get a glimpse of his teeth, smeared with red.

Snow crunches behind me.

"Aw, hell," Jesse says, getting a good look at Reece. Kate is waddling over too, a blanket slung over her shoulders.

Jesse squints down the trail. "Were you followed?" The path is silent, no movement except for the falling snow.

"Nah," Reece says.

"Yer sure?"

Reece nods, blinks snow from his eyes. "I got jumped before I could get a word out to 'em. But it's all good. They rode out first. I watched 'em go."

There's a collective sigh among the rest of us, and Reece closes his eyes, exhausted. For a moment the clearing is so silent I can hear the crystallized snow ping and plink as it joins what's already gathered on the ground.

Jesse grabs Silver's reins. "Charlotte, can you get Reece inside while I see to Silver?"

I nod.

"I'll help," Kate says.

"You'll go sit by the fire and not tax yerself," Jesse says.

"I'm sick of being fretted over and treated like a delicate doll," Kate grumbles. "The baby's gonna come eventually, even if I do nothing but lie in bed for the next week. I can't keep it in forever."

Jesse gives her a pleading look, and she reluctantly complies, plodding for the house.

"Reece?" I crouch down beside him.

"Yer using my name," he says.

I guess I am. I take one of his arms and guide it behind my neck. "Just stand with me, all right?" I push to my feet, and he manages to aid in the process. I am too short to properly assist him, and so most of his weight ends up slumped into me, threatening to push me over, his feet dragging clumsily through the snow as we make for the house.

"I know this is part of the plan," I mutter as we walk, "but it doesn't look very promising."

"It'll pan out. You'll see."

"All I see is the infamous Rose Kid looking beat to hell."

"And ain't that what you always wanted?" He cocks his head toward me, and the brim of his hat skims my forehead. "To see me suffering and hurt?"

I jerk my gaze back to the house. "I never said that."

You'll hang for this, " he says, mimicking my voice with an uncanny likeness. "That's what you said in the coach. I know that rope you were making were meant for my neck."

"You held me against my will then."

"And now?"

There's an anguished tone to his voice. Perhaps it is the result of being beaten so badly. Perhaps it is also desperation, a need to have someone validate the good that exists in him, despite all the bad he has done. Whatever it is, I can't ignore it, and I foolishly look him in the eye.

The one not swollen shut doesn't appear hollow or lifeless, but deliriously hopeful.

And now things are different.

This is the answer he is waiting for, and I can't give it

to him. Things are indeed different, but not in the way he hopes. Against all odds, I trust him somewhat. But not wholly, and I don't know if I ever could. Not after he attempted to rob me at gunpoint. Not after that trip in the stagecoach. I cannot forget these things, and he should never forget that I intended to strangle him with a rope made of my own undergarments.

If he longs for forgiveness, I can give that. But I fear he is looking for more.

"That's what I figured," he says suddenly. "I'll see myself in."

He withdraws his arm from my neck and wearily ascends the stoop. He did not feel warm when he was beside me, but as he steps into the house, I feel his absence, the winter air cold and piercing where our bodies had touched.

Kate fills a bowl with water, and after she's helped Reece sponge most of the blood from his face and neck, I stuff a sock with snow and hand it over. He applies it to his swollen eye. There's a nasty gash above it that may need some needle and thread, but it's hard to tell with his skin so puffed up.

When Jesse comes in from dealing with Silver, we all sit at the kitchen table and Reece tells us what happened. Luther Rose took the bait, but not before Reece took a beating.

Jesse begins talking about Sunday—what time he

and Reece should ride to town, if they should travel to-gether or separate, how they plan to take the gang out on the train. Reece suggests that Jesse remain hidden, in a cargo car if possible. After meeting up with the gang, Reece could then lead them into a surprise ambush.

"You can't do it, Jesse," Kate says suddenly, her eyes glossy in the firelight.

"Course I can," he argues. "It's a good, smart con. Damn near foolproof."

"Maybe it's better to just tip off the Law, let 'em know the Riders'll be on the train."

"And risk 'em screwing it up and Rose getting away? Nohow. That puts Reece at risk, too."

I nod in agreement. If even one member of the gang gets away, they'll know Reece crossed them. They'll make good on the offer to torture his poor mother, and then they'll kill him, too, if they manage to find him again. Plus, they have Jesse's name now, which means the Coltons are indefinitely at risk. Even still, Kate is shaking her head like a spooked child.

"No. I won't have it."

"Kate . . ." Jesse reaches for her.

"You can't," she repeats, slapping the table. "I won't let you go risk yer life when it ain't you Rose wants."

Reece and I glance at each other quickly, then back to Kate.

"What the devil are you talking about?" Reece asks, but I think I might know. In fact, I feel foolish that I hadn't considered it before.

Everything she said to me that day she taught me to

handle the rifle . . . How her youth was founded on acting before thinking, how her brashness cost lives and loss, how Nate sounds so much like Kate, and how that person is now dead. Because that part of her died. She left it behind.

"There never was a gunslinger," I say quietly. "It was you, Kate. You killed Waylan Rose."

"Guilty." Her lip quivers, caught between a smile and tears.

"But you were . . . what? Eighteen?" Reece balks.

"Is it so hard to believe a girl mighta bested Waylan Rose and his boys?" Kate snaps. "Yer look of shock says *yes*. I walked into the sheriff's office in Phoenix a decade back and told 'em the Rose Riders were dead. It was them that chose to see a young man in my place, to assume I were a hired gun. And I never corrected the rumors. Why would I? I wanted to stay hidden, and that was easiest when I were just some sad orphaned girl."

I don't doubt any of it. She is brash and bold, quick enough with her rifle and sharp enough to not miss, certainly not one to be trifled with. I imagine she was only more tenacious as a kid, when she did not carry life inside her and sought only revenge for her father's murder.

"Kate, I ain't exactly innocent," Jesse says. "I helped."

"But I pulled the trigger—"

"Wait," Reece cuts in. "Kate told me she'd seen the rose mark carved on her father, and also yer brother. If'n she didn't hire you to be her gunslinger, how'd yer brother get caught up with Rose?"

"My father were killed for a journal that showed the way to a rich gold mine," Kate explains, hanging her head slightly. "I went to Jesse's father for help, only he'd passed on. Once Jesse knew I were chasing Rose toward a mine, him and his brother offered their help so long as they could take some of the prize."

"Only Will never wanted that gold," Jesse says.

"Is this the same gold you offered to pay me with?" Reece says.

"Yeah, and it's just as well that you don't want it," Kate says. "It ain't clean money. Too much blood and hate surrounding it. Might even be cursed. Like I said, we don't touch it if we can manage."

I recline in my chair, trying to digest this development. No reporter on earth could ask for a better story. This is an epic—lost gold and a female gunslinger and a quest for revenge that catches up with her ten years later, when the Rose Kid finds his boss's brother's killer, but instead of seeking retribution, the Kid turns on his own to help the enemy and thereby win his freedom. It sounds like the stuff of fiction, the kind of tale that would have townsfolk talking and a paper going back for reprints.

"Do you think Rose knows the Coltons have the gold?" I ask Reece.

He shakes his head.

"It don't matter one way or another," Jesse says. "There's only one way outta this mess, and I gotta be involved." He turns toward Kate. "I already lost Will to the Rose Riders. I can't lose you and the little one, too. I couldn't live with myself."

"And I'm supposed to live without you?" she says. "That ain't fair."

Jesse's mouth presses into a sly smile. "That's insulting, Kate. I ain't gonna miss."

CHAPTER THIRTY-FIVE

REECE

I peel my clothes off in the bedroom, cringing with each layer shed. What ain't wet with snow is still damp with blood and clings to my limbs. Even the stuff that don't cling—like my boots—are hell to remove. Every muscle I got is racked with exhaustion. Bending hurts. Tugging aches. Breathing deep stings. I pray I don't got a cracked rib. Diaz sure kicked me enough.

When I manage to get fully undressed, I step into the shallow bathing tub. It's been filled since yesterday, but the water's still cold enough to make me gasp, and then I'm cursing myself for gasping, 'cus that makes my whole body thrum with pain.

I splash my face, sponge water over my neck and shoulders. Blood and dirt lift free, swirling in the tub. What don't come clean I scrub free, slowly and carefully, 'cus every bit of pressure hurts. I imagine that Vaughn's silence at my question is also something I can wash away.

And now?

What a ridiculous thing to ask. I ain't surprised by the way she turned her attention to the house, avoided answering. I ain't nothing but embarrassed that I thought things might be different suddenly, that her calling me Reece these last few days might mean something. I've held all the power since our meeting. She was a mark for theft. She was a prisoner in a coach. She was a mouse and I were the cat, and I can see why that is so unfair, why it is wrong and greedy of me to hope that she sees us as equals.

And still I'd hoped.

I don't know what's gotten into me. I ain't looked at a girl twice these past few years. Hell, I never wanted to lay eyes on a girl, period. I saw how Rose used my mother to keep me loyal, and I knew fancying someone would only give him more ammunition to use against me. So I been keeping my head down. Till now, I guess. Just a little bit of distance from him, a chance at a new life, and I've let myself get sloppy.

I finish washing and step outta the tub. While drying, I catch sight of myself in the small mirror above the dresser. I look as bad as Vaughn implied. I've regained some visibility outta my right eye, but it's still badly swollen, and while the gash on my brow has stopped bleeding, it don't look pretty. There's a shadow of a bruise already showing on my chest, too, and I reckon it'll be joined by more come morning.

I fish my clothes from the floor. With some cringing, I get my socks and underthings on. The pants are harder, but I manage to wrestle 'em on and have just finished with the button when there's a knock at the door.

Before I can say nothing, it cracks open.

"Jesse said you could borrow one of his — oh!" Vaughn's gaze lifts from the clean shirt she's carrying, and she blushes. "I'm sorry. I'll . . ."

"Just give it here." I snatch up the shirt and struggle to put it on. I hate how I can't move without cringing, that the simplest tasks have become a challenge. I can feel Vaughn watching, and when I look, she's focused on the bruise on my chest. The way her eyes dart away from my skin only to flit back makes me wonder if maybe I were wrong before. Maybe I pulled away too soon, didn't give her a chance to answer. I ain't been with many women, but I know they don't blush for no reason. Then again, most don't enter a room when the occupant ain't had a chance to respond to their knocking, neither. I go to work fastening the shirt's buttons.

"So what happened, precisely?" Vaughn asks. "The confrontation and the fight?"

"I told you already."

"Yes, but the details. Were you not terrified? How did you think so quickly in a situation like that?"

Her tone is so serious, concerned. There's even a bit of awe.

My hands fall to my sides, the shirt buttons forgotten. Something *has* changed; she just couldn't find the words to express it. Her eyes leave the bruises to meet my gaze.

She seems closer now than she did as she helped me into the house, which is crazy, 'cus we're standing several feet apart. A bit of my blood still stains the collar of her dress. I remember how her frame strained beneath the weight of mine, how I were a burden she couldn't bear and yet she tried nonetheless.

Vaughn gives me the most innocent, carefree smile as she breathes out a laugh. Something careens 'gainst my ribs.

Then she flips open a journal I hadn't noticed her carrying, and as her expression steels, I see my mistake.

"What does Rose look like?" she continues. "Give me his likeness. And the others. I want their names again and a description of each." She is no longer looking at me, but at the pencil she's brought to paper.

I'm a damned fool. I am so naively stupid.

"Get out," I say, throwing a hand at the door.

"What?" Her face snaps up, and she's so confused it's almost comical. *Almost.*

"Get out!"

"But—"

"This ain't a story, Vaughn, it's our lives! Mine and Kate's and Jesse's. It ain't something for you to treat like a game or to write up with fancy, romantic words, alls so you can sell it to some sensational paper and line yer own pocket. Our misfortunes ain't yer ticket to success."

"I thought that—"

"You didn't think nothing, dammit. You've never had to! You gone through yer whole life getting everything you want, prolly even taking some of it. Well, you can't take this! Have some decency, for Christ's sake."

She glares at me a moment, a violent crease between her brows, pencil gripped so hard her knuckles go white. Then, like the child she is, she leaves and slams the door.

That night, I pace the kitchen, unable to sleep.

Do you think Rose knows the Coltons have the gold? Vaughn asked.

I'd shaken my head truthfully in that moment, but now a memory haunts me: Luther Rose showing me a coin that looked exactly like the one he'd pulled from my pocket that day at the Lloyds'.

"They're twins, see," he'd said. Like my piece, the currency marking had also been shaved off, but the eagle gleamed in the firelight. "Waylan and me grew up in an orphanage. When he ran off, he swore he'd return for me once he had the means to provide a decent life. I begged to go with him then and there, but he were eight years my senior and I'd've only slowed him down. He said there were nothing like these coins in the world, not with the way he'd done shaved off some of the details, and so long as I had mine and he had his, it would be like we were together." He laid the two coins 'gainst his palm, tracing the faces with a thumb. "Waylan came back for me, like he promised, but he were different. Quieter, keener. He stood straighter and smiled more, only the smile were crooked and a little empty. When the orphanage director tried to stop him from taking me, he shot her in the chest, then emptied the donation box before we fled."

"Why're you telling me this?" I'd asked. It was but a few days after my attempted escape from the whorehouse. I was bruised and sore, my limbs still tight and tender.

"'Cus I want you to understand that love makes us do odd things, son. Remember that."

He worried his palm with his thumb. The coins had disappeared into his jacket.

"Do you think he ever found it? The cache he was after in the Superstitions?"

"Gold," Rose clarified. "It were solid gold ore—rumored to be enough for a man to become a king. Or to disappear."

His expression were difficult to read in the firelight, but it looked almost like longing. I got the feeling it were his brother who wanted the kingdom, but that Luther wanted to disappear, to make a life for himself. Maybe even an honest one, with a family and a respectable career.

"So do you think he found the gold?" I asked.

"Yeah. I think it's what killed him."

Before, I thought he meant that the quest had killed his brother, that Waylan had led his men into the heartless, cursed depths of the Superstition Mountains, and though they'd found the gold, they'd been too weak to make their way out. Maybe they got lost. Maybe they starved. Maybe even it was Indians who got the best of 'em.

But as I sit before the Coltons' fire, I fear I heard Luther Rose wrong. Or misunderstood. Perhaps he meant that his brother found the gold and then was killed *for* it. Kate wanted revenge, after all, and she got it. With it, she inherited an enormous fortune, one she's kept hidden and quiet because it ties her to so much blood.

And prolly Rose suspects this.

Which means he'll want more than vengeance. He'll want the gunslinger who killed his brother, and then he'll want all that gunslinger's gold, too.

I straighten from the chair, peer out the window. The snow is undisturbed, pale and gleaming beneath the moon.

I weren't followed. I know I weren't. My head were heavy as Silver carried me back, but I'd managed to look over my shoulder a few times. There were nothing but snow and wind on my tail. This house is still safe, secure.

But if Jesse fails on Sunday . . . if he dies when Rose lives, I'll be asked to show the way to this house. If I run, I'll be followed. If anything goes wrong, this clearing *will* fall.

I consider telling the Coltons that Rose likely knows 'bout their gold. I consider, also, the fear it'll evoke, the way the plan might crumble, and I can't run no more. Neither can the Coltons. The Rose Riders won't stop coming. They'll track us to the gates of Hell.

So we'll do what needs being done. We'll board that train, shoot clean and true. And if Jesse Colton misses, I'll finish what's been started.

CHAPTER THIRTY-SIX

CHARLOTTE

The snow stays on the trees through the night. There is no breeze, and so it rests there, blanketing the limbs like slender white dress gloves come morning.

It is only after I have descended the worst of the chilly mountains and am leaving the barely visible trail that signs of the storm fade. To the south, the plains are a patchwork of dusty gold-brown and muddy snow, unfolding toward Prescott.

I left at dawn, and I did not tell a soul.

Reece never came to bed, and when I crept into the kitchen after a night of fitful dreams, I found him before the fire, asleep in a chair, his head at an awkward angle. Without his hat, I could see the whole of his beaten face. He looked younger in sleep, and peaceful, too. He so often confronts the world glowering, his demons etched across his brow, a sullen expression held tight in the muscles of his tanned cheeks. Asleep, he did not look like the young man who had ordered me from the bedroom the evening prior, his eyes flashing with anger. Instead, he looked like someone I should wake to bid farewell.

But I knew better.

I'd spent the evening avoiding him. Kate must have heard the entire affair, or at least his outburst, because as I dried dishes, she said, "When folks tell us our own faults, it's only natural to deny 'em. The things Jesse threw in my face! And the things I threw back! Sometimes we see others more clearly than we see ourselves. At least 'bout the stuff that matters most."

I hated that she was defending him instead of nursing my hurt. Worse still, I hated that she was right. That Reece was right.

I *was* using their story—their life—as a step to climb. That much I can admit. But it was for reasons more complex than my own ambitions. The only way I've been able to keep that pool of blood beneath Parker's head from spreading before my eyes has been to throw my efforts into comforts, into writing. I did it to cope, not realizing the damage and hurt I caused others in the process.

This whole time I have wanted nothing but to silence my uncle, and Reece is correct when he says I have put my family's quandaries above those of the Coltons. I have been so intent on having someone else solve the problem for me, I failed to see that I had the power to solve it myself.

And so I will leave them to their story—Reece and Kate and Jesse—the tale I am not entitled to tell. I will see to mine instead.

It will not be easy, or free of risk. After all, folks entering the lions' den rarely emerge unscathed. But I have watched Reece face his demons, and I am willing to face the devil in my own life. I carry on for Prescott.

It is a Saturday, exactly a week after the gala that welcomed the rail to the capital, and the streets are painfully quiet compared with the last time I was in town. Snow lingers in the shadowy recesses of windowsills and rooflines, hiding where the sun cannot reach it. Everything else has melted, and the sorrel's shoes leave prints in the damp streets.

A block from the post office, I pull out my journal and retrieve Uncle's ledger sheets from where I'd tucked them for safekeeping. I copy the numbers into the journal, then tear out a fresh page and draft a letter. When I'm finished, I flag down a young boy who has a bag of salt tucked under his arm. He jogs across the street to meet me, his nose pink from the cold.

"Will you take this to the post office"—I hand him my note—"and have it mailed to this address?" I pass him another scrap of paper bearing the address for the *Yuma Inquirer,* with attention to the editor, Ruth Dodson.

"Mail it with what money?" the boy asks. "Look, miss, I

ain't got time for games. Ma'll have my ear if I ain't home with this salt soon."

I give him enough to cover the postage. "Come back when the job's done, and I'll give you a full dollar."

He looks at the coin in his palm. I took it from a pitcher on Kate's mantel, where, dusting with her the very day we first arrived at the clearing, I'd discovered that she stores a bit of spare change. I feel guilty about swiping the money, but have every intention of paying it back.

The boy snatches up the note and turns briskly on his heel, heading for the post office. I'd expected him to question why I couldn't mail the letter myself, but I suppose the prize was too pretty.

A carriage rumbles by.

A bird warbles out of view.

The courthouse clock strikes the hour.

The boy is taking too long.

Just as I'm certain my identity has been discovered, the post office door opens and he steps back onto the street. Relief floods me. I can be recognized in time, but not yet. There is one more thing I need to do.

"It's mailed?" I ask when the boy jogs over.

He nods. "Gimme the dollar."

"Only if you promise to not speak of this to anyone."

He shrugs, unconcerned. "Whatever you say, miss."

I pass him the coin he's earned, and he tucks it into his pocket, then walks off without a goodbye. I glance up and down the street. No one seems to have noticed our transaction.

A stagecoach pulls up alongside the post office. A canvas bag full of letters and parcels is loaded. Even if someone were to search the letters, it's the boy's handwriting on that fateful envelope, not mine, but still I linger, waiting for the coach to drive off. I watch as its wheels leave narrow lines in the dirt streets, and then I wait an extra minute once it turns from view. Five minutes. Maybe ten. Enough that it has exited the city proper.

Satisfied, I ride to the offices of the *Morning Courier,* barely a block from the courthouse. The streets are busier now, and more than one set of eyes drifts in my direction as I stop before the two-story brick building. A proud whitewashed sign boasting the word COURIER looks down on me from above an arched window. I secure the sorrel and head inside. Even before the door swings shut behind me, a man in dusty work clothes has rushed over to inspect Uncle's horse. He glances my way, and I give him a sheepish grin. The snakelike smile he shoots back betrays him, as does the speed at which he rushes off.

He does not realize he is playing right into my hand.

I hurry up to the second floor, where Mr. Marion has set up his office and printing press. A daily paper is a rarity in this part of the country, and already typesetters are hard at work, lining their composing sticks with tomorrow's stories, letter by letter. The cases the men labor at are tall, like podiums, but several times wider — a sight both intimidating and inspiring at once. To think that every page of printed word is possible because of the individual letters housed in each case's drawers.

One of the men catches me watching and jerks his

head toward a slightly ajar office door. Of course I must be here to see the editor. Why else would a woman visit a press?

I nod my thanks and knock on the door. A voice calls for me to enter.

Nudging the door open, I find John Marion bent over his desk, scribbling frantically. When he looks up to greet me, I am not prepared for his plainness. The editor writes with such force and fanfare I presumed him to be a striking man or, at the very least, a man who exuded authority, but he has a patchy beard and an unassuming narrow face. His dark hair is swept back, so when he looks up to greet me, I can clearly see the puzzlement in his eyes.

"Can I help you?"

"I'm sorry to bother you, Mr. Marion. I know you're a busy man, and based on the staff you keep, I can see that what I'm about to ask you is not customary, but—"

"Spit it out already," he says. While his tone is gruff, his expression is not. This is just his demeanor, I realize. Much like the words he prints, Mr. Marion is not one to dance around his point or waste time on pleasantries.

I smooth my disheveled dress. "I come asking for a job."

His forehead furrows.

"I want to write for the paper, but I understand that I might need to start as a typesetter and work my way up."

He sets his pen down and looks at me pointedly. "And you assume I will turn you down because there are no women on my staff?"

"I saw the composers on the way in, sir."

"I have hired female typesetters before. My wife was one."

"Well, I have no intention of marrying you."

He lets out a belly laugh, and his plainness pales with it. Father was by far a more handsome man, but Mr. Marion reminds me of him in this moment, bright-eyed and smiling.

"Nor am I searching for a bride. My wife is retired, not deceased. But I like your wit. A paper needs a sharp sensibility to succeed. Not even having read your work, I can see that you'll do well. Here, or with another press."

I try not to show my confusion. Mr. Marion is different from what I anticipated. I expected to be dismissed immediately, not entertained. I believed him to think women incapable of such a role, but perhaps it is only Uncle Gerald who has told me this. Perhaps I am unfairly combining his beliefs with those of Mr. Marion.

"That said," the editor continues, "I do not even know with whom I'm speaking."

"Charlotte Vaughn, sir."

He frowns. "A relation to Gerald Vaughn, I presume?"

I nod. "I'm his niece."

Now Mr. Marion looks deeply conflicted. I do not match the image Uncle has surely painted of me.

"Does your uncle know you're in town? I believe he's been looking for you."

There's a commotion in the hallway, followed by a bang as Uncle Gerald barrels into the office and the door rattles against the wall.

I knew he'd be arriving, yet when I turn to face him,

I'm still not prepared for the way his presence makes my breath pinch off. He is dressed well despite the fact that he should be spending today at the mines with the workers. If he were anything like Father, he would be in slacks and suspenders, a work shirt and cap.

"Charlotte, thank goodness," Uncle croons, gathering me into a hug as though he truly cares for my well-being. "My apologies about the interruption, John," he says to Mr. Marion. "It won't happen again." He gives the editor a parting nod and ushers me out of the room, acting as though I am too weak to stand on my own feet. By the time we enter the stairwell, the act vanishes, along with his caring tone.

"I was relieved to see my horse is well. As for you . . ." His gaze dips to my feet. "You've found shoes. How unfortunate."

We burst into the morning sunshine.

A small crowd has gathered on the opposite side of the street, and so the act resumes. Uncle with an arm over my shoulder, for I'm a sick, troubled girl. A hand gripping tightly about my wrist in case I get a notion to run.

The spectators watch as Uncle escorts me toward his steed. One woman clutches the front of her dress in relief. Another has a look of pity in her eyes. They are all concerned for me, pleased to see me home. Uncle's stories have spread like wildfire over the dry plains.

I look the part, too, I realize. My dress is far from clean. Reece's blood still stains the collar. My hair is greasy and unwashed, hanging stringy and wild around my face. In hindsight, it's a wonder Mr. Marion even listened to a word I had to say. He likely printed a piece about my kidnapping on Uncle's behalf after all, citing my poor mental state and the reward that would be given for my safe return home.

Uncle Gerald heaves me onto his horse. I could scream and writhe for the show, but I go willingly. The more cooperative my entrance, the less adamantly townsfolk will cling to stories that I am unwell, and the less they will miss me when I disappear again. For I have no intention of staying longer than necessary.

Uncle's knees hold me in place, his arms imprisoning me as he grabs the reins of his mare, plus those of the sorrel. He rides his horse harder than necessary, and because I've a bad seat in the saddle, I jolt and bump against him. It is the worst bit of contact yet—crueler, somehow, than his grabbing my arm or wrestling me onto the horse. I need him, the support he provides, or I'll fall from the saddle.

I do not want to need him.

When we arrive at the house, a curtain at the bay window is drawn aside and, like an eye blinking, quickly drops into place. Then the front door flies open and Mother stumbles into view.

"Charlotte, how could you?" she screeches. "Why would you come back? Why!"

She has deteriorated in my absence. Her skin has gone ashy and her hair lost its shine. Wrinkles around her eyes seem to have spread. She looks like the unhinged woman my uncle paints her to be.

I've been gone too long. I never should have left.

"Lillian, get in the house," Uncle Gerald orders.

Ignoring him, she races forward, gathers me in her arms. She hugs me to her chest and I breathe in the scent of her. She is softer than a pillow, more familiar than any bed. Her hands grip my cheeks, and she moves my face back so she can look at me properly. Tears cling to the corners of her eyes.

"You foolish girl. You've only made things worse."

She pulls me nearer once more.

"I have a plan," I whisper into her hair.

"Lillian," Uncle barks.

She slinks to his side, takes his hand. And that's when I see it—the ring on her finger.

It is not the one she wore to honor her vows to my father, but a thinner, duller band. It is the shackle my uncle has used to bind her.

They have already wed.

CHAPTER THIRTY-SEVEN

REECE

When I wake in the morning, Vaughn's missing.

"We gotta find her," I say, palms pressed to the kitchen table. Kate's clutching a mug of hot tea like her life depends on it while Jesse checks the simmering porridge. "She don't know what she's doing, and she ain't fit for it."

"She's fit for just 'bout anything," Kate says. She sets her mug down and starts unfurling fingers. "She tried to shoot you on the train. She turned Rose's men over in Wickenburg. She weathered yer ill-treatment in the coach till she could make a run for it. Then she came to me looking for a gunslinger. And nearly shot you again in my kitchen." Kate moves on to her second hand. "She caught Jesse entering the clearing while we slept." Another finger. "She wiggled outta a bind with a bounty hunter. Should I keep going?"

"Nah, I get yer point."

"I reckon that girl might not be able to shoot like you, but she sure as hell's cunning enough to do damn near anything she sets her mind to. Besides, you don't even know where she went."

"I'm just worried, all right? What if she went to find a gunslinger again, only it pans out worse than last time? Besides, ain't you guys bothered by her up and vanishing, that she might get spotted or give us away somehow?"

Jesse stops stirring the porridge. "Why'd she be spotted? You said you weren't followed, and it ain't like there's folk in these mountains to spot her tracks."

I take a long slug of coffee. Kate's right 'bout Vaughn being resourceful. She's proved it several times over, and I don't know why I feel this urge to run after her. But if she's gone to confront her uncle without any backup, I pray she's got a solid plan. If she don't, there's a good chance I won't never see her again. I mighta said some harsh words last night, but that don't mean I wanted her gone permanently. Hell, I woke desperate to talk to her, to tell her I meant what I said, but I wish I'd gone about it differently. Kept my tone even. Made my point without insulting her so boldly. I get right furious when folks assume things 'bout me—presume to know my entire life story—and that's exactly what I did to her.

"You positive you don't want payment for tomorrow's train job?" Jesse asks.

"Right positive," I say. "But speaking of gold . . . It ain't squirreled away here at the hideout, is it?"

"Not knowing something can be a blessing," Kate says pointedly.

"I reckon it's here. Gold ain't an easy thing to transport, and you'd wanna keep it in a safe place, not the claim you call home in Prescott. Maybe it's buried out back or folded into the floorboards or hiding between horse stalls."

Jesse slops some porridge into my bowl. "You got a mind made for thievery and stealing. It's like yer supposed to be an outlaw or something."

"Here, read this," Kate says, tossing a clothbound book on the table. "You oughta keep yer mind busy, and Charlotte seemed to be enjoying that the other night."

I glance at the cover. *Around the World in Eighty Days.*

There ain't no time for reading, but to appease the both of 'em, I tuck the book into the large interior pocket of my jacket.

Later that afternoon, Kate finds me while I'm seeing to the horses. Jesse and I ride for the P&AC early tomorrow, and we can't risk a loose shoe or lamed horse.

"Why you so curious 'bout the gold, Reece?"

I lower the horse's leg and brush my palm 'long her flanks. "No reason."

"You seem to care where we keep it."

"I don't," I insist.

Kate rolls her eyes and settles awkwardly onto the saddle stand. Her belly's somehow grown even larger in the past week, and I ain't sure she's gonna be able to get back up without help.

"You remind me of Jesse a bit, when he were younger," she says. "You got this giant black cloud of regret and guilt hovering over you, and if you don't let it rain here and there, it's gonna part one day and you'll drown in the downpour."

"What the devil does that mean?"

"Just that no matter what you do, that cloud's prolly still gonna be there, hovering. You gotta learn to exist with it." She brushes a section of dark hair over her shoulder, and for a moment it's like she's swatting her own cloud, ordering it to keep its distance.

"You got one too?" I ask. "A cloud?"

"Don't we all?" She smiles, and it's the same conflicted kinda smile I seen when she admitted to killing Waylan Rose.

The pigs grunt and squeal out by the tank, and I take a few rushed steps forward so I can see 'round the stable. It's only Jesse, come out to fill a bucket.

"She'll be back," Kate says.

"You don't know that."

Suddenly the thought of not being able to properly part ways with Vaughn feels like a knife pressed to my skin. After the train job's done, I ain't dawdling. I'm riding for the sunset before the Law can show up and make my life hell all over again.

"I *do* know it," Kate says, "'cus I reckon this is her story, too."

I cringe, embarrassed. "You heard all that last night?"

"You were shouting something fierce. I think I coulda heard from much farther away than the kitchen."

I lift my hat and wipe at my brow with my forearm.

Kate goes on. "This story started as mine and became Jesse's and then yers, and now I think in a way it's Charlotte's, too. She got involved 'cus she needed a gunslinger and desired a feature for the paper, but it's bigger than just that now. If'n she wants to stay, it'll be up to you to allow it."

"Is this some kinda religious sermon I ain't fully getting?"

"I'm more spiritual than religious," she says, "and no. It's just . . . we ain't nothing but human, Reece. Most folks are good, but even the good can be greedy and selfish and scheming. Our motives ain't always virtuous, 'specially at first, but they can become so, if'n you give 'em time to change and grow."

I exhale through my nose, shaking my head. "Vaughn and I don't got nothing in common. We been at each other's throats since the day we met, and that ain't gonna grow into something more civil."

"Sounds like me and Jesse 'bout ten years back, and look at us now." She braces a hand 'gainst the saddle bench and pushes awkwardly to her feet. "Plus, you might try calling Vaughn by her name. There's a lot of power in that. I know from being an ass on this subject myself."

"I ain't a poet, and all this cryptic, symbolic talk is confusing my simple ears."

She laughs. "You know, I used to hate poetry, too. So much fluff and pomp. But it's kinda been growing on me over the years. Ain't that amazing—how a person can change?"

She shuffles for the house, her hands pressed to her lower back. I finish with the horses, grumbling to myself as Kate's words echo in my head.

How a person can change.

And just like that, I know why I started looking at Vaughn—Charlotte—differently. She'd stopped calling me the Rose Kid and instead addressed me as Reece. We started talking—having real conversations 'bout the past and the future and the road we're both walking now. She challenged me, and I challenged her right in return, and maybe we've both grown from that.

How a person can change.

Me. Her. Jesse. Kate.

I reckon she could be onto something. That this is all of our story.

Suddenly I want Charlotte to return more than ever. 'Cus it's only gonna be her story if'n she's here to play a part.

CHAPTER THIRTY-EIGHT

CHARLOTTE

They wed just yesterday afternoon, a quick ceremony while the snow fell outside. Mother tells me this as we're ushered into the house. The only reason she is not dead is because the marriage is so recent. For her to die on their first evening as man and wife would have looked suspicious. Still, I can barely hold her gaze. I know what she endured last night in Uncle's bed, and the guilt slams into me like a hammer spiking a rail tie.

I could have spared her this. If I'd returned sooner, if I'd never gone to Banghart's for a gunslinger and instead come straight to Prescott. But now Uncle has the inheritance, and he will surely dispose of Mother at the earliest convenience. Perhaps both of us, if he can manage it.

My plan no longer seems so foolproof.

I clench the armrests of the chair Uncle has shoved me into. Outside his office, Mother is banging on the door, desperate to gain entrance, but Uncle locked it. Now he sets his pistol on the mahogany desk and angles the barrel my way. My heart pounds wildly. Uncle presses his palms to the desk, leaning forward, towering before me. He is trying to intimidate me.

I hate that it is working.

"Where have you been?"

"Away."

"That's no answer."

I keep my gaze focused straight ahead, as though I am staring through him. If I look him in the eye, I fear I may lose all my nerve.

His arm sweeps out violently, knocking papers and books from the desk. A bottle of ink crashes. Black weeps onto the carpet.

"Where the hell have you been?" he screams.

"What should concern you," I say slowly, "is where you will be tomorrow."

He is around his desk so quickly, it is as if he walked through it. Fingers pinch my chin and jerk up hard, so that I'm forced to look at him.

"You don't get to threaten me, Charlotte. I always told your father that he didn't keep a tight enough rein on you. Let a woman dream too openly and she gets all types of wild notions, becomes unruly—as useless as an unbroken horse." He shoves my chin to the side and folds his arms over his chest. "You ran only to come back. Why?"

"I'm sure you noticed your ledger has been compromised."

He stills. Fear dances in his eyes. He hasn't noticed.

"I took a few pages with me."

He sifts through the mess of paper he pushed to the floor, finds the ledgers, flips them open. He rifles through them, pausing when his fingers find the rough, short edges of the year-old pages I tore out.

"Where are these sheets?"

"I gave them to Mr. Marion."

Uncle Gerald shoots up. "What?"

"I reckon it will make an intriguing story, no? *Local business owner commits fraud; lies about profits and pockets difference.* Your miners will be up in arms. Anyone you've done business with will question if you've shortchanged them. Surely your word will not be held in the same esteem throughout all of Prescott."

He grabs his pistol from the desk and races off, not even bothering to retrieve his jacket from where it is slung over his desk chair. Mother tumbles into the office as he yanks open the door. He drags her into the hall and slams the door aggressively. I hear a key turn, locking me inside.

Footsteps, another door slamming, then silence.

"Charlotte?" my mother ventures a moment later. "Charlotte, talk to me!"

I want to—Lord, do I want to—but I worry if I let my guard drop, the tears will break free and I will never regain composure.

I can hear her shuffling about in the hallway, and a moment later, a scrap of paper is shoved beneath the office door. I retrieve it and find a newspaper clipping from the *Morning Courier* in which I am reported as missing, a victim of the Rose Kid whose sanity is to be questioned.

Still, there is a reward for my return. My dear uncle wants nothing more than to see me safely home.

I love you, Mother has scrawled across the top of the paper.

It is an incredible feat to blink back the tears. I feel thirteen again, when I first declared my aspirations of being a journalist. Father had been supportive, but Mother had told me to pursue midwifing or a good marriage. Those were my options.

"Your father encourages you because the world turns in his favor," she told me. "Men do not understand what it is like to be a woman attempting a 'man's' job. I love you too much to watch your dreams crushed beneath the unfair nature of the world."

I hadn't believed her, and she'd known it. She started sliding newspaper clippings of stories she believed might interest me under my bedroom door. They always read *I love you* at the top. Just like this one now.

"I love you, too," I whisper through the door. "I'm sorry I didn't come sooner. I could have prevented all of this. I could have spared you from—"

"Do not take blame for what's happened for one second, Charlotte Vaughn," she says. "There is only one guilty party here, and it is your uncle."

"Did he change his will yet?"

"No. He plans to do it later today. Mr. Douglas is to visit."

"So the Gulch Mine and all of Father's businesses are strictly yours—ours?"

"For a few more hours, yes."

I breathe a sigh of relief.

"Where have you been?" Mother asks.

I tell her how I went to see Kate Colton the night I ran, how every moment since leaving I have been trying to find an impartial gunslinger to help us break free of Uncle. How it was slow and difficult because the Coltons were forced to go into hiding after the boy the Territory knows as the Rose Kid left them exposed to the wrath of the Rose Riders, and I found myself caught in the middle of it. I even mention the incident with Parker, carrying on quickly as Mother tries to interject.

"But we don't need a gunslinger, and we don't need the Law," I insist. "All we need is the truth about Uncle Gerald, and the threat it imposes if printed. When he comes back, he will see that I've finished him. He will flee the Territory immediately."

"Charlotte, I do not think you comprehend how thoroughly your uncle has purchased people in town. There is no winning with—"

The sound of the front door flying open and cracking against the wall sends me jumping to my feet.

"You lying, deceitful brat!" Uncle screams as he flings the office door open. I get the briefest glimpse of Mother in the hall—her face white with concern—before he slams the door shut and locks it once more. The back of his hand connects with my cheek, and I stumble away, grabbing the chair to keep from falling.

"Was this your plan—to trick me into confessing to an editor?" he roars. "To tie my own noose? John Marion is an old friend and an honest reporter. He won't print a story when there is no proof."

"But you did confess?" One look at Uncle's face—the sweat beading along his brow, the flighty state of his eyes—and I know it is true. He barged into Mr. Marion's office asking to explain himself.

About the ledgers, I can imagine him saying. *They're falsified. Please don't print anything. Charlotte isn't well. I run a fair business.*

No matter the argument, it is enough to plant seeds of doubt.

"He may not print anything, but will he keep your story in confidence?" I ask. "Can you guarantee he won't mention your strange plea to a friend, who might tell another, perhaps someone you haven't bought or bribed? Imagine the rage at the mine if your workers hear of this. Imagine what might happen if the story reaches the *Weekly Miner* and *they* choose to print something in the *Courier*'s silence!"

"They won't!" Uncle Gerald roars, spit flying from his mouth. "I own this town!"

"Then it's good that I sent the ledgers to the offices of the *Yuma Inquirer.*"

He draws his pistol and presses the barrel to the underside of my chin. "I could silence you right now," he snarls.

"That won't stop the story from printing. And killing your niece surely won't make you look more innocent in the eyes of readers."

"You forget that everyone thinks you're crazy, Charlotte. They'll think you killed yourself."

I swallow, trying to ignore the cold metal against my skin. "But will people in Yuma, who know me and Mother? People who trusted Father and respected our family? The Gulch Mine may be here in the Prescott area, but its business partners extend along the Colorado, into Yuma, and beyond. If they learn of your true nature, you will have no future in this Territory."

He leans closer, the barrel pressing harder into my throat. "That's assuming they buy the story. And the *Inquirer?*" He barks out a laugh. "A paper run entirely by women? No one will believe a word they print."

"Are you willing to bet on that?" I say.

Fear flickers over his face. He can see the dominoes lined up, the way they will each topple when the *Inquirer* prints the story. It will be there in black and white, confirming any rumors and whispers that have started to circulate throughout Prescott. The miners will be furious. If they don't kill him, the repercussions will. Mr. Marion may feel bold enough to print his own story. The Law may come calling.

Uncle's influence will crumple. His honor will vanish, his reputation shatter.

He will be ruined.

This one article will ruin him.

He deflates, the pistol falling away from my skin as he slumps against his desk. "How could you do this to me?" he asks.

"You did it to yourself," I respond. "The key?" I hold my hand out and he drops it into my palm.

I leave him standing there, slack-jawed and stunned, and unlock the door. In the hallway, Mother pulls me into an embrace. Not a heartbeat later, a gunshot rips through the house. I push away from Mother, looking down at my body—at her—certain that Uncle has just fired on us.

We are well. The house is silent, save for the ringing in my ears.

I turn back toward the office.

I already suspect what I might find, but I nudge the door open anyway.

Uncle Gerald is slumped face forward on his desk, having put a bullet through his brain.

"You can't stay here," Mother says, setting a steaming cup of tea before me. "Paul might not believe our story, and if he goes to the sheriff, there's no guarantee they'll listen to our side of things. At least not until the story you mentioned is printed and people reconsider the lies Gerald has spread about us here in town. There's also Parker to worry about. Dead at your hands. How did it ever come to this?"

Her expression is wrought with worry, and rightly so. She is absolutely correct. While one problem is solved, another has surfaced, and I never anticipated Uncle choosing the path he did. I'd expected him to run, starting over as a new person miles away where no one knew him. I'd banked on him experiencing shame and regret. I'd wanted him to suffer, to scrape by, to toil. Just once, I wanted him to truly labor for the things he might call his own. He was supposed to *pay* for his crimes, not escape them, but I suppose retribution and justice are merely cousins.

"Charlotte?" Mother says.

I take a sip of my tea, trying to blink away the image of Uncle Gerald's body. It reminds me too much of Parker, only instead of the blood creeping across floorboards, this time it seeped into ledger papers.

"Charlotte, do you hear what I'm saying? Paul will be back tomorrow. He only went to Jerome to check affairs at the mine. And if the people at Banghart's are looking for Parker's killer . . ." She exhales heavily. "You need to be gone when he returns."

"And leave you to be charged with Uncle's death?"

"Then what do you propose?"

I set the teacup down, tracing the floral pattern on the saucer with my thumb as I weigh our options.

"You should return to Yuma," I say finally, "but visit Mr. Marion first. Tell him I've been staying with the Coltons this past week, and that anyone claiming the death of a bounty hunter in Banghart's was done at my hands must be mistaken. The Coltons will vouch for me. I'll have them write him a letter. But if Mr. Marion's agreeable, urge him to print a story saying as much with haste, and also to cover Uncle's fraudulent business practices. I had suspected Mr. Marion to be in Uncle's pocket, but after today, I believe he will do what's right. I sent the original ledger sheets to Ruth Dodson, but I copied everything into my journal first. I'll give you those pages before I leave. If it's not enough for Mr. Marion, have him contact Mrs. Dodson to confirm the story. Once everything prints in the *Courier*—plus the *Inquirer* back home—we should be fully cleared. People will believe the suicide was legitimate, not a story we used to cover up a murder. I'll come home then."

"And in the meantime?" Mother asks, her brow wrinkled.

"I'll stay with the Coltons. Kate is pregnant and approaching her time. She'll need help delivering the baby, and I've learned from one of the best."

A smile flicks over Mother's face, and I glance away. The light is changing beyond the kitchen window, warning of approaching dusk. I need to leave now. The Rose Riders will board a train in Seligman come dawn, which means they are likely traveling north or already near the depot, and this is the safest time to travel.

I flip open my journal to the pages where I copied Uncle's ledgers. Tearing them free, I slide them across the table to Mother.

"Stay one night, please," she urges.

"I have to go. Please just trust me on this."

"I've always trusted you, Charlotte."

"See you in Yuma?" I ask as we hug.

She smoothes my wild hair, lays a kiss on my forehead. "See you in Yuma."

CHAPTER THIRTY-NINE

REECE

Jesse and me spend the afternoon going over our plans.

He'll board the train at the depot, and I'll chase it down on my horse later. The gang don't know what Jesse looks like, and that will be the key to duping 'em. Jesse and me can't be seen together till we're ready to fire our pistols.

We walk through countless scenarios: if'n all the boys are waiting in the dining car like I requested, if Rose's got 'em spread throughout the train, who we take out and in what order if'n something goes wrong. (Rose first. Always Rose first.) Kate butts into our planning all afternoon, sometimes offering advice, other times pleading with Jesse to reconsider, and by the time we sit for dinner, she's rattled something fierce.

"Quit pacing, Kate, please," Jesse begs.

"I don't want you to do this."

"It ain't about want, it's about need." He looks to me for support.

"Don't put me in the middle of this," I say.

But I think even Kate knows there ain't much can be done otherwise, not if they want a normal life. They need the Rose Riders gone. I need 'em gone. The whole Territory'll be safer with 'em buried, too.

The Coltons argue a bit more, till Jesse takes Kate's hand and pulls her onto his lap. He presses his lips to her forehead. It's just the one kiss, but I feel like I ain't supposed to be present. I retreat to the bedroom and shut the door.

As a kid, I were good at becoming invisible. Whenever Pa went for the bottle, I'd slink into the shadows and move 'bout our house like a ghost, keeping my back pressed to walls, trying not to breathe too loudly. Above all else, I never entered the room he occupied 'less it was absolutely necessary.

This is how I act now, only it ain't outta fear, but respect.

I want the Coltons to have their own moment, their own room, their own world. They only face the coming dawn 'cus of the blood I brought to their doorstep.

I reckon this is the dark cloud Kate were talking 'bout. I carry deep wells of guilt inside me, and yes, I ain't innocent in the path I'll walk tomorrow with Jesse. But Kate also knew what she were doing ten years back when she shot Waylan Rose between the eyes. She killed him and every last boy riding beside him. She believed them all dead, and still her and Jesse took precautions, built a hideaway, knew a day might come when they'd need to flee. The ghosts of our misdeeds can haunt us till we lie in our own graves, and it ain't helping me to lug my guilt 'round everywhere. I think 'bout Kate, brushing her hair over her shoulder, batting away that cloud of regret. I imagine mine the same, trailing behind like a cape, reminding me of what I done and all the ways I can do better. I'll tolerate it. Some days I might even wear it. But no matter what, from this day forward, it will not wear me.

I can hear Kate out in the kitchen, reading aloud from *Little Women*—to the babe inside her or Jesse. Maybe both. I collapse on the bed, still fully clothed. The pillow smells like Charlotte. I weren't even aware I knew what she smelled like, but this is her, surrounding me. The mattress is stiff, but still so much softer than the floor.

My eyelids flutter shut.

When I jolt awake, the sun's set and the house is dark. Kate ain't reading no more, but Mutt's growling low in the kitchen. I can make out a pair of voices, whispering too soft for me to hear nothing useful.

Then there's the muffled creak of floorboards. The handle of the bedroom door turns.

I lunge for the nightstand, only to remember my pistol's out on the Coltons' table along with my belt and knife.

"It's me," Charlotte says from the doorway.

"Jesus Christ." I sink into the pillow, my chest hammering. "You scared me."

"I'm sorry."

"It's fine. You just . . . you can't go sneaking up on someone like that."

"I mean about the other day," she says. "How I asked for details. You were right. It's not my story to tell."

Jesse passes by the door, heading back to bed with a candle in hand and Mutt on his heels. When his door shuts, the light dies with it, and I turn toward the night-stand. After rousing the lantern, I twist back to Charlotte. And freeze. There's a welt on her cheek, and her coat's hanging open and askew on her shoulders. She's still wearing the brown dress I last saw her in. There's blood on it.

I jump from the bed, and my hands push the coat down her arms till it catches at the crook of her elbows. Then I'm inspecting her—brushing her hair back to see her neck, the side of her head—searching for whatever injuries left the dress collar stained.

"It's yours," she says. "Reece, it's your blood."

From when she helped me into the house. I realize my hands are cupping her face, and I step away quickly.

"Why'd you come back?"

"Kate will need help with the labor," she says, but she's looking at me like maybe that ain't the only reason. "I need to lie low for a few days, also."

"Yer uncle's been seen to?"

She nods.

"How?"

"I'm tired, Reece. I'd like to sleep."

She shuffles for the bed and moves one of the two

pillows to the foot of the mattress so her feet will be up near the head. Then she sheds her coat and shoes and crawls beneath the covers.

"You ain't gonna strangle me with a noose while I sleep?" I joke when I realize what she's suggesting.

"Do you plan to steal my earrings?"

I smile, and she gives me a crooked, closed-lip grin in return. I douse the lantern and ease onto the bed, staying above the quilt. It's a cool night, but I don't got a need for it. Not with her hip just barely grazing my leg, making the bedding between us feel as hot as coals.

"He shot himself," Charlotte whispers a moment later. She goes on to explain it all. It were a good plan, a sneaky angle. Tie the noose and let the man hang himself. It ain't all that different than the con I'm pulling on Rose.

"I thought he'd just run, disappear," she continues. "Maybe try to make a name for himself in a new town where no one knew him and he could change his name. But he's always been a leech, my uncle. He only knew how to follow a trail already blazed by others."

"I'm sorry I didn't help more."

"You helped plenty," she says.

"That ain't true."

"You said everything I needed to hear. Trust me, Reece."

"All right, Charlotte Vaughn. If you say so."

I ain't got the slightest what she's really driving at. I been gruff and closed off and judgmental. The things I said to her most recently weren't exactly kind. She ventured to Kate's claim 'cus she wanted a gunslinger, and when none of us provided it, she made her own luck, executed her own plan. She don't owe us nothing. Kate's tough enough to make do without a midwife when the time comes. I reckon Charlotte knows this same as me, and if she truly needed somewhere to hole up a few days till the papers clear her and her ma's names, she coulda done just that at the Coltons' Prescott place. Coming all the way to the hideout after losing the day's light couldn't've been an easy ride, but perhaps this is just a decency she wants to offer. She's a good person, Charlotte. She ain't chasing a story no longer, so maybe it's like Kate said. Maybe there's just something *more*.

CHAPTER FORTY

CHARLOTTE

I am envious of the speed at which Reece falls asleep. Barely a few minutes after we cease talking, his breathing falls into a peaceful, languid rhythm, and though the house is silent, I can't find sleep myself.

And Lord am I tired.

Still, my mind keeps reliving the same moment: the look of surprise on Reece's face when he woke to find me entering the bedroom, then the storm that spread across his features when he thought I might be injured. He was out of the bed in one fluid moment, his hands on my shoulders and neck, then cupping my face.

I hadn't recoiled.

He moved as quickly—perhaps even faster—than he had in those days I spent in the stagecoach, but I felt no fear from the movement this time, no threat. He was deliberate but concerned, his touch gentle. When I think of it now, the places he touched seem to tingle with heat. His thumbs on my cheeks, his palms on my jaw, his fingers grazing the nape of my neck.

I flex my feet beneath the blankets, clench and unclench my hands.

I try to tell myself I am reliving this moment because it is kind and warm and good. Because it is a welcome change from the nightmares of the bounty hunter's blood or my uncle's vacant eyes. But then I'm feeling the ghost of Reece's touch again—the jacket slipping from my shoulders, his hands tracing my jaw—and I know it's more than that.

Why'd you come back?

Because I needed to disappear for a little while.

Because Kate will need my help.

And because maybe I wasn't ready to say goodbye to Reece Murphy.

Dreams find me eventually, and they are not pleasant. Uncle's cooling body. His lifeless eyes. His blood covering the ledgers, seeping into the grain of the desk.

"Charlotte," someone says, shaking me at the shoulder. "Charlotte!" I jolt awake to find Jesse crouched beside me. "The baby's coming."

He looks as though he's seen a ghost, and suddenly the words come together for me, the fog of sleep rolling off.

The baby. Kate.

I stumble out of bed, reaching for my shoes. Reece is

awake now, too, and he watches us leave, concern etched in his features.

In the Coltons' bedroom, Kate is pacing. Her nightgown is wet from the waist down.

"I told him not to wake you," she says. "It's just the waters breaking. I ain't even felt nothing yet and—*oh*." She puts a hand to the bed frame. For a few seconds she is elsewhere; then she looks up at me. "That weren't half bad."

"They'll get . . ." Not worse. What was the way Mother always put it? "More intense."

Jesse's energy is tight and frenzied, so I send him to stoke the fire and tell him to get Kate some water. I walk with her in small circles at the foot of the bed, letting her pause whenever a new wave strikes. The rhythm becomes almost peaceful, and we carry on like that, our fingers threaded together as we pace.

By dawn, Kate's gone into herself, seemingly unaware that the rest of us move about the house. As each new wave builds, she pauses and bends over, moaning through the worst of the pressure.

"What's wrong?" Jesse keeps asking. "Something's wrong."

"Everything is fine," I insist.

I've aided Mother through enough labors to know that this is normal. The waves are predictable, growing more intense with each pass. Kate is sweaty and tired, but it's called labor for a reason. All Jesse sees, however, is the blood on Kate's nightgown and how she continually buckles over to breathe through a wave, as though it might split her in two. I finally shoo him from the bedroom so Kate can focus, telling him to keep Mutt outside, too. The dog is just as excitable as Jesse, and Kate does not need distractions.

But a few minutes later Kate waves me away as well, wanting a moment of true solitude, and I slip into the kitchen. Jesse and Reece are hovering at the table, looking spooked. They're both wearing their pistol belts, ammunition crammed into every last hold.

"I can't leave her like this," Jesse says.

"I'll be with her," I say, "and we'll be fine. It's you two we ought to worry after."

He must hear a truth in my argument because he plucks his hat from the table, claps Reece on the shoulder, and goes to saddle his horse. But Reece lingers, even after the door slaps shut behind Jesse.

"You have to get him, Reece. Rose and all the others."

"That's the plan."

"I can't bear to see bad men keep winning."

He gazes at his boots, then back at me, bringing the brim of that ridiculous hat up so that I can see his eyes. They're brown. I spent so much time scrutinizing their hollowness that I never noticed their color.

"So that's why you came back?" he says. "'Cus you wanted to see how this all ends?"

"It also didn't feel right to part without a proper farewell."

"Well, don't go saying no goodbyes," he says with a smile. "I'll be back by dusk." He tips his hat at me like a gentleman.

"You return, and I'll buy you a new hat," I say. "That one is hideous."

"If this goes well, I'll buy my own hat. Hell, I'll buy *you* a hat. What do you want? A fancy bonnet?"

"You don't know me at all, do you? We might have to change that."

"If you say so, Charlotte Vaughn."

I watch him jog for the stable and wave him and Jesse off from the stoop. Reece looks back only once, and his eyes are nowhere near hollow or lifeless. I'm not sure if he's changed or if the way I view him has.

The men disappear into the trees, and I return to Kate.

CHAPTER FORTY-ONE

REECE

The train chugs into Banghart's round high noon, and I'm shaking like a goddamn sinner at confession. Jesse said it were only visible in my hands, but I swear it's gotten worse since we split on the way into town.

I scour the depot. Like we planned, Jesse's boarding the third car. Could be a Rose Rider is in there too, but Jesse's safe so long as I ain't with him. Once the train departs, he'll make his way back a car, where he'll hide among some cargo, and then it'll be my job to lead Rose to him. I'll say I got Jesse handcuffed and bound, when really, Jesse'll just be waiting for Rose's head to come into view.

It ain't a fair way to die—shot in the back and betrayed by yer own man—but no one ever said life were fair, certainly not 'mongst outlaws, and besides, it ain't like Luther Rose has lived a life that demands fair treatment.

"All aboard!" someone shouts.

I tense in the saddle. The thought of having to chase this train and ditch my horse to pull myself aboard ain't comforting. I've only stormed stationary locomotives, but Jesse and me agreed this was the safest approach. If'n Rose and his boys think I missed the departure, I can approach 'em on my own terms. And that's what this is all about, staying in charge, keeping a firm hand on the reins. Soon as we lose control, everything'll run away from us.

A whistle scream pierces the afternoon.

The train starts chugging.

"Don't let me down, son," Jesse had said when we split. "I ain't in the habit of shooting kids, but I'll do it if'n I got to."

Even after all this, a part of him still doubts me, and that hurts worse than I care to admit. 'Cus I don't much mind Jesse calling me *son*. Rose used that word to make me feel small and powerless, to remind me that I was indebted to him. But with Jesse, it feels like a declaration of respect.

I ain't gonna let him down, and it's time to prove it.

I kick the sorrel I been riding—the same mare Charlotte stole from her uncle—to action. Jesse loaned me a spare pistol belt so I could holster my piece properly, and for that I'm glad. I'm riding the sorrel fast as possible, and last thing I need to worry 'bout is a weapon slipping from my waistband.

Somewhere between Banghart's and the tracks, my hands quit shaking. I bring the horse alongside the steadily quickening train. Cars drift by, rattling and rocking on the rough rail, which startles the mare some. I struggle to keep her steady, and as the handle of a door slips into view, I lean out and grab hold. My legs slip from the stirrups, and my shoulders ache in protest. I'm pulled away from the sorrel. Swinging and grunting, I wrestle myself onto the lip of the car. The mare immediately slows and veers away from the tracks. Perhaps she'll go back to Banghart's, where we left the bay Jesse rode into town, or maybe she'll find her way back to the mountain trail, where Jesse left Rebel tethered. We'll share her saddle back to the house if'n we make it outta this whole thing alive.

The sorrel grows smaller as the train speeds on, and I go to meet the devil.

The P&AC rails prove as rough as a washboard. I'm jostled and jolted as I make my way up the aisle, the bruises from my run-in with Diaz flaring with each step. This passenger car ain't nothing like the refined ones we often rob on the Southern Pacific, but the local folk seem impressed nonetheless. I keep an eye peeled for any of the boys, but don't see no one till I reach the dining car. I slide the door open, and there he is—Luther Rose, seated at a small table set for two.

He looks up when he sees me enter, and he smiles—the widest, brightest smile I've ever seen from him. He even plucks the cigar from his mouth to do so, making sure he shows me every last tooth. Then he motions at the place setting opposite him. There ain't any food in sight, but whiskey has been poured to the brim of stout glasses, some of it sloshing free when the train rocks over a particularly harsh section of rail.

"Murphy," Rose says, setting his glass down. "I were beginning to think you might not show."

"It weren't an easy con to pull off," I say as I sit.

The few folk eating nearby are busy with their own meals and conversations and ain't concerned 'bout us in the slightest. The only two men that appear to be listening, their heads tilted just so, sit directly behind Boss —Crawford and Barrera.

"Where's Diaz?" I ask.

"Where's Colton?"

"I asked first."

It's a bold statement, 'specially with Rose, but he shakes me off with a smile, his brows rising almost lazily. "What's it matter where he's at, son? Here, have a cigar."

He passes me one, plus a book of matches.

"I said to bring everyone. Where is he?"

Rose takes a long pull from his glass and sets it down. And then, finally, ever so slowly, he says, "With DeSoto."

I freeze, a burning match held just inches from the cigar I were aiming to light.

DeSoto. He weren't with the lot of 'em when I searched 'em out on the plains. At least not nowhere where I could see him. But he were around. He were hiding. He had to be. And when I were too beat to notice, when just holding my head up to see the trail ahead were a struggle, he followed.

He followed, and he saw everything. The way to the Coltons' hideout and how the path don't bottleneck and how the house's just sitting there for the taking. He brought that info back to the gang. DeSoto, who never says a word 'less addressed directly. DeSoto, who always fades into the background, brings up the rear, hangs in the shadows. DeSoto, always quiet and always forgotten.

I forgot 'bout him, too. I got greedy and tried to con the devil, forgetting that the devil can't be conned 'cus he plays by his own rules and those rules're always changing. The devil is patient and sly and willing to bide his time till we lay our weakness bare before him.

Rose coulda had them attack that very night I returned with half my blood on my front. He coulda attacked any day since. But he told the boys to pull back and keep their distance. He's been waiting for this moment right now, when the Coltons are separated and the prize will be easy to take. Luther Rose aims to win two pots in the same hand: one made of revenge, the other of gold.

Flames bite at my fingers, and I shake out the match.

"We're gonna be very rich men when this is over, Murphy." Rose thumbs the lip of his whiskey glass, smiling. "I'll take that cowboy's life while Diaz and DeSoto take his gold. Everything Jesse Colton took from my brother, I'm winning back."

I think of Charlotte in the doorway and how I told her I'd return by dusk. I think of Kate and the baby that may or may not be in the world yet. I think of both their guards down and attention elsewhere and how they ain't gonna see it coming, ain't gonna stand a chance. I think till the images of the result surface in my mind and I start feeling sick.

"That sounds like something worth celebrating," I say, numb.

"Don't it? So let's get on with it. Where's the cowboy?"

"Not here."

"Yer lying."

The car rattles hard. More whiskey slops over the edge of my untouched glass.

"He were too spooked when I returned beat half to death that day. I couldn't convince him to get on the train. But he'll be in Prescott. He had errands to see to, and I'll walk you to each and every place he planned to visit."

"Murphy . . ." Rose says, slow.

I fumble for another light.

"Murphy." This one said sharp, like a warning.

I strike the match.

Rose inches a finger toward his pistol belt. "Son, you better straighten yer story before—"

I flick the match onto the whiskey-drenched table before he can pull, and the surface springs to life with flames.

CHAPTER FORTY-TWO

CHARLOTTE

By midmorning I am tired. I don't dare complain because Kate works harder.

She seems unaware of the hours that have passed, whereas I am quite aware of my growling belly and bleary eyes. I have a newfound respect for my mother, who has been called to a house and sometimes not returned for nearly forty-eight hours.

Kate's close at least.

I can feel the baby's head.

I tell her she's doing wonderfully, that every wave is bringing the baby closer, that soon she'll get to meet the little one and it will all have been worthwhile.

I repeat everything I've heard my mother say and try not to think on the heartbreaking outcomes that can also occur: babies who arrive in the world stillborn, mothers who bleed inwardly and never finish the birthing.

Kate seems too stubborn for anything like that to happen.

But then again, life is rarely fair.

After an hour of pushing, the babe has still not come.

Kate's forehead is slick with sweat, her hair sticking to her shoulders.

"You're close."

"You been saying that for hours," she grunts.

"This time I mean it. Just a little more."

She breathes and waits, and at the next wave she pushes and pushes and pushes. And I'm there waiting at the foot of bed. I've got my hands out and ready, and still the baby nearly shoots between my fingers, slick with blood and fluids. I turn the small soul over.

"It's a boy."

But he's not crying.

He's purple, too.

I think they all look purple at first. I can't remember. It's been so long since I assisted my mother.

I give the baby a little tap on the back, and he coughs. Mucus shoots from his nose and mouth, landing on my arms, and I don't care in the slightest because he's started crying—a raw, screeching, beautiful sound.

I pass him to Kate, and the instant that baby touches

her skin, he quiets. It's now Kate who's crying, silent tears streaming down her cheeks as she smiles. "Oh my God," she mutters. "Oh my God." Then she kisses the baby's forehead and whispers, "Hello, William."

"William?" It's a good name. A strong name.

"After Jesse's brother. Jesse were so certain it were gonna to be a boy, too. He's gotta be right 'bout everything." Her eyes dart around the room. "Where is he? Send him in."

"He's gone, Kate. He went with Reece."

"To the train," she says, remembering.

"Yeah, but he'll be back. They both will."

I take a fresh towel and wipe the baby clean as best I can while he rests on Kate's chest. After I've seen to the cord, I tell Kate she should try feeding him. She nods, stroking the little bit of dark hair on the baby's crown, almost oblivious to my presence. I excuse myself to fetch some water. The afterbirth will come soon, and then I'll help Kate move to the second bed so I can go about stripping the first and washing the bloody sheets.

"Hey, Charlotte," Kate says when I reach the doorway. "Thanks for being here."

"You could have done it alone."

"That ain't the point."

She looks beat, yet she's still glowing. I smile back, finally understanding why my mother never gave up her job. Even once Father had secured a comfortable life for us, she didn't want to miss this. Some days, she'd come home heartbroken. But there were many days like this one with Kate. It's a miracle, really. A common yet always dazzling miracle.

I grab the bucket from the dry sink and head outside. Mutt follows, nipping at my heels, but in a friendly manner. I think he's finally starting to approve of me.

The sun is high overhead. Little William's been born on a beautiful January day. The same day, perhaps, that his parents will finally win their freedom from the Rose Riders. My pulse kicks a little, thinking of Reece and Jesse, and I strain my hearing, as if it were possible to catch a locomotive's whistle from where I stand.

I submerge the bucket in the tank, heave it out. Halfway to the house, Mutt's tail goes ramrod straight. He turns for the trail, growling.

I freeze. This time I can make something out after all. But it is not a train whistle.

Hooves.

My pulse kicks harder.

It's a half-day ride to Banghart's, where they planned to board the train. They can't be back so quickly. And if they were, Mutt wouldn't be growling.

I feel the wrongness down in my bones.

I don't wait to see the horse or the rider atop it. I drop the bucket, water splashing, and sprint for the house.

The first gunshot screams when I'm almost to the stoop. It sends dirt flying near my ankles. The next bullet takes a bite from the wooden step.

Mutt bolts inside, and then I'm scrambling through the entrance too, slamming the door behind me. Lunging for Kate's Winchester, which Jesse had moved to its holding place above the entrance before leaving. It's kept loaded, so I crank the rifle's lever, and then shove the barrel out the window.

Lord, do I wish Kate had let me shoot at targets, not just practice form and aim.

I sweep the clearing and find the shooter.

He's dismounted near the tank and is standing behind his horse for shelter. As he leads the steed closer, step by step, a beam of early-afternoon light catches his pistol. It's aimed at the house.

CHAPTER FORTY-THREE

REECE

I bolt from the flaming table. No sooner have I set foot on the landing beyond the dining car than a bullet nicks the door frame I just squeezed through.

"Don't shoot him!" Rose shouts. "Just—"

The door slams shut, cutting off his words.

Just catch him . . . follow him?

Prolly both. He needs me alive to find Jesse, and that's all that's keeping me breathing.

There's a ladder running 'longside the door to the next car. I take hold of a rung and start climbing. As I'm heaving myself onto the top of the car, Barrera grabs my ankle.

"Come on, Murphy," he croons from below. "We only wanna talk."

I kick with my free leg, and my boot connects with his chin. He goes stumbling outta sight. I don't waste time seeing if he fell from the train or merely clattered to the landing. I run.

Or rather, I try to.

Soon as I stand, the wind becomes a roar, a gale force pushing at my back, making my feet wanna move too quickly. My hat nearly lifts off my head. I clamp a hand down on it and crouch low, shuffling toward the rear of the train.

Chino Valley races by in the corners of my vision — pale yellows and browns. I keep my sights on the next few feet of railcar ahead, otherwise my stomach twists in knots.

"Murphy!" Barrera yells behind me.

He didn't fall then. Shame.

I run, and when I reach the end of the passenger car, I leap to the next. The whole of the P&AC line seems to be an oldfangled, barely pieced together mess, so I prolly shouldn't be shocked to find the roof of the second passenger car more sloped than the first. But I am. My boots connect with the pitched plane, and my right ankle buckles with surprise. At the same moment, there's a slight bend in the rail, and I'm thrown from my feet. I hit the roof on my side, but can't find purchase. The momentum of the turning train's got a hold on me, and I roll toward the edge of the roof, arms flailing, fingers grasping.

I find nothing but slick wood. My legs go over the edge. I hear the scream of air curving 'round the train cars, feel the tug of gravity . . .

And my hand closes down on the lip of the car's roof.

I cling there, swaying. One boot knocks 'gainst the passenger car window below. I use it to my advantage, pushing and kicking off the glass. I get an elbow onto the roof, then another. But now my feet ain't able to kick off the window no more and I'm stuck hanging, the fight draining from me. Heat laces through my arms. Something digs into my ribs—the book Kate gave me, still tucked inside my jacket. My palms are sweaty, and the surface beneath them slick. I can't hold on much longer. Just as my elbow begins to slide out—right as I'm bracing for what's sure to be a deadly fall—hands clamp down on my wrists.

Barrera.

He drags me to safety and slams me down onto the roof in one violent motion. My head hits with an ugly crack. My vision wobbles, and then my breath cuts off as he grabs my throat.

He shoulda let me fall. God, I wish he let me fall.

With a spare hand, he draws his pistol and presses the barrel to the underside of my chin.

"Rose said not to shoot," I choke out.

"Maybe I didn't have a choice." Barrera cocks the weapon. "Maybe you shot first."

The wind screams in my ears. The air smells like smoke and coal. Barrera drops the pistol to see to strangling me with both hands.

"I can't . . . breathe. Barrera, I can't—"

"Diaz said you strangled Hobbs. How could you do that?"

I kick and flail beneath him, scrape at his fingers, try

reaching for my holstered gun. I don't got the energy, and he won't let up.

"How could you do that to yer own crew?"

I grapple for his pistol, forgotten somewhere near my head.

"How?"

I ain't even gasping no more, I'm plain out of air. My lips form shapes 'round nothing. This is how I'm gonna die. Jesse will be all right, at least. That is, till he returns to the house and finds whatever remains of Kate and Charlotte and the baby. God, the baby.

I'm gonna die right here with Barrera's hands on my neck and the deep blue sky framing his angry, murderous face. Maybe this is exactly what I deserve.

There's a gunshot, and Barrera falls away, relinquishing his grip on me. I cough and sputter, sit up. Barrera's unblinking eyes stare up at the heavens. Jesse stands at the other end of the car, pistol smoking. He just saved me. I'm trying to figure how he appeared outta nowhere like an angel, when I remember he boarded the very car we're now standing atop. He was supposed to be making his way back to the cargo car, but he coulda heard the struggle, maybe even saw my boots dangling outside the window.

"What the hell happened?" he shouts.

"Rose lied 'bout—"

There's movement behind Jesse. A hand coming into view, clinging to the top of the ladder. Then a face— Crawford—and his pistol.

"Jesse, duck!"

He does—just barely in the nick of time—and Crawford's shot sails over his head. I fire back, and that's when Crawford puts it together. I ain't on their side. I've joined with the enemy, and he's outnumbered on this roof. He slides down the ladder.

"Get off the train!" I yell to Jesse, and I dart past him and follow Crawford. "Get off the train and go back to Kate!"

"What?"

"Just do it, Jesse. They're in trouble."

I throw a leg over the edge of the car, grappling for the ladder. Crawford's already transferred to the ladder of the next car—a boxcar—and is climbing to safety. I can't let him get away, not when he's seen Jesse and has a description he can give Rose.

I stow my pistol and leap to the boxcar's ladder. I connect with it hard, nearly missing my grip. I slide a rung or two. When I grab tight, my shoulder flares with heat and my bruises ache, the rails flying by below. I pull myself against the rungs and draw one quick breath before scrambling to the top of the car.

Unlike the passenger cars, the boxcar roof is flatter than an open plain. This is like running across the floor of a barn, and I gain on Crawford, who's still limping from his injury in Wickenburg.

He jumps to the following boxcar, the wind snatching his hat as he goes. It floats over Chino Valley and I lose sight of it as I jump to follow him. This second boxcar's got its side door open, and Crawford swings over the edge, propelling himself through the doorway.

I don't got a notion where he thinks he'll go next. There ain't nothing but two flatcars left to the train. He's as good as trapped.

I do as he did, grabbing the lip of the boxcar above the open door and swinging myself down and inside.

My feet hit the floor of the strangest boxcar I've ever seen. Half the bed's been converted into what can only be described as a portable hog ranch. The place stinks of pigs and rotten food, and the beasts are mulling about in an honest-to-god pen, built right here in what otherwise looks like a work car. A maintenance foreman's tools fill the rest of the bed, hanging on the walls and lying atop cargo crates.

Crawford's standing barely two paces away, a sledge-hammer in his hands.

He knew what he'd find in these tight quarters. Him and the boys got on the train way up north, had plenty of time to case every last car. It ain't him that's trapped. It's me.

He swings the sledgehammer, and I dive to the side, rolling past Crawford and deeper into the crowded car. The hammer collides with the door frame. Wood goes flying. I go for my pistol, but before I can draw, the sledge-hammer's coming at me again. I dive a second time, losing my hat, grappling like mad for a weapon of any kind as I regain my footing. There's a crate of rail ties. My hand closes over one of the iron spikes, and I barely got time to yank my hand clear of Crawford's next blow. He swings again, and the sledgehammer crushes the wooden crate. Spikes go spilling free.

"I told him you weren't worth it the very first day!" he screams. "But God does he love you. Yer the worst out of any of us, and still he cares for you most."

I dodge another blow, find my back up 'gainst the far wall of the train.

"What happened, Murphy? Did ya find their gold and think you could take it all for yerself? Or maybe you started fancying that city girl. Diaz is gonna gut her, you know that?"

He raises the hammer again, but it's growing heavy, and I can see his aim. I sidestep it quickly, and when the hammer strikes the wall of the car, it lodges in the wood. He yanks, trying to retrieve it. I drive the iron spike into the back of his hand. As he roars in pain, I kick him in the gut. The force is enough to yank the hammer free of the wall, but his grip slips from the handle. The sledge-hammer clatters to the floor of the car as Crawford topples backwards, colliding with the hogs' pen.

Finally, I got time to go for my pistol, but so does Crawford. We both pause, fingers frozen beside our holsters.

"You might fool Boss," Crawford snarls, "but you ain't fooling me. Yer as sinful as the rest of us, Murphy, maybe more so."

"Yer right," I tell him. "I'm a killer. I'll prolly burn in hell with the rest of y'all. But I'm gonna go out doing the right thing."

I draw my weapon, same time as him.

I can immediately see he's got me beat, and I dive to the side, squeezing my trigger even though I know my aim's off. But he counters my move, trying to sight me as I lunge away, and he leans into the line of my shot. His bullet flies wide, and mine catches him in the neck.

Eyes flashing, Crawford falls against the wooden pen. It creaks under his weight, then buckles completely, and the mob of hungry pigs closes in. It's the same burial as Hobbs's and Jones's, and while Crawford mighta deserved it, that don't make it any easier to watch.

I holster my pistol and turn away. The open doors of the boxcar are reinforced with slats of wood that create a giant X, and using 'em as foot- and handholds, I'm able to work my way back toward the car's roof. When I pull myself up, I find myself face to face with Jesse.

"Yer still here?"

"What?" he shouts.

"I told you to go back!"

"Back where? I couldn't hear you over the wind."

I grab him at the arm and tug him toward the rear of the car. "Climb down!"

He tries to protest, and I shove him hard. He obliges.

On the flatbed, we're sheltered from the worst of the wind. I peer 'round the boxcar. Prescott waits to the south, still hidden from view, but we're coming up on the stretch of trail that leads to the hideaway.

"You gotta jump," I say to Jesse. "Rose sent two men to the house."

The color blows clear outta Jesse's face. It's like he's been shot in the gut. "You said you weren't followed."

"I didn't think I were, but he tricked me, Jesse. That's

what he does. I shoulda seen it coming. I'm sorry. But you gotta go now. Jump, and you can make it to the horse easy, ride back."

"Not in time, though," he says. "Not if he sent 'em this morning."

"So you ain't gonna try?"

His Remington is in his hand faster than I can blink. "Is this a double cross?" He holds the weapon in close to his chest, barrel pointed at mine. "You send me into a trap while you waltz off with Rose?"

"What? No! Crawford's dead in that boxcar, I swear it."

A wrinkle forms on his brow—there just a second and gone. He's putting it together. I got no reason to lie. If it were a trap, I'd have shot him already or walked him straight to the enemy.

"And you'll . . ." His gaze drifts toward the boxcar, toward wherever Luther Rose is prowling.

I nod. "I promise I'm telling the truth, Jesse. I promise it on my mother's life. On yer unborn child's."

He stuffs the pistol away and claps the side of my face with a palm. "You done good, kid." For the briefest moment I feel like I've found the father I always wished for. The kind that challenged me, but in ways that make me better, not in ways that beat me down.

But then there's the gunshot.

And the blood that flies from Jesse's shoulder.

And his hand falling away from my cheek as he falls.

I whip 'round to see Rose standing on the boxcar roof. "Murphy—son!" he shouts over the wind. "You draw your pistol and shoot that bastard in the head."

I crouch low beside Jesse. He's exhaling in short bursts through the pain, but it ain't a fatal blow, not if he gets to help.

Do it, Murphy, I hear. *Do it right now, and all will be forgiven.*

I can feel Rose's weapon aimed at my back.

I grab the front of Jesse's shirt, heave him to his feet.

I draw my pistol.

"Reece?" Jesse asks, his eyes as desperate as his voice is fearful.

"I'm sorry. This is gonna hurt."

I shove him off the train.

CHAPTER FORTY-FOUR

CHARLOTTE

I stare down the barrel.

There is no way I am going to make this shot. He's too far away, the bulk of him hidden behind the horse. Even if I *had* been given an opportunity to practice with bullets, I don't think I'd stand a chance. At this distance, the Rose Rider's head is smaller than the bucket I used during target practice.

But the horse . . . I could probably hit the horse.

I *can't* hit the horse. The poor creature didn't pick its rider. It didn't choose to trot into this clearing, to serve as this outlaw's shield. It's just an innocent animal and—

The Rider fires his pistol.

A bullet slices through the shutter. I flinch, feeling the sting of wood splinters on my cheek.

"Charlotte?" Kate yells from the bedroom.

Another gunshot.

This one misses the shutter altogether and instead hits the section of wall between the window and the door. It lodges in the wood and doesn't enter the kitchen.

"Charlotte!"

The baby is crying now too.

I bring the rifle barrel back up to my eye, hold the butt firm to my shoulder as Reece taught me. I sight the man.

Yer shooting the rifle, the rifle ain't shooting you.

All that remains is the one step I've never practiced. I pull the trigger.

The rifle recoils, sending a jolt of pain through my shoulder.

The bullet bites into the dirt just shy of my target, but the horse goes wild, whinnying and rearing. Its hooves slide along the sloped bank of the reservoir until the creature loses purchase and topples onto its side, pinning the Rose Rider in place. His screams rattle the afternoon. The horse rocks there for momentum and, after finally regaining its footing, runs off and disappears behind the house.

Cursing, the outlaw fires blindly in my direction. I duck for cover. Three more shots hit the walls before he's empty.

Then I'm back on my feet, scanning out the shutter. The man is crawling for the shelter of some shrubs, what's sure to be a broken leg dragging behind him. I fire again, but the severity of the situation has finally caught up to me and my hands shake against my will. Though the Rider is moving as slow as molasses, it proves too difficult. The rifle is empty before I've had any success, and by the time I reload, the man has dragged himself behind the shrubs and fallen still. I watch a few seconds, but he doesn't move. Perhaps he's dead.

I pull the rifle back from the shutter and check on Kate. The afterbirth has come and the bed is a mess. William is crying in her arms, and she looks as though she's seen the devil.

"They're here?" she gasps out.

"One Rider. I think I got him."

"Check."

There is nothing I want more than to stay in this room with her, door bolted and curtains drawn.

"Charlotte—" she urges.

Outside, a horse whinnies. At first I believe it to be the outlaw's steed, returning to find its rider. But then comes the crackling snap of fire, the horse's cry again. It's coming from the direction of the stable.

The man I shot is not nearly as injured as I first thought if he's managed to start a fire.

"Maybe I should just tell him where the gold is," I say to Kate. "That's why he's here."

"Yer a fool if you think that's all he'll want. That he'll take the gold and just ride out."

"It's worth trying."

"It ain't."

The horse's screams get more frantic. If'n the wind picks up or the flames get strong enough, the house'll be at risk. I grab the rifle and leave Kate with the baby.

I toe the front door open, wait a moment, then step onto the porch cautiously. Pulse pounding, I scan the

whole of the clearing, only to find that the man is no longer behind the shrubs. I never should have turned away
from the window. I should have unloaded the rifle into
the brush until he was most certainly, undeniably dead.

I home in on the stable, where flames continue to
spread. Reece and Jesse took three mares with them this
morning—Rebel, Uncle's sorrel, and a bay quarter—but
Kate's horse, Silver, remains. Her stall is farthest from the
house, and also farthest from the fire, but she can smell
the smoke and hear the crackling flames, and it's worked
her into a frenzy. She prods the earth with her front hoof,
throws her head.

I run before I lose my nerve. Straight to her stall. When
I throw open the door, she bolts, nearly trampling me and
causing me to drop the rifle as I dive aside.

That's when a bullet hits the dirt near my hand.

My head snaps up, searching for the shooter.

The very thing that protects this little clearing is now
protecting my assailant. He is hidden somewhere among
the pines and rocks and shrubs, as good as invisible. And
I've foolishly run into the center of the gauntlet, with
nothing to protect me but a wooden structure already
aflame.

As I reach for the rifle, a bullet battles me back again. I
shuffle into the safety of the stall. It is thick with smoke,
and flames from the neighboring stall are starting to lick
their way in. I cough, feeling blindly through the smoke
for the rifle. Instead, I find only a heavy blanket Silver uses
in the evenings. I use it to bat at the attacking flames, but
for each tongue of fire that I smother, another seems to

spring to life in its place. My lungs are starting to protest the dirty air. If I don't run for it now, I'll be trapped in this stall not just by enemy bullets, but by flames.

I turn and see a figure pushing through the thick smoke.

It is not the outlaw I shot at from the house. It's a second Rose Rider. There are two.

This one wears a blood-red jacket and a bandanna over his mouth and nose. Beneath the brim of his black hat, dark eyes smile at me.

I bolt to the right. He trips me with his rifle, and I crash to all fours. A hand closes on my ankle, and I kick out wildly, catching him in the chest or face. I don't pause to look. I scramble for the house and get only one stall closer before his grip closes over my ankle a second time.

He pulls me nearer. Dirt and pebbles lodge beneath my nails as I attempt to grab hold of something—anything. My skirt gets caught beneath my weight, bunching up around my hips.

Hands flip me over, and I kick and scream, but he straddles me, pinning me easily in place. Flames from the stable dance behind him, around us. The heat is unbearable.

"Where's the gold, girlie?"

"I don't know."

He grabs at my chin, angling my face so that I'm forced to look at him. "Where's the gold?"

"They never told me." He pinches my mouth so tightly I stumble on my own words. Tears stream down my cheeks. "Please," I beg. "I don't know where it is."

He has a knife now, drawn somewhere along his waist.

He brandishes it in front of me, touching it to my nose, lips, the underside of my chin. He slips it beneath the collar of my dress and then yanks wide. The fabric rips, exposing my shoulder.

"Last chance."

"I don't know, I don't know. Please, I don't know anything."

His head cocks to the side, his eyes shining with amusement. "I remember you from the Jail Tree," he says, and my blood goes cold. "Look who's bound and jailed now. Look who's begging for mercy."

I flail wildly, searching for the rifle I know I won't find, praying I might discover a rock in the dirt instead. My fingers graze something so hot, I recoil. A horseshoe, baking in the heat of the fire. He wrestles with my skirt, fingers scraping my thighs, and I grab the blistering steel. Swinging it up, I shove it into his face.

He screams, leaps back.

And then I'm on my feet, running, my burned palm throbbing in pain. Just beyond the stable, I find my only chance of a weapon—a pitchfork stuck in a bale of hay that's set to go ablaze any moment.

The man is screaming threats at me, his footsteps pounding nearer.

I grab the pitchfork and spin. He doesn't have time to stop. He was running too hard, intent on tackling me. I grip the handle with all my strength as he collides with the fork. My burned skin screaming in protest, I shove harder.

His eyes bulge, and his gaze drops to his chest, where his jacket is turning a deeper shade of red around each prong of the fork.

He grabs at the handle, tries to pull it out.

I stagger back, watching as he falls to his knees and then flops to the side, unmoving. I step nearer and nudge him with my boot. His body rocks from my prodding, but his eyes do not blink.

I stumble away. Fight the urge to be sick.

But I had to check, had to be sure. I couldn't make the same mistake twice, not like with the first man.

The first man!

My gaze snaps up just in time to see the back of a gray jacket limping into the house.

I sprint for the rifle. It's hot from sitting so near the fire, and the palm of my hand is blistering from the horseshoe. My thighs feel hot, too, in the places where the dead man's fingers crawled at my underthings.

Winchester in hand, I run for the house.

A trail of blood leads the way onto the stoop and through the door. I crank the rifle's lever, ejecting a shell. Step onto the stoop. Take aim.

The man is hobbling for Kate's doorway, oblivious of me.

I will not miss this time. Even if the bullet goes straight through him, the bed is offset. Kate and the baby will be fine. The shot will find a home in the wall.

I take a deep breath.

Steady my aim.

And just before I can squeeze the trigger—a gunshot.

My head snaps up from the barrel. The Rose Rider is still standing there.

No.

But then a blot of blood appears on his back. It blossoms and blooms, spreading across the fabric of his jacket, and he topples forward, not moving once he hits the floorboards.

I race inside, burst into the bedroom.

Kate's arm is still extended, one of her twin Colts smoking while William cries in the crook of her other arm.

CHAPTER FORTY-FIVE

REECE

For what seems like ages, Jesse is airborne, floating like a feather. Then time slams back to speed and he's tucking, rolling as he crashes to the ground, tumbling and flailing through the brush and thorns and hard earth, shrinking as the train races on.

Rose leaps down to the flatcar. Instinctively I throw my forearm up to deflect the blow, but the punch never comes. Instead, he grabs the front of my shirt.

I barely have the sense to holster my pistol before the world turns upside down.

There's an instant of weightlessness, the roar of the train speeding off, and then impact. The air goes outta my lungs. I try to do what Jesse did and roll up, but the worst of the crash has already happened, and it's easier to be limp. Stones cut at my shirt and slice into my skin. Dirt stings my eyes. Prickers and shrub claw and scrape, the book in my pocket jabbing at my flesh all the while.

Then, as quickly as it started, it stops.

I sag into the cold winter earth.

Up, Luther Rose tells me. *Get up, you worthless excuse of a man!*

I lift my head.

He's struggling to his feet, drawing his gun. I follow his aim. *Jesse.* He's running for Rebel, still tethered to a mesquite in the distance where we left her at the start of the trail. His bad shoulder hangs, the arm limp and dark with his blood.

Get up, Reece.

It's so startling to hear my name—not Murphy, or son, or kid—that it takes me a second to realize it ain't Rose's voice in my head, but my own.

Get up, get up, get up.

I push onto my hands and knees, sit back on my heels.

Rose starts shooting. The bullets cut through cacti and shrub, each one biting closer to Jesse's heels.

I draw my pistol. Take aim. Fire.

Luther Rose drops his weapon and falls to one knee, my bullet having found a home in his thigh.

"Get up!" I shout at him. "Get up, you worthless excuse of a man!"

Jesse's on the horse now, riding into the woods. The shrub and trees swallow him. He's safe.

Rose shoves to his feet, his weight planted firmly

through the uninjured leg. "Murphy," he says, "I know why you think I wronged you. And I'm sorry."

"No, you ain't."

"I failed you. Lemme make it right."

He's giving me that look I've seen so many times, the one that always comes when he calls me *son*. He don't even appear shocked that I've betrayed him. He just seems sad.

"You can't right this," I tell him. "It's too far gone to save."

A corner of his mouth quirks. "Don't preach to me 'bout evils, son. Not when you done struck down yer own brothers."

"They ain't my family, and I ain't never been yer son."

He nods, like he believes he can understand my position. "Family's the most powerful witchcraft, ain't it? I been doing this all for my brother, and he ain't even here no more. But I'll let it go for you, Murphy. I'll let that Jesse fella live if you come with me right now. We can leave, just the two of us. Go start again somewhere else, lead the quiet life we both always wanted."

"You know *nothing* 'bout what I want!" I scream. I'm aiming my revolver at him now, the weapon quivering in my grasp. "I never wanted any of this. You forced it on me. You *made* me into the Rose Kid."

"And so what?" he asks, throwing his palms at the heavens. "The Rose Kid dies today?"

"Maybe."

I never intended to face off with him like this, but if this is how it's gotta be, then I'm ready. Only one person's gonna walk away from this section of rail.

He understands what I mean, and just like that, the world seems to narrow.

CHAPTER FORTY-SIX

CHARLOTTE

I take Silver and ride.

We can deal with the bodies later. Same with the soiled sheets and birthing mess. Kate swears she is strong enough to battle the fire if it manages to spread to the house. For now, we'll let the stable burn. It can be rebuilt. Most things can. But Reece and Jesse, not in the slightest, and something with the train setup has gone horribly wrong.

Both of the Riders' horses follow me, and I'm in too much of a hurry to bother chasing them off. It's roughly an hour to the rails, and I need to make time. My hastily bandaged palm stings with each slap of the reins, and the torn fabric of my dress flaps against my shoulder. I should have changed or taken a jacket, gathered more ammunition. I should have done a lot of things, but I left too quickly, driven by fear, with nothing but the Winchester and a few more rounds.

The mountains become a blur, a whirring tunnel of dirt and rock and green pines. And then, in the middle of the trail, just before it opens onto the plain, is Jesse, slumped forward on his horse.

"Jesse!" I pull up alongside him. His shoulder is slick with blood, and when he raises his head to greet my gaze, he can barely keep his eyes from rolling. He is likely swimming in pain, perhaps on the verge of losing consciousness. "What happened? Where's Reece?"

"Kate . . ." he says. "The baby."

"They're fine."

"Two men. At the house. Reece said—"

"They're taken care of. Kate's fine. William, too."

"Will." He says the name as if it is the greatest treasure.

"Where's Reece?"

"With Rose."

With him? That can't be right. He wouldn't betray us. Not after everything.

"Stay here," I tell Jesse. "Or keep riding if you can manage. I'll catch up in a moment."

I nudge Silver again, and we surge forward.

CHAPTER FORTY-SEVEN

REECE

Rose pushes his jacket back, slow, tucking it behind his holsters. Only the left piece is stowed there, its grip gleaming in the sunlight. The other still lies where he dropped it after my bullet found his leg.

I lost my hat back in the boxcar and am left squinting hard in the sun. Rose's face is a blank canvas, mouth and nose bright, eyes and brow dark from the shadow cast by his hat. The day is deathly still—no wind, breeze, nothing. Blades of grass stand like tombstones. Our jackets hang by our knees like iron shields.

Even with my weapon already drawn and his in a holster, I know he can best me.

So when he moves, I'm struck through with shock, 'cus it's slow and cautious, the kind of harmless draw I seen many men do in the gang's presence.

Palm showing, he lowers his left hand till the web of

skin between his thumb and forefinger can lift the revolver from his belt. The barrel stays pointed at the ground, the grip resting on the back of his hand as he holds it before him. With it balancing like that, he surrenders.

I ain't never seen Luther Rose surrender to no one. But here he stands, offering his weapon to me.

Ain't that amazing—how a person can change.

The slightest breeze skims over the plain. My bangs snag in my lashes. Rose's jacket ripples at his knees. Just as suddenly as it started, the breeze dies, and the peacefulness of the moment goes with it. The air 'round Rose is suddenly laced with tension.

"I'm sorry," he says, and I know I been wrong 'bout everything.

He moves fast as lightning, and the pistol comes up, grip sliding into his palm.

I aim and he aims, and two shots rattle the stillness of the valley.

Luther Rose drops to the dirt
and I
feel
invincible.

CHAPTER FORTY-EIGHT

CHARLOTTE

They stand apart in the distance, connected only by the dark shape of the tracks, which seems to string them together like beads on a cord. I draw Silver's rein, frozen with surprise.

Reece's weapon is aimed at Rose, who appears to be surrendering, but I somehow know it will not be that simple. The devil wears wings at all the right times and then casts them aside when we believe him to be an angel.

Don't fall for it, Reece. Whatever he's telling you, don't believe it.

Reece's gun dips just slightly—he thinks it's over, that the devil has come clean. That's when Rose's hand twitches and Reece sees the truth.

Their weapons come up.

There are two gunshots.

And they both fall.

CHAPTER FORTY-NINE

REECE

I feel the cold, burning pain only after I've slumped to my knees.

There's a hole near the pocket of my jacket, a gaping wound just above my hip. There ain't enough blood, not to match the pain.

I slump to my side and roll back to look at the sky. It is the biggest blanket, the most peaceful quilt. The earth beneath me is cold.

You did it, Reece. You did it.

The Rose Kid is dead.

Reece Murphy is free.

CHAPTER FIFTY

CHARLOTTE

Silver carries me into the valley, over thorny burrs, around angry shrub. It must take a good five minutes to reach them. I draw rein beside Rose and check him first. I will never make the mistake of not checking again.

He is dead. The bullet has punched a hole into his chest, right over his heart, and he doesn't look as if he felt even an ounce of pain. His lips are barely parted.

One of the horses that followed Silver nudges the body with her muzzle. Rose's steed, perhaps.

"Reece?" I run to him. He's staring up at the sky, clearly in pain. Rose commits a lifetime of atrocities and blinks out like a candle, but Reece is forced to endure this after all he's already weathered. It doesn't seem fair. It isn't.

"It's you," he says, surprised. His eyes find the ripped state of my sleeve, and then realization dawns on his face. "Did Jesse—? I sent him to . . ."

"No. I passed him on the trail. But Kate's fine. And I'll make sure Jesse is, too."

"Are you hurt?"

He means it—this ridiculous question when I am whole and he's been shot. There's blood above his hip, a hole in the pocket of his jacket. Beneath, his shirt is wet —stained red—and when I pull the fabric back, I can see the bullet lodged there, his skin swelling around the lead. Blood seeps with each breath he takes.

"I'm fine," I tell him, though it is only partially true. I lay the jacket back in place and find his hand, guide it to the wound and help him apply pressure. "Where are the others?"

"Dead," he grunts out. "Jesse and me took care of 'em."

"Can you get up? We need to get you to the house."

"Nah," he says. "Leave me here."

"What? No. Get up, Reece Murphy. You get up right now."

"I don't reckon I can."

"That's not fair. You don't get to come this far and quit. Not when they're all gone. Not when it's your turn to finally live. You're not supposed to die today."

"Maybe I am." His eyes roll a little. "Hey, Charlotte? I'm sorry 'bout everything."

I can't help it. I start crying. Because he's right to apologize for some things, yet I don't want him to feel this way. Not now. Not at the end.

"You think," he continues, "that we mighta been friends in a different life? You and me?"

"We're already friends in this one," I tell him.

He manages a smile.

"Now come on, Reece. Get up. I'll bring the horse."

"I can't even sit." He looks up at the sky, his breathing labored. Reaching blindly, he finds my hand, threads his fingers through mine. "Charlotte, I want you to tell the story, all right? 'Bout the Rose Kid. And how he died here today. But how he became Reece Murphy again first. Can you do that?"

I blink back tears. "Of course."

He squeezes my hand and I squeeze back.

"Please go help Jesse," he says when I don't move. "No one else gets to die 'cus of me. No one."

I see the argument he's making, I do. Jesse needs help and has only a shoulder wound. Reece has been shot in the gut, and I know how deadly stomach wounds can be. With the rough state of the trail, it's about an hour back to the hideout, less if I ride at a good clip, but he'll only slow me down. It's lose one of them or potentially lose them both. Still, I try to lug him to a sitting position. He's too heavy. I put his arm behind my shoulder and try to stand as I did that day in the snow. I can't move him even an inch.

"I'll return with help," I say. I'm not certain Kate will be strong enough for the ride, not after twelve hours of hard labor, but that is a problem for when I reach the house. "Just hold on till I get back."

"All right, Charlotte Vaughn," he grits out. "If you say so."

I am unfair to Silver, urging her constantly faster up the trail. I catch up to Jesse about halfway to the house; he's slumped over in the saddle and barely conscious. I grab hold of Rebel's lead and guide the mare on.

By the time we enter the clearing, Jesse is fading fast, and Kate comes shuffling to help. We manage to lug him into the house, where he goes straight onto the kitchen table. I rock William while Kate sees to the injury. Probably she has experience with gunshot wounds. She's a bit slow on her feet, but she sterilizes some tools from her sewing kit and uses them to dig out the bullet. It's not the bullet that often kills folk, she tells me, but infection. She pulls out a small square of fabric—a bit of Jesse's shirt torn free and dragged into the wound by the force of the shot. Then she goes about bandaging his shoulder. It's likely he'll lose use of the arm or, at best, experience limited mobility, but Kate's confident he'll live. "And what need's he got to lasso a bull no more? The rail's killing the ranching industry. This just puts him outta his misery quicker." She says it all jokingly, but there's a pained look in her eyes. I figure it doesn't matter much if your livelihood is stripped from you by injury or chance or fate; it still hurts all the same.

We move Jesse to the second bedroom, and as his eyes wink shut in sleep, I turn to Kate.

"We have to go back for Reece."

"He's alive?"

I quickly tell her about the shootout, how Reece shot Rose but also took a bullet to the stomach in the process.

"I couldn't move him on my own. I need another set of hands."

Kate glances at Jesse. Their future is bright now. Because Reece took care of Rose, they no longer have to live in fear. She understands the complexity of the situation—how Reece brought this tragedy to her door but also kept it at bay—because in the end, she simply nods.

I do not know how she finds the strength to sit in the saddle. But she leaves William sleeping snugly beside Jesse and mounts Silver without a protest. I take Jesse's horse, and we ride.

Kate quickly falls behind. She can't fly at the same speed as I can, not after all she's been through, but so long as she makes it to the rails, all will be well.

When the tracks come into view, both bodies are gone. So are the Rose Riders' horses that followed me originally.

At first I think I have seen it wrong. It is hard to tell what is shrub or rock at a distance, but then I'm down in the valley, pacing the place where it happened beneath the late afternoon sun, and they are nowhere to be found.

I stare at their blood in the dirt. Rose's is thick and dark in the place he'd fallen. Reece's is not as prominent where he lay, but there are dribs and drabs showing that his body moved over near Rose's, then disappeared. The entire area is awash with boot prints and the markings of hooves. And then there are the marks of a wagon, arriving from and disappearing in the same direction—toward Prescott.

Oh God.

I know what happened. The train arrived in town.

Passengers spoke of a fight that took place onboard. Maybe someone peering from a window even saw two figures resembling Luther Rose and the Rose Kid leaping from the train. A posse was assembled, and they rode this way to chase the outlaws.

There is no sign of a struggle in the dirt.

Reece was too weak to put up a fight. The Law came while I was gone, and they took him. They took him, and now he'll hang.

CHAPTER FIFTY-ONE

CHARLOTTE

I shout a frantic farewell to Kate and am immediately back in the saddle, riding for Prescott as fast as Rebel will take me.

I don't know what I intend to do. It is unlikely that anyone will listen to my word compared with everything the Territory believes to be true about the outlaw known as Reece Murphy, but I know I have to try.

I make excellent time on the open plains, following the rail, but twilight is falling by the time I enter the city. My seat is numb from the saddle. The bandage on my burnt hand feels wet, too. I never bothered to grab gloves when leaving the Coltons', and I would not be surprised to learn that my palm is now bleeding. I don't stop to check. Riding directly to the sheriff's office, I come upon a throng of people huddled out front, their incessant chatter punctuated by a striking hammer. At the rear of the group, a cameraman is breaking down a tripod stand.

"What happened here?" I ask him.

"Three Rose Riders are dead, Luther Rose and the Rose Kid among them."

My heart drops. "Are you sure?"

"I better be! I just took the picture for the paper. They had the coffins propped up on the hitching post and everything." He points for emphasis, and through the dispersing crowd I get my first unobstructed view of the sheriff's office.

Three coffins lie on the ground. Two are sealed shut, and a man is hunched over the third, putting the final nail in place.

And that's when I see it—Reece's pompous, broad-brimmed, Montana-pinched dark felt hat resting atop one of the coffins.

"It can't be," I mutter.

"You sound like half the town." The photographer chuckles. "I reckon some folk believed those devils would never be in the ground, but the Law won today. About time, really."

He keeps prattling, but I've already turned away, unable to watch as the coffins are loaded onto a wagon.

Reece died alone.

I promised him I'd return, and then I was too late. It's bad enough that he had to take his last breath with no one there to comfort him, but to be lugged off by the Law, too? To be made a spectacle of, even in death? He'll end up a photo in the paper now, the subject of sensational headlines and stories that recount all his wretched misdeeds and wax lyrical about his demise. And he'll share all that coverage with Luther Rose, the shadow he spent the last few years trying to escape.

I should have been there to retrieve his body. He deserved a quiet burial. At least that much—that little— he'd earned.

Not knowing what else to do, I go to Uncle Gerald's house. Mother must have returned to Yuma at some point today, and Paul is either still at the mine or staying with a friend, because the house is silent. Too silent. I keep hearing my final words to Reece—*I'll return with help, just hold on till I get back*—followed by his weak reply. *All right, Charlotte Vaughn. If you say so.*

It's getting late. The light is all but lost, and the ride will not be easy. But I can't stay here tonight—not alone —and I've traveled this way after sunset before.

Kate is up feeding the baby when I enter the clearing, and she rushes out to meet me. "Reece?" she asks from the front stoop.

I shake my head.

"I'm so sorry," she says.

"For what? You didn't kill him."

"No, but it still hurts when we lose folk we care 'bout. For yer loss, I'm sorry."

I didn't care for him in the way she's implying. This gaping hole in my chest cannot possibly be for that reason.

It's simply that I envisioned a different ending. This is the wrong outcome, and yet it's reality. The powerlessness that overwhelms me is frighteningly vast and seemingly endless, so much so that even tears seem pointless. I wonder if perhaps it was this very feeling that made Reece's eyes appear so hollow.

Kate says to come inside.

Kate says it's cold and very late and I should sleep.

Kate says, "Charlotte, do you hear me, Charlotte? Please come in the house."

"All right," I mutter. But I stand there a moment longer, staring at the trail, imagining I can see all the way to that desolate stretch of rail where Reece Murphy faced his demons.

Maybe I cared for him after all. Maybe, with more time, I could have cared for him quite deeply. I guess I'll never know.

The evening is long and restless.

The stable has more or less burned to the ground, so I secure Rebel to a shrub for the night, as Kate has done with Silver. I brought a second horse from Uncle's, so I have the means of returning home tomorrow, and I tie her out for the night as well. Then I join the Coltons inside, where we're all stuck in the second bedroom because no one's had time to see to the soiled sheets in the first. The Coltons have the bed, and I have some blankets on the floor beside William's cradle.

Each time the baby wakes—hollering and wailing—Kate feeds him, and I check on Jesse, changing his bandages as necessary. I get little sleep, but being busy distracts me from all the things I'd rather not think about. It's the quiet moments between interruptions from William when the nightmares creep in . . .

Parker. Uncle Gerald. That Rose Rider in the red jacket. His fingers scraping my thighs. The throbbing of my burnt palm. How my shoulder still feels exposed.

And then Reece.

Reece speaking through the pain.

Reece telling me to leave.

Reece squeezing my hand before I left him there to die.

I cry for the first time, my back to the Coltons' bed. They are not loud tears, nor many, but I thought unleashing them might lift a sense of burden from my shoulders. Instead, I just feel weaker.

Come morning, Jesse manages to surface from his ebbing state of oblivion and ask after Reece. Kate tells him the unfortunate news, and his mouth pulls into a conflicted grimace. But then she lifts William from the cradle and sets the baby in his arms, and any ache Jesse was feeling immediately vanishes. His face lights up. He holds the baby as if the child is made of glass. He stares while the baby gapes back, and Kate watches both of them, glowing. Everything about the image is warm and bright and promising.

Kate lifts the covers and slides into the bed. Jesse presses a kiss to her temple. From the doorway, I feel as if I am witnessing a private affair, a moment made only for the three of them. I have overstayed my welcome.

I am saddling the borrowed horse when Kate catches up to me.

"Say, Charlotte? Yer gonna be some bigtime journalist, right?"

"One can only hope."

"If'n you ever write 'bout the gang or Reece, can you do us a favor and not never mention me or Jesse by name? And don't bring up our fortune neither, or how Rose was after it. Gold makes monsters of men, and folk'll stop at nothing to get their hands on it. Weave a few false yarns, if you can. Print the truth, but not every last drop. Fair?"

Just two weeks earlier I would have rejected this plea, turned my nose up at the entire argument. I would have rebutted that a journalist aims to report fact and that nothing is more sacred than the truth. In some instances I still believe this. But in others . . . Well, the truth people want and the truth they need to hear can be two different things.

"I'll leave you out of any story," I tell her. "You have my word."

"We owe you, Charlotte. I mean that. We ain't got much to offer, but if you ever need a favor in return, you just write."

"Write even if you don't need a favor!" Jesse calls. He's appeared in the doorway, leaning on the jamb for support with William tucked into the crook of his uninjured arm. "Kate likes letters nearly as much as her books."

"Will you return to Prescott?" I ask.

"I ain't so fond of people," Kate says, "but this clearing ain't no place to raise a child. Too isolated. Isolation breeds ignorance. I reckon we'll head home once Jesse's healed up."

"Then I'll send any letters there."

"Safe travels," Kate says as I step into the saddle.

I give the Coltons a parting wave and ride from the clearing for the final time.

Heading for the stage stop around noon, I pass the *Courier* office. A boy on the street holds a stack of newspapers, shouting, "Luther Rose, killed by the Law! The infamous Rose Kid, dead!"

Having found a bit of money beneath Uncle's mattress after dropping off the horse, I hurry to pay for a paper. There's the photo of the open coffins propped up outside the sheriff's office, and the lawmen stand around the deceased, gripping their suspenders proudly. Luther Rose is front and center, his arms folded over his chest. The coffin to his left reveals a man I do not recognize, but the third coffin—Reece's—is sealed shut. His hat rests on the hitching post nearby.

According to the story, passengers aboard the train recognized Luther Rose when a fight erupted in the dining car. The Law surmised that there was a struggle among the Rose Riders, potentially one of the lower men —maybe even Reece—trying to take control of the gang. At the Prescott depot, one of the outlaws was found shot dead atop a passenger car, and Reece was discovered in a boxcar, his body mutilated almost beyond recognition. But being that his hat was one of a kind and found in the very same car, identifying the remains was easy. Meanwhile, a group of lawmen rode out along the tracks, following up on a passenger's report that he saw someone jump from the train. It was along a barren stretch of Chino Valley where the Law engaged in a shootout with Luther Rose.

This story is a bald-faced lie. I stood there and watched Reece shoot Rose without a soul in sight, yet here is this falsified story, printed right in the *Morning Courier*—a story that lifts up the badge-wearing men who did nothing but collect dead outlaws. I cannot fault Mr. Marion too severely, as the posse likely gave him this tale, touting themselves as heroes and speaking of a thrilling gunfight. The editor took their word as fact, for who would expect a lawman to lie?

Even still, it makes no sense. The details don't add up.

If the Law wanted to claim responsibility for *killing* Luther Rose, I could understand the doctored facts. But why not claim to have killed the "infamous Rose Kid," too? Why not show his face for all the Territory to see? He wasn't in the boxcar. He was just lying there on the plains, perfectly identifiable.

Unless . . .

The ground seems to shift beneath me.

There was no sign of a struggle when I returned to the site of the shootout. Reece said he couldn't sit, but what if he'd found the strength? What if he'd managed not only to sit, but to stand? To mount the horse that had followed me from the clearing earlier and lingered near Rose? What if he'd managed to disappear?

The posse had stamped hooves all over that site. I could have easily missed a set of hooves riding in the opposite direction when I returned with Kate. If the Law was sloppy, overly excited at having found Luther Rose's body, they might have missed them too. They could have assumed Rose died alone, succumbing to injuries sustained on the train, and misidentified Reece. A *different* Rose Rider could have met a grisly fate in that work car while Reece managed to slip away.

Of course, if he'd managed to mount a horse, there's no explanation for why he wouldn't have ridden directly for the Coltons'. Their residence was the closest bit of help for miles. Perhaps he'd gotten lost, too delirious to steer the horse. Or maybe he heard the posse coming and hid in a panic, only to find he didn't have the strength to continue on after they rode out.

It is still quite likely that Reece is dead—that he died alone, just not in the place I first imagined—but if he's alive . . .

If there's even the slightest chance he's out there . . .

I know what I have to do. I promised to do it, regardless.

I've a story to write.

354

I take a backbreaking stagecoach to Maricopa, then a westbound train to Yuma.

In the passenger car, I delay because the task seems impossible. I stare out the window. I read the rest of the paper. There's a story on Uncle Gerald's suicide and reports of his illegal bookkeeping. Mother and I are referred to as perfectly sane and the victims of "slanderous character attacks by the late businessman." There it is, in black and white. It is printed, and so it will be believed to be true.

My pencil feels heavier than ever. Words have great power, unbelievable impact. I cannot abuse that.

I open my journal and begin writing. The words come slowly at first because they are heavy and burdensome, and I'm not sure how to string them together. But when I keep at the page long enough and write from the heart, they begin to flow. Soon I can't seem to write quickly enough.

I try to capture the person I knew to be Reece Murphy. He was not a saint, but he was not evil. He was tortured by his past. He was forced to make difficult decisions, often between two equally poor choices, but when it mattered most, he made the right ones.

Reece Murphy was a boy who became a man while riding with the devil.

I write his story in a train car identical to the one in which our lives intersected, where the story, in many ways, began. And when I arrive in Yuma, the first thing I do after reconciling with my mother is visit the printing offices of the *Inquirer*.

CHAPTER FIFTY-TWO

CHARLOTTE

"*The True Story* of the Rose Kid" prints only a week after the initial reports of Reece's death.

Within days, the piece is all over the Territory, with reprinting requests coming to the *Inquirer* office by wire. Locals are abuzz. Many people reconsider what they know about the infamous Rose Kid. They question the validity of the Law's identification of that mutilated body from the work car and speculate about Reece dying alone on the plains, ultimately redeemed. Some even whisper that he may still be alive.

But for every reader who has this hopeful, receptive reaction, another questions my sanity. I am called a liar and a sensationalist, a sympathizer of murderers and thieves. My motives are criticized. I receive threats, encouragements to quit, suggestions that I stick to writing fiction, not fact. But the story is bigger than I am, and after years of listening to Uncle Gerald tell me that a woman has no place in journalism, I am not persuaded to accept such nonsense because droves of men think just as he did.

The print requests keep coming, and barely two weeks later the story's been available in more places than I ever imagined. Cousin Eliza even writes to tell me that she saw my work in the *Pittsburg Dispatch,* which makes me think of Nellie Bly and nearly causes me to burst with pride.

Then, about a month after the story is published, when the frenzy and fanfare surrounding the piece is finally dying down, an envelope arrives at the *Inquirer* office directed to me. I open it hesitantly, bracing for another hateful rant. On the sheet of paper within, there is just one line of writing.

I liked the story. Thank you. — RM

I drop the note and fly to the window, throwing it open. In the distance, a locomotive exhales at the depot. Passengers climb aboard. Carts and carriages rattle by on the street below as folk go about their business. But of course he's nowhere to be seen. Of *course.*

I duck back inside, feeling foolish, hot.

I knew that he harbored great demons and regret, that in many ways he thought himself unworthy of a normal life, even if it was all he ever dreamed of. But I thought clearing his name would help him move on, see past the image people had of him and the feelings of inadequacy he suffered as a result. Instead, he's just remained in hiding. He's still running from the past.

It is perhaps unfair of me to expect anything different. If he needs time alone, he's earned it. Besides, what am I hoping for, truly? That night before Kate went into labor, I returned to the Coltons' because I admitted I had unfinished business with Reece Murphy. I owed him a farewell. That was all—a proper goodbye, a parting of ways.

He wanted a fresh slate, a new life.

I wanted a safe family, a promising career.

I cleared his name with my story, and my own name was cleared from the reports about Uncle and with a bit of help from the Coltons regarding my whereabouts the day Parker died. I still harbor some guilt about that. I never intended to kill him, and yet it happened at my hands. Perhaps I will always be haunted by those events. Perhaps this is the same type of fog that continues to haunt Reece.

But we both got our dreams, and this note is our goodbye. Justice has been served, and a deserving person earned a second chance. All is as it should be.

I stow the letter in my desk drawer and do not read it again. But, against my better judgment, I start glancing over my shoulder, searching for his face among crowds.

The wet season comes, and then the dry, endless stretch of summer.

I write in the stuffy *Inquirer* offices, windows open,

surrounded by Ruth Dodson and my new family of female journalists and typesetters, the noise of a whirring printer always within earshot.

Mother holds on to the Gulch Mine but entrusts management of it to Paul. He reports weekly by wire and proves a fair and decent man, the type Uncle Gerald never was, which reminds me that family is fickle and blood alone does not define character. We vacation in Prescott come August, making sure to check in with Paul and his affairs. The rail has done good things for the mine, and the whole of the city, too. Prescott is bustling, and goods are shipped in at fairer costs. Numerous copper claims have been reopened now that materials can be transported with such ease. The P&AC seems plagued by delays, mudslides, and slipping rails, yet Father would be proud. Like him, the people seem to adore the inconsistent line, going so far as to call her Old Reliable. It brings new people to the capital, folks looking to settle and spread roots in the Territory.

I search for Reece among these faces, but with less determination than before.

As the weeks pass, multiple Territory papers begin theorizing that any surviving Rose Riders have fled Arizona or are, in fact, deceased. There have been no sightings of the outlaws in towns, nor train heists by men who match their descriptions. Still, mention of the gang makes people discuss Reece. In his disappearance, he becomes almost mythical, a legend I hear children whispering about on the streets. "I get to be the Rose Kid!" they argue as they reenact an epic shootout, thumbs cocking imaginary hammers.

It makes me smile.

He's become bigger than himself, an entity people assume to know, when really, humans are far too complex to fit into one newspaper story. But at least some folk seem to think on him positively now, which is all he'd ever asked for.

Come October, the *Inquirer* office is abuzz with the news of Nellie Bly, who, having taken a job at the *New York Post*, went undercover in an insane asylum for ten days and published her findings on the treatment—and mistreatment—of patients. We talk about her late into the evening, our eyes wide with wonder, like little girls. My pieces covering life in the southern portion of the Territory—reports on politics and the rail and city developments—seem generic by comparison, but I stay focused and meet my deadlines. The truth is important, and even the smallest stories, if reported irresponsibly, can wreak havoc.

A week or so later, a letter with familiar script arrives on my desk. After so many months of silence, it is entirely unexpected. I tear it open so impatiently that I slice my finger on the stiff paper.

Firstly, I read the Bly piece. Yours are better.
Secondly, I bought a new hat. I know you hated the first,

and it were lost on the train that day anyways, so it were time. I also cut my hair. I reckon I look different these days, but it's still me, at least in all the ways that matter.

I miss you. — RM

My stories are not better, and he knows it. Some days I worry that I peaked with my debut article.

I read the note again, smiling. It sounds like him, I realize. After all this time, I can still hear his voice in my head.

I save the letter, but stop looking for him. He seems happy now, at peace, and I cannot spend my whole life searching for a shadow. I have stories to write and places to visit, and legends are like the wind—intangible and fleeting.

As November comes to a close and the chill of winter evenings settles over Yuma, I accept a journalist position in Pittsburgh. Cousin Eliza—or rather, her mother—has graciously opened her house to me, and Mother gives me her blessing to relocate. I am to write for the very paper Nellie Bly vacated in favor of the *New York Post,* and it feels as if fate has set the wheels in motion.

Standing at the depot on the first of December, I hold a small suitcase against my knees. I imagine I will greatly miss this Territory—its beauty and its harshness. It is wild in a way Pittsburgh is surely not, but it is also changing. The world seems to be closing in wherever I look, trains connecting even the smallest of towns. I have a feeling I'll end up back here someday, after several years in the big city, maybe less. I am not certain I am cut out for reporting—at least not exclusively. Even at the *Inquirer* I favored the small stories to those of politics and campaigns. I'd find myself tempted to embellish details and give people dramatic flair—a blazer they did not don, a feature they hadn't possessed. Perhaps I should try my hand at novels.

It's funny, I think as the train approaches, how a person can spend so long chasing the truth only to find they love fabricated stories just as fiercely.

Maybe legends are tangible after all.

Perhaps they are created on the page.

CHAPTER FIFTY-THREE

REECE

I spot her the moment she arrives at the depot.

She ain't changed much in the past eleven months, and still the sight of her in the flesh makes my heart kick a little faster. I were worried maybe I'd feel nothing. Maybe all that time away would've changed things.

'Cus it sure changed me.

Somehow I got on one of the horses that day. I knew it were only matter of time before the train chugged into Prescott and the Law came crawling over the plains. Charlotte were taking too long, and fearing help wouldn't return for me in time, I found the strength to get in the saddle. Problem was, I promptly blacked out. The horse traveled for home without my guidance, and by the time I came to and realized home for the steed was wherever the Rose Riders had been holed up in Chino Valley—not the Coltons'—we were practically to Banghart's. Fading in and out of consciousness, I managed to get myself to the nearest claim, where a puzzled old man stepped from his home to greet me. I mighta been sick on his boots as he helped me inside.

He said it were the book in my pocket that saved me, and he placed *Around the World in Eighty Days* in my hands. I'd forgotten I'd been carrying it, which were ironic, really, seeing as the whole time on the train I were cursing it for jabbing my ribs. There were a hole clear through one cover and out the other, but 'parently the bullet slowed enough that it only lodged in my flesh, didn't dig deep enough to hit nothing vital. The man kept saying I were lucky as he dug out the lead and stitched up my skin, and I kept saying that even with luck, it still hurt like hell.

Little more than a week after the shootout, he set a paper clipping on my bedside table. "The True Story of the Rose Kid," the headline declared. I drafted a note to Charlotte immediately, but I weren't able to mail it to the printing office till a few days later, after sneaking off in the night. Prolly the old man suspected my identity by then, and though it seemed like he bought Charlotte's word in the paper, I weren't 'bout to linger and find out otherwise. I left him a note with directions to one of the gang's old hideouts, where he could find a bit of money for his troubles.

I headed to another hideout of Rose's and stayed there till late March, when I were healed real strong. I even considered staying permanently, but it were too quiet and so damn lonely. I took just enough of the coin to get by, then wandered.

I thought 'bout visiting the Coltons, to thank 'em, but I'd brought 'em enough trouble already. I went west instead, thinking 'bout Charlotte. She was a tune I couldn't get outta my head, but instead of turning to Yuma, I kept on till I hit the Colorado River.

Using a fake name, I went into La Paz and asked after my folks, only to learn my father were in a grave and my ma done eloped with a banker from California. That was all the closure I shoulda needed—Ma were safe, Pa were gone—but still I couldn't sit tight, couldn't settle down.

I kept wandering, kept running.

I read Charlotte's articles, read every paper I could get my hands on, read *Around the World in Eighty Days,* too.

I bought a plain hat and dragged a blade over my skull.

First time I glanced in a mirror following that shaving were the first time I didn't see my father staring back. Or any piece of Rose or the Kid or them Riders. It was like I were a new man.

I wrote her again that very moment, though I couldn't pinpoint why 'till a few days later. It were simple, really. I wanted to see her again, had to. Not 'cus I expected nothing, but 'cus she were the only soul who knew me as both people—who met me as the Rose Kid and saw me teetering on death's doorstep as Reece Murphy. Moving forward—*truly* living—only felt possible if I owned up to that.

By the time I made it to Yuma and stopped by the *Inquirer* office, she'd already resigned. A typesetter told me she were headed east, that the train were due to leave sometime that afternoon. I couldn't bring myself to search out her home, go opening up old wounds if it weren't something she wanted or were prepared for. So I went to the depot and waited.

I'll leave it up to her.

I might be able to make do as an invisible man if I keep working at it. I been doing it these past eleven months, and it gets a little easier each day. The rest of the world can think I'm dead or nothing but a legend, but I gotta know if she sees me.

She watches the train chug into the depot.

The passenger car doors slide open. Folks start stepping on, and I hang back, letting her board with the others.

It's familiar, this Southern Pacific railcar, full of dark memories and bad deeds. I ain't that person no more, but ugly pasts make for permanent scars.

I board last.

She's seated near the rear of the car, glancing out the window like she ain't certain she's made the right choice, like maybe she's leaving something important behind.

I walk forward. Her gaze drifts up the aisle. It floats over me, through me, beyond . . . But then it snaps back. She catches something beneath the brim of my new hat —something she recognizes—and her eyes lock firm with mine.

She lurches upright, fingers pressed 'gainst her lips. Behind 'em, a smile blooms. Ever so slowly, she nods at the cushion beside her, as if to say *Sit*.

And I reply, "All right, Charlotte Vaughn. If you say so."

AUTHOR'S NOTE

The events of *Retribution Rails* unfold ten years after
the events of its companion novel, *Vengeance Road*, and
in that single decade, the landscape of Arizona changed
greatly, with trains crisscrossing much of the Territory,
connecting towns and altering the way of life.

In some regards, this was a positive thing. Goods
could be more quickly transported to towns and cit-
ies. Shipping rates became more reasonable. New jobs
and industries ventured west. But much of this growth
came at disastrous costs. To make way for the rail, Na-
tive Americans were driven from their homes, forced to
relocate to reservations or killed in cold blood over the
disputed land. When lines were built, it was mainly at the
hands of minorities—Chinese and Mexicans in Arizona
—who made significantly less than white foremen and
laborers. And even once the rail was completed, other

groups continued to see detrimental effects. Cowboys and ranchers, in particular, faced dwindling job offers. Instead of beef being driven across the plains over the course of months, it could now be shipped by train in a matter of days. In many cases, railroads even cut across cattle routes. The ever-expanding web of rail lines, combined with the winter blizzard of 1887, decimated the cattle industry. It never fully recovered.

While *Vengeance Road* was inspired by a legend, *Retribution Rails* was inspired by these rails—the lines that disrupted some lives while connecting others, and the innovation that birthed new industries while killing the old. A great deal of manpower (and money) was put into developing America's rail systems, many of which did not stand the test of time. The Prescott and Arizona Central, for instance, was completed on New Year's Eve, 1886, and abandoned a mere seven years later. Built on a shoestring, the P&AC was always plagued by problems —mudslides, washouts, delayed trains, and more—and it was never rebuilt after a spring storm washed out a large section of track in March 1893.

Many of the details regarding this line are historically accurate within *Retribution Rails*. When Reece and Charlotte arrive in Prescott on January 1, 1887, a celebratory gala was indeed making its way through the streets. The speech Charlotte listens to from her family's carriage is quoted from one of the many speakers who addressed the crowd before the rail director, Thomas Bullock, brought the celebration to a close. Even the half-hog-ranch, half-work-car that Reece enters to face off with Crawford during the climax of the novel is factual. A crafty maintenance foreman built the pen when realizing that his tools only took up half the bed, allowing the work crew fresh pork while keeping the stench of pigs confined to a small space. Truth really is stranger than fiction. However, you may now be scratching your head at the dining car scene, wondering why such a car would exist on a shoestring operation. It likely didn't. But this is where I pull out my artistic license card and admit that I doctored things to work for my story.

Another creative liberty? The *Yuma Inquirer*. No such paper existed, but the market for newspapers was present in almost every frontier town and a newly established one run exclusively by women did not seem that far a stretch. After all, starting a paper was the easy part. The trouble was keeping it running.

The *Prescott Morning Courier* was one of Arizona's literary success stories. Its editor, John Marion, worked first for the *Arizona Miner* (owning it for a period of time) and later the *Courier,* which he founded in 1882. He was described as tenacious and full of vigor, and his style of reporting was viewed as bullying and slanderous by some, with complaints that Marion relied too heavily on opinion while drafting his pieces. Others maintained Marion's paper was as reputable as any, that he was simply blunt and ruthless. Regardless, Marion was a staunch supporter of the P&AC and his writing helped rally the people of Prescott behind the rail. Whether the real John Marion would have helped Charlotte as my fictitious version did is hard to say. But had a female-run paper like the *Yuma*

Inquirer existed, I feel strongly that they would have done some fact-checking and then come to Charlotte's aid as quickly as they could line their composing sticks.

As for Nellie Bly, she would have most certainly been an inspiration for someone in Charlotte's position. Though Bly was not renowned until the publication of *Ten Days in the Madhouse* (October 1887) and her subsequent *Around the World in Seventy-Two Days* (1890), any young girl trying to break in to the male-dominated field of journalism would likely have adored the example set by Nellie Bly, so long as that girl had access to the reporter's writing.

While Reece and Charlotte are fictitious, the world they navigate in *Retribution Rails* is not. Despite my many hours of research, it is possible I have overlooked something and a historical inaccuracy has snuck in to this finished copy. Any such errors are mine alone.

Writing this novel felt like standing on a precipice. The West was "wild" in part because it was lawless, but also because nothing was constant. As railroads expanded and modern conveniences closed in, the Wild West slowly died. In many ways, the rail killed the frontier. I'll leave where Reece and Charlotte land in this strange, shifting world up to your imagination.

ACKNOWLEDGMENTS

Publishing a novel is a team effort and I tend to rely on the same group of champions with each book, both in the publishing world and in my personal life.

On the publishing end, many thanks to my agent, Sara Crowe, as well as the gang at Houghton Mifflin Harcourt: Kate O'Sullivan, Catherine Onder, Mary Wilcox, Linda Magram, Lisa DiSarro, Karen Walsh, Tara Sonin, Cara Llewellyn, Mary Magrisso, Dalia Geffen, Sophie Kittredge, and everyone who touched this project in some way or another. I'm so lucky to have you guys. Also, much love to Teagan White for another beautiful cover.

Thanks to my many writing friends (you know who you are) who stood by me as I struggled to draft and revise this novel. In particular, I owe Mindy McGinnis an incredible debt for her ruthless critiques and lengthy email brainstorms, and I'd be lost without Susan Dennard and

Alex Bracken. Thanks for the judgment-free, endlessly supportive, always-there-to-lean-on friendship, ladies. Now let's get back to work! (#cattleprod) And of course, my utmost gratitude to Ryan Graudin, Mackenzi Lee, and Tamora Pierce, who all read *Retribution Rails* prior to publication and shared such kind words about it.

To the members of my *Vengeance Road* posse: I am so grateful for every ounce of support that you have shown me and these Western stories. You keep me inspired, motivated, and determined to grow with each book I write. Thank you.

Buckets of gratitude to my family as well. My parents, sister, in-laws, relatives . . . Your undying support and love is the stuff of legends.

To my husband, Rob, for staying calm and encouraging throughout my many panicked moments these past eighteen months. I know now that I bit off more than I could chew. Two contracted novels plus a short story with schedules that all overlapped? I didn't even do this much *before* we had a kid. I'm still not quite sure how I managed it, only that without you I definitely would have failed.

Casey, my love. Since you've been in the world, I've written two Westerns, this one dedicated to you. It's strange because this lawless, wild tale is filled with the types of hardships I hope you never have to endure. And yet this book is for you. They're all for you. I love you, and I mean it when I say you are my wildest, grandest, most amazing adventure.

And last, to the lovers of books—the readers and

reviewers, the librarians and educators, the booksellers and book-stockers: You guys make the bookish world go 'round. You make my career possible. Thank you for picking up this novel. Thank you, thank you, *thank you*.